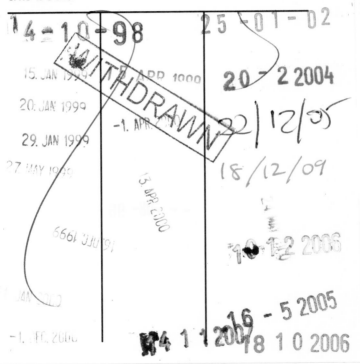

Approaches to Teaching Kafka's Short Fiction

Approaches to Teaching World Literature

Joseph Gibaldi, series editor

For a complete listing of titles,
see the last pages of this book.

Approaches to
Teaching Kafka's
Short Fiction

Edited by
Richard T. Gray

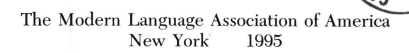

The Modern Language Association of America
New York   1995

© 1995 by The Modern Language Association of America. All rights reserved
Printed in the United States of America

Library of Congress Cataloging-in-Publication Data

Approaches to teaching Kafka's short fiction / edited by Richard T.
  Gray.
      p.   cm.—(Approaches to teaching world literature : 51)
    Includes bibliographical references and index.
    ISBN 0-87352-725-9—ISBN 0-87352-726-7   (pbk.)
    1. Kafka, Franz, 1883–1924—Criticism and interpretation.
  2. German literature—Study and teaching.   I. Gray, Richard T.
  II. Series.
  PT2621.A26Z5745   1995
  833'.912—dc20   94-34520

Excerpt from *Invisible Cities* by Italo Calvino, © 1972 by Giulio Einaudi editore
s.p.a., English translation © 1974 by Harcourt Brace & Company. Reprinted by
permission of Harcourt Brace & Company.

"The Wall and the Books," from Jorge Luis Borges, *Labyrinths*, © 1966 by New
Directions Pub. Corp. Reprinted by permission of New Directions.

A version of Henry Sussman's essay appeared in *Modern Language Notes* 100
(1985): 138–50. Used by permission of Johns Hopkins University Press.

Cover illustration of the paperback edition: "Man, Encaged" ("Mann,
eingezäumt"), an illustration by Franz Kafka for *The Trial*. Archiv für Kunst und
Geschichte, Berlin.

Published by The Modern Language Association of America
10 Astor Place, New York, New York 10003-6981

Set in Caledonia. Printed on recycled paper

CONTENTS

PREFACE TO THE SERIES

In *The Art of Teaching* Gilbert Highet wrote, "Bad teaching wastes a great deal of effort, and spoils many lives which might have been full of energy and happiness." All too many teachers have failed in their work, Highet argued, simply "because they have not thought about it." We hope that the Approaches to Teaching World Literature series, sponsored by the Modern Language Association's Publications Committee, will not only improve the craft—as well as the art—of teaching but also encourage serious and continuing discussion of the aims and methods of teaching literature.

The principal objective of the series is to collect within each volume different points of view on teaching a specific literary work, a literary tradition, or a writer widely taught at the undergraduate level. The preparation of each volume begins with a wide-ranging survey of instructors, thus enabling us to include in the volume the philosophies and approaches, thoughts and methods of scores of experienced teachers. The result is a sourcebook of material, information, and ideas on teaching the subject of the volume to undergraduates.

The series is intended to serve nonspecialists as well as specialists, inexperienced as well as experienced teachers, graduate students who wish to learn effective ways of teaching as well as senior professors who wish to compare their own approaches with the approaches of colleagues in other schools. Of course, no volume in the series can ever substitute for erudition, intelligence, creativity, and sensitivity in teaching. We hope merely that each book will point readers in useful directions; at most each will offer only a first step in the long journey to successful teaching.

Joseph Gibaldi
Series Editor

PREFACE TO THE VOLUME

In a 1981 essay with the tantalizing title "Why Read Kafka?" the British Germanist Martin Swales cites the biographical emphasis of much current Kafka criticism as a symptom that the linguistic utterances constituting Kafka's fiction have "in some way broken down": the shunning of explication in favor of mere explanation in critical studies of Kafka demonstrates for Swales the failure of Kafka's fiction "to work as public communication" (357). To be sure, Swales refuses to ascribe this failure to Kafka's works themselves, attributing it instead to what he views as "a general malaise in Kafka criticism" (358), and his essay argues against that critical syndrome which perceives Kafka's literature exclusively as the product of a hermeneutically inscrutable private code, while arguing for its interpretive relevance within the context of the multiple public codes of contemporary society. Swales's remarks strike me as significant for undergraduate teachers of Kafka for three reasons. First, they point to the oscillation between imaginative explication and sober explanation that has continually determined the extremes of Kafka reception. Second, Swales's admonition that Kafka's fiction not be limited to explanation by means of biographical or other "private" codes but be opened up to explication according to various public codes provides a fundamental rule of thumb for the exploration of Kafka's texts in the undergraduate classroom. Finally, that Swales even found it necessary to pose the question Why read Kafka? signals and historically locates an emergent crisis in the Anglo-American reception of one of the preeminent modernist writers.

From the time of the Anglo-American "discovery" of Kafka in the 1950s through the early 1970s, not only did Kafka's works assume their place as a cornerstone of the undergraduate world literature curriculum, but an acquaintance with his writing was considered de rigueur for the general sensibility of all those who wished to be considered "intellectuals." During this period in which Kafka was valorized in both his critical and his popular reception, the question Why read Kafka? could thus only be regarded as either superfluous or senseless. While Kafka has remained a central figure in literary criticism, perhaps receiving even more scholarly attention in the wake of the recent pluralistic explosion of literary theory, since the 1980s his popular reception has begun to show signs of decline. This situation presents today's undergraduate teachers of Kafka's fiction with specific problems. I have little doubt that college and university professors currently still hold the conviction that a familiarity with Kafka's writings is fundamental to a liberal arts education, and the frequency with which his fiction has been and continues to be anthologized in readers and textbooks of various sorts indicates that educators continue to assign him a cardinal place in the canon of world literature. However, where questioning the status of canonical literature is concerned, undergraduate students today are far ahead of us as teachers and scholars—even if their questioning often seems to us improperly motivated. Nevertheless, my own teaching experience frequently confirms that contemporary students tend to be somewhat skeptical of the value of reading Kafka; indeed, that they often need to be persuaded of his significance and "relevance" for their more pragmatic conception of education. In this sense the question Why read Kafka? not only marks the legitimation crisis currently sensed by undergraduate teachers of Kafka but is a symptom of the overriding crisis in humanistic education that characterizes the last decade.

Education is perhaps one of the only spheres of human endeavor in which one can sometimes effect a cure to an affliction merely by treating the symptoms. As teachers we certainly know no more rewarding experience than witnessing that general transformation in students' attitudes that sometimes occurs once they have been "inspired" by a certain author, a style of writing, an unfamiliar manner of thought, or a novel weltanschauung. While it is the uniqueness of Kafka's fiction—a uniqueness corroborated by the necessity of coining the adjective *Kafkaesque* to designate the peculiar mood his texts evoke—that defines the inordinate challenge he presents to undergraduates, this same uniqueness constitutes his potential for generating that "aha" experience of intellectual self-satisfaction which is so paramount to the motivation of their *self*-education.

The purpose of the present volume, consistent with that of the series as a whole, is to provide undergraduate instructors with background information, resources, ideas, critical perspectives, and pedagogical techniques that will help them make Kafka and the modernist writing he represents more accessible to their students. If it is true, as one of the anonymous consultant readers of this volume maintained, that "Kafka remains one of the most taught and least understood writers of our century," then the appropriateness of such a teacher's guide seems beyond question. At the same time, the materials presented here make no claim to dispel misunderstandings of Kafka's texts by providing a key for their "correct" interpretation; indeed, such a goal would necessarily be grounded in an objectivist hermeneutics that presupposes that all texts have a specific, unequivocal significance, and it is precisely the resistance to such unequivocality that has come to be cited as one of the most characteristic and significant aspects of Kafka's fiction. For this reason we should formulate our pedagogical objectives in the teaching of Kafka more circumspectly, not so much insisting on a "proper" understanding of his texts as aiming at the provision of conditions that will make it possible for students to experience them in an intellectually productive manner. The goal of the present volume is thus decidedly not to advance a narrow view either of Kafka the writer or of his individual works but, rather, to address as many critical, intellectual, and contextual perspectives as possible—given, of course, the limitations required by adherence to the framework established for this series. Especially considering the multiplicity of cultural con-texts in which Kafka's literature can be and has been fruitfully interpreted, the present volume advances no claim to completeness. By the same token, it sets out to document those positions most representative of the primary directions of Kafka scholarship, supplementing them with the pedagogical strategies and classroom experiences of insightful and practiced teachers.

The scope of the present work differs from that of the majority of the volumes previously published in the Approaches to Teaching World Litera-ture series in that it focuses on a selected group of short texts rather than on one long opus. Especially when, considering Kafka's oeuvre, one could easily justify a volume dealing with *The Trial* or *The Castle*, novels that are frequently taught in undergraduate courses, the decision to focus instead on a selection of stories requires some explanation. The preference for a concentration on selected pieces of Kafka's short fiction over one of the novels stems from both pedagogical and literary-critical considerations. Par-ticularly for undergraduates who are getting their first taste of Kafka's fiction, reading the novels can prove to be an exercise in frustration and futility, and it is therefore often difficult for them as untrained readers to sustain enough energy and attention to turn such an extended reading into an educationally productive experience. The stories, which present the essen-tials of Kafka's fiction in a more concentrated form, hence represent a peda-gogical vehicle that is better suited for introducing undergraduate students to his literature. As eminently manageable textual units, these stories can not only be read at a single sitting but, perhaps more important, also allow teachers to require rereading without placing unreasonable demands on their students' study time and attentiveness. But beyond being pedagogically more "economical," the short fictional works are perhaps more representa-tive of Kafka's oeuvre than the novels are. First, all three novels remained fragments, implying not only that Kafka was dissatisfied with their thematic development and aesthetic structure but also that he himself did not possess those specific talents requisite for a writer of novels. As Kafka was only too well aware, his literature derived its energy from spontaneous inspiration rather than from strategic, long-term deliberation, and hence he found him-self incapable of sustaining this creative intensity over the extensive period of time that the writing of novels demands. For this reason, short works of fiction proved ultimately to be the genre optimally suited to Kafka's creativ-ity, as he himself noted in the famous diary entry of 23 September 1912 (*Diaries, 1910–1913* 275–76), written in response to the successful composi-tion of "The Judgment." It is in these shorter works, then, that Kafka's literary genius came into its full expressive fruition. Indeed, one could argue that the episodic quality so typical of Kafka's novels derives from their structure as a kind of chain reaction of short stories, joined together by a common protagonist.

Second, the decision to focus on selected stories rather than on one of the novels has the advantage of presenting a broader cross section of Kafka's writing. While early Kafka research tended to view his texts more or less monolithically, more-recent scholarship has stressed the diversity of forms, structures, and narrative techniques that make up the body of Kafka's fiction. In fact, it is possible to distinguish three distinct periods in Kafka's mature style, each of which is represented by a characteristic narrative stance. The first period (c. 1912–14) is marked by the production of "perspectival" narratives, tales that, while primarily grounded in the figural perspective of the protagonist common to first-person narratives, are yet told in the third person; the second period (c. 1914–16) is a transitional phase, marked by the introduction of first-person narratives, in which a tendency toward an ironizing objectivity begins to make itself evident; the third phase (c. 1917–24), finally, is represented by Kafka's "parabolic" stories, in which the narrated events are related with an almost alienating distance. By examining a selection of Kafka's short fictional works, one may thus highlight the inherent diversity of his fiction, and by selecting pieces from each phase of Kafka's creativity, one may also track his evolution as artist. In addition, because the short stories manifest the gamut of sophisticated literary forms and techniques Kafka employs, they provide material appropriate to the classroom study of narrative structure and its influence on the conditions that shape the readers' reception of fictional texts.

The choice of "The Judgment," *The Metamorphosis*, "In the Penal Colony," "A Country Doctor," and "A Hunger Artist" as the focal texts of the present volume is motivated by the desire to present works representative of these distinct stages of Kafka's literary production. "The Judgment," written on the night of 22–23 September 1912, is universally recognized as that story whose composition initiates Kafka's "breakthrough" to his own unique literary voice. *The Metamorphosis*, written in November and December of the same year, replicates in many respects the narrative techniques and thematic issues dealt with in "The Judgment," and thus it corroborated for Kafka the belief that he had found the literary style appropriate to the portrayal of what he called his "dreamlike inner life" (*Diaries, 1914–1923* 77). As the work by Kafka most frequently anthologized and most often read by undergraduates, its aptness for the present volume can scarcely be contested. "In the Penal Colony," written in October 1914, is likewise widely read in undergraduate courses, and as the text in which Kafka's transition from perspectivistic to parabolic narration first makes itself manifest, it marks one of the crucial turning points in his literary development. "A Country Doctor," composed in January and February 1916, is a striking example of Kafka's employment of a "timeless" first-person narrative as part of the transition to the universalizing parables of his late period. Finally, "A Hunger Artist," written in February 1922, is exemplary of Kafka's late parabolic style. It is further significant that each of these texts was published by Kafka himself during his lifetime, some more than once. Against the backdrop of

Kafka's overwhelming diffidence toward the products of his pen—a diffidence that gives way to the extreme of self-effacement in the writer's infamous request to his friend Max Brod that he destroy all Kafka's extant unpublished manuscripts on their author's death—their very publication indicates that Kafka viewed them with relative approval. Our focus on works published by the author himself thus also suspends most of those problems of textual authenticity and accuracy that are intrinsic to any examination of the novels and stories published posthumously from Kafka's diaries and notebooks.

Regarding the makeup and scope of the present volume, a few more remarks are necessary. While the five stories named above provide the primary focus for the majority of the essays that compose the "Approaches" section of this work, other representative pieces of Kafka's short fiction have been included, especially where they help elucidate Kafka's embeddedness in broader literary and cultural contexts. Each of the five essays with which the volume closes, however, provides an interpretive or pedagogical perspective on one of the five focal texts, and these essays are intended to serve teachers as potential models. With regard to the "Materials" section, it is obvious that, given the vast scholarship on Kafka, no claim to completeness can be made. "The Instructor's Library," however, begins with a discussion of bibliographies and reference works that can serve teachers as resource tools to help guide their further studies. While the volume is intended for those who teach Kafka in either German or English, the selection of critical materials favors, wherever possible, works written in English or available in English translation.

Needless to say, without the initiative and effort of numerous individuals, a book such as this one could never take shape. Special recognition must be given to Thomas Barry, who formulated the initial plan for this volume and did much of the groundwork before withdrawing from the project for personal reasons. Because plans for the volume lay idle for some time before I took over editorship and because the original outline required substantial revision and supplementation, this book has had an unusually long gestation period. For that reason I particularly want to thank the early contributors, some of whom have waited several years for their essays to appear, for their patience and understanding. I wish further to express my gratitude to all those who so generously invested their pedagogical creativity and critical energy in the essays that make up the "Approaches" section, as well as to all those colleagues, listed at the end of the volume, who took the time to give detailed answers to the preliminary questionnaires. The "Materials" section relies heavily on their comments, insights, and suggestions.

It seems appropriate to recognize here those individuals who made significant contributions to my development as a teacher and scholar. Special thanks to Anne F. Baecker, my mentor and counselor during my undergraduate years; to Jane K. Brown, Jerry Glenn, Jens Rieckmann, and Frank Ryder for their commitment as graduate teachers and their subsequent collegial support; and finally to my *Doktorvater*, Walter H. Sokel, to whom I dedicate this volume. His pedagogical commitment and scholarly guidance have shaped much more than just my understanding of Kafka. Last but not least, I want to express my gratitude to my wife, Sabine Wilke, who as companion and colleague has supplied endless encouragement and support not only during the preparation of this volume but throughout my career.

Richard T. Gray
University of Washington

Part One

MATERIALS

Editions and Translations

German Editions

Critically edited texts in German for the five stories that form the focus of this volume are relatively reliable in their authenticity since all five texts were published by Kafka himself during his lifetime. To date, the standard edition is the volume *Erzählungen* in Max Brod's edition of the *Gesammelte Werke*, which collects all the short stories whose publication Kafka himself arranged. In the Brod edition the posthumously published stories are gathered in two separate volumes, *Beschreibung eines Kampfes* and *Hochzeitsvorbereitungen auf dem Lande*. Unfortunately, the texts of these stories as printed in the Brod edition are not always fully reliable, and only with the publication of the critical edition of Kafka's complete works, presently being issued by Fischer Verlag under the editorship of Jürgen Born and Malcolm Pasley, will teachers and scholars of Kafka have access to dependable, critically edited texts for all of Kafka's short fiction. As of this writing, however, the volumes of the critical edition that will contain the stories, whether published in Kafka's lifetime or posthumously, have not yet appeared.

In the survey conducted for this book, respondents cited the Fischer paperback editions of Kafka's stories as those most frequently used in the classroom. Most often named was Paul Raabe's edition of the *Sämtliche Erzählungen*, the only book that assembles the entirety of Kafka's short fiction in a single, affordable paperback. Also popular among teachers is the Fischer paperback *Das Urteil und andere Erzählungen*, which gives a good cross section of Kafka's fiction, including all five of the texts accentuated here. Both of these editions have been frequently reprinted, making them easily accessible as well as moderately priced. Teachers must be aware, however, that these editions were published for the German market and hence include no reading aids or other supplementary materials aimed at the needs of North American undergraduates. Consequently, they can be recommended only for advanced students who are fluent readers of German.

A critically edited text of "Das Urteil" ("The Judgment"), which Kafka published three times in slightly different versions, is made available by Gerhard Neumann in his volume containing notes and commentary to this story. Neumann not only lists textual variants but also prints those passages Kafka deleted from the text before publication. The detailed physical description of the manuscript supplied by Neumann gives important clues to the compositional practice Kafka employed during the writing of this central text. The critical apparatus of the volume includes a detailed commentary on the story, a discussion of the biographical and historical contexts that influenced its composition, and an exposition of its relations to the motifs Kafka addressed in "Letter to His Father." In addition, Neumann provides analyses of specific motifs and motific complexes, examines the position of the story vis-à-vis Kafka's oeuvre, and reviews its receptive history. For those who do not read German, portions of Neumann's study have been published in Mark Anderson's *Reading Kafka: Prague, Politics, and the Fin de Siècle*. As a critical tool, Neumann's volume is indispensable for those who teach "The Judgment" in German, especially in upper-division literature courses. Teachers who prefer to use an edited version of "Das Urteil" that provides textual glosses and German-English vocabulary may turn to Robert Spaethling and Eugene Weber's *A Reader in German Literature* or to *Sechs kleine Morde*, by Kimberley Sparks and Constance Kenna.

A surprisingly inexpensive edition of *Die Verwandlung (The Metamorphosis)* is available in the Reclam Universal-Bibliothek. This edition may also be used in conjunction with the companion volume *Erläuterungen und Dokumente*, edited by Peter Beicken. While this supplementary volume, whose notes are keyed by line and page to the Reclam edition of the text, is not specifically intended for non-German readers and thus provides no glosses or vocabulary aids for North American students, it does contain a highly informative commentary and critical apparatus. Beicken documents the text's motific structure and its myriad allusions to the tradition of Western literature, outlines the biographical background against which the story evolved, and details the history of its critical reception. The volume concludes with a collection of brief excerpts from secondary sources that are intended to provide impulses and guidance for classroom discussions. *Die Verwandlung* is also available in a variety of glossed versions edited specifically for use in the classroom. Several of the survey participants expressed a preference for the Norton edition, edited by Marjorie Hoover, commending in particular its availability and the useful German-English vocabulary at the back of the volume. In addition, *Die Verwandlung* has been published in a student edition with notes and vocabulary by Peter Hutchinson. Moreover, this story has been anthologized in readers intended for use by students who require linguistic and literary guidance—for example in Anna Otten's *Meistererzählungen* and in an anthology compiled by Marjorie Hoover, Charles Hoffmann, and Richard Plant.

A critically edited German text of "In der Strafkolonie" ("In the Penal Colony") is supplied in Klaus Wagenbach's commentated edition, which includes textual variants and a history of the story's publication. This volume is supplemented by a chronology of the period in which the story was composed and a historical examination of the institution of penal colonies. For readers of German, Wagenbach's volume provides the essential background to this text. Surprisingly, this story has not yet been made available in a version edited for North American students. This is not the case for "Ein Landarzt" ("A Country Doctor"), which is published and interpreted in Franz Baumer's *Sieben Prosastücke* and also available, glossed and edited, in John Michalski's *Deutsche Dichter und Denker*. A glossed and edited text of "Ein Hungerkünstler" ("A Hunger Artist"), finally, appears in Spaethling and Weber's *Reader*.

Dual-Language Editions

Of the five stories that form the central concern of the present volume, only *The Metamorphosis* and "A Country Doctor" are available in bilingual editions, the latter in Harry Steinhauer's *German Stories/Deutsche Novellen*, the former in book form published by Schocken. Schocken has also issued two dual-language editions of other works by Kafka that may be of general interest to teachers of undergraduates: *Parables and Paradoxes* (short parabolic pieces) and *Letter to His Father*. These volumes present important primary materials that teachers may wish to assign as supplementary or background readings to the stories. *Letter*, for instance, offers significant insights into Kafka's family life, while readings of selected aphorisms and brief parables from *Parables and Paradoxes* may serve as springboards for the interpretation of Kafka's short stories, especially since they often reiterate motifs and structures common to his fiction.

Translations

Kafka's popularity in the English-speaking world has made him a profitable venture for publishers, giving rise to a plethora of English editions of his short fiction. Despite some stiltedness and general inadequacies, the translations by Willa Muir and Edwin Muir have retained their dominance over the past four decades. This situation could change in the not too distant future, since in the wake of German publication of the critical edition of Kafka's complete works, Schocken is planning a new English-language edition that will present fresh or revised translations based on the critically reconstructed versions of the texts. The volume now used most frequently by teachers, however, is the Muirs' translation in Schocken's *The Complete Stories* (also available in a British edition, *The Penguin Complete Short Stories of Franz Kafka*). Those specifying a preference for this edition cited completeness, availability, and reasonable price as its principal virtues. Another popular edition is the collection *"The Penal Colony,"* also published by Schocken, which assembles the Muir translations of selected stories, including all five of the texts highlighted in the present volume. The Schocken edition *Dearest Father: Stories and Other Writings* also was cited by several respondents as the edition of choice. Other teachers favor the Pocket edition *The Basic Kafka* (which includes an introductory essay by Erich Heller), primarily because it is remarkably inexpensive. But while it does offer a wide selection of Kafka's texts, it does not represent a complete edition of Kafka's short fiction; indeed, some of the seminal stories are notably absent.

For those seeking alternatives to the Muir translations for the five texts principally under discussion here, a number of options are available. Malcolm Pasley, who has devoted considerable energy to textual scholarship of Kafka and is one of the editors of the critical edition, has translated a collection titled *Shorter Works of Franz Kafka.* His excellent translation of "The Judgment," moreover, is printed in Angel Flores's *The Problem of "The Judgment."* The early translation of *The Metamorphosis* by A. L. Lloyd is out of print, but one respondent, who believes it to be more accurate in places than currently available translations, recommends putting it on reserve for students. Most survey participants who teach *The Metamorphosis,* however, prefer Stanley Corngold's Bantam edition; aside from supplying a superb translation completed by a critic who has devoted much scholarship to Kafka in general and this text in particular, the Bantam edition also includes notes and provocative critical materials that are helpful classroom aids. For an alternative or supplemental translation of "In the Penal Colony," respondents recommend Eugene Jolas's version, which appeared in the *Partisan Review* in 1941. Both "A Country Doctor" and "A Hunger Artist" are obtainable in translations by Steinhauer, the former in the dual-language edition cited above and the latter in his *Twelve German Novellas.*

Kafka is represented in the widely used *Norton Anthology of World Masterpieces* by the Corngold translation of *The Metamorphosis. The Norton Anthology of Short Fiction* includes both this story and "A Hunger Artist." All five of the texts addressed in the present volume have been anthologized so frequently in English translation that to list each publication separately here would be impossible. However, the anthologies containing these and other texts by Kafka are cited by Marie Luise Caputo-Mayr and Julius Herz in their bibliography of Kafka's primary works. They devote to each story a separate entry that lists every publication until 1980, both in the original German and in translation. A thorough alphabetical index, which supplies both German and English titles of Kafka's works, makes this bibliographical compendium especially easy to use.

The Instructor's Library

Bibliographies and Reference Works

Kafka studies have profited substantially from a number of outstanding bibliographical and reference works, which also represent significant tools for teachers of undergraduates. In 1961 Harry Järv published the first substantial bibliography of secondary literature on Kafka, a compilation that, now dated, has been superseded by the Caputo-Mayr–Herz bibliography of secondary literature. This catalog, which covers the years 1955–85, is divided into five sections: bibliographies, essay collections, dissertations, articles, and book-length studies. Since it is supplemented by an index that cross-references Kafka's individual texts with the bibliographical entries, one can easily track down the body of secondary literature relevant to any single story. The functionality of this reference work is heightened by the inclusion of brief commentaries (in German) describing the focus and thrust of each work cited. An updated second edition of this indispensable bibliography, covering material published through 1992, is forthcoming. The authors are also working on an English-language version of their bibliography that will incorporate a selection of the secondary sources with English commentaries. A third bibliography, compiled by Angel Flores, is neither as up-to-date nor as complete as that of Caputo-Mayr and Herz, but because it was written with an English-speaking audience in mind, it also represents an important reference tool for teachers of undergraduates. Covering the years 1908 to 1976, this volume contains both a list of publications by Kafka, including English translations, and an alphabetically organized bibliography of secondary materials. Its usefulness is enhanced by the inclusion of two cross-reference indices: one summarizes background and biographical materials, and the other lists under a separate heading for each of Kafka's texts the critical interpretations, including relevant pages in book-length studies covering his entire oeuvre. The Flores bibliography will probably have outlived its usefulness once Caputo-Mayr and Herz's English-language edition has appeared. To keep abreast of more recent publications, one can follow the bibliographical updates that appear regularly in the *Journal of the Kafka Society of America*. The Caputo-Mayr–Herz bibliography of primary materials, finally, supplies all the necessary information about German and English publications and reprints of Kafka's writings through 1980.

For teachers who read German, Peter Beicken's *Franz Kafka: Eine kritische Einführung in die Forschung* provides an essential introduction to the primary currents of Kafka interpretation. In addition to informative chapters on the general reception of Kafka, the hermeneutical problems specific to his texts, and the major lines of interpretation, Beicken includes segments treating the directions characteristic for the interpretation of the major texts, including sections on each of the five stories highlighted in the present volume. Another valuable reference tool is Hartmut Binder's *Kafka-Kommentar zu sämtlichen Erzählungen*, which supplies background information and textual commentaries on each of Kafka's stories. Numerous respondents also named the two-volume *Kafka-Handbuch*, edited by Binder, as an indispensable reference guide. These volumes collect critical summaries of issues that have dominated the history of Kafka research, written by some of the world's leading Kafka scholars. The first volume contains an extensive cultural-historical description of Bohemia during the Austro-Hungarian monarchy; an examination of the history, sociology, and culture of Kafka's Prague;

and a detailed, authoritative Kafka biography written by Binder himself, the undisputed expert on the biographical facts of Kafka's life and their relations to his fiction. The first half of the second volume comprises a kind of critical survey of Kafka's work and its reception, including examinations of language and metaphor, narratological characteristics, and typical structures and forms. The second half, in which an extensive chapter is devoted to Kafka's short fiction, covers each of his works separately, tracing the fundamental interpretive positions and controversies. Each section includes a bibliography of secondary materials relevant to the topic addressed, and the entire work concludes with an index that references names and the titles of Kafka's works. Unfortunately, there are no equivalent reference tools available for those who do not read German. Teachers interested in a brief outline of the trends of Kafka criticism may turn to H. R. Reiss's survey. For some individual texts, good bibliographies and summaries are available. Those who teach *The Metamorphosis* may refer to the bibliography in Corngold's *The Commentators' Despair*; for "The Judgment," one can rely on Angel Flores's collection *The Problem of "The Judgment"*; for "A Hunger Artist," Gerhard Dünnhaupt's survey of criticism is recommended.

Background and Biographical Studies

The wide-ranging relationships between Kafka and individual writers or philosophers clearly cannot be documented here, and several survey participants remarked that the best introduction to Kafka's intellectual background can be provided by general cultural histories of Europe from 1850 to the First World War. For those seeking a somewhat narrower focus, William Johnston's superb intellectual history of Austria from 1848 to 1938 portrays the cultural-intellectual environment that helped breed Kafka's thought. Julius Herz's "Franz Kafka and Austria: National Background and Ethnic Identity" supplies a brief introduction to this sociocultural context, while Wolfdietrich Rasch's essay on turn-of-the-century literature provides insights into the literary scene in which Kafka participated. Because Kafka's fiction has extensive connections to the literature and philosophy of the Austrian *fin de siècle*, Carl Schorske's celebrated book on Vienna in this period portrays well the cultural background to Kafka's thought. Those interested in information about the intellectual and artistic atmosphere of Austria at the turn of the century should also consult *Wittgenstein's Vienna*, by Allan Janik and Stephen Toulmin. This extraordinary intellectual history elucidates the close bonds that linked diverse areas of cultural production in Austria at this time, citing the influence of such thinkers as Ernst Mach and Karl Kraus. Kafka, one must remember, was in tune with the cultural events of Austria throughout his life. Walter Sokel's *The Writer in Extremis*, which sketches the intellectual and artistic currents of German literary expressionism, also outlines a significant literary-historical context for the understanding of

Kafka's fiction. Kafka's relation to expressionism is likewise treated in an essay by Paul Raabe and in a book-length study by Walter Falk. Readers of English interested in this subject will want to turn to the chapter entitled "Kafka as Expressionist" in Corngold's *Franz Kafka: The Necessity of Form* (250–88). Readers of German can refer as well to Silvio Vietta and Hans-Georg Kemper's volume on expressionism, which includes an informative analysis of "The Judgment" that orients this story within the context of this broader aesthetic movement.

Evelyn Beck's study of the impact of the Yiddish theater on Kafka provides a further significant context for an understanding of structure and style of his fiction. The extensive relations between Kafka and the broader traditions of Western literature are documented in detail in Bert Nagel's study of Kafka and world literature. Kafka's relation to the specifics of Prague's sociohistorical context, especially to the role of its Jews, is presented in Christoph Stölzl's *Kafkas böses Böhmen*, the main points of which are reiterated in the same author's contribution to the historical section of the *Kafka-Handbuch* (Binder 1: 40–100). Wagenbach's biography of the young Kafka also supplies basic information. Mark Anderson's 1989 collection *Reading Kafka* contains, among other valuable materials, an entire section on the topic of Kafka and Prague as well as English translations of segments from Stölzl's and Wagenbach's studies. Eduard Goldstücker's essay "On Prague as Background" can serve as a brief introduction to Kafka's Prague. Useful in this context as well, especially because of its numerous photographs, is Johann Bauer's *Kafka and Prague*. Marthe Robert's monograph *As Lonely as Franz Kafka* concentrates on the relations between the environment of Prague and Kafka's fiction. Those wishing to examine more closely Prague as historical and cultural context, especially with regard to its German-speaking Jews, will want to consult Ritchie Robertson's study of Kafka, Gary Cohen's excellent history of the Germans in Prague, and Josef Fraenkel's collection of essays on and by the Jews of Austria. Those interested in the broader conflicts of European Jewry may want to turn to Sander Gilman's study *Jewish Self-Hatred*. Margot Norris's essay on Kafka and the problem of mimesis analyzes intellectual-historical relations between Kafka's art and the thought of Charles Darwin and Friedrich Nietzsche, and Kenneth Hughes's collection of Marxist criticism on Kafka provides a background for those interested in connections between Kafka and Marxian social thought.

The peculiarities of Kafka's existence in the so-called multiple ghetto of the German-speaking Jew in Prague have from the outset greatly influenced our understanding of his literature. It is precisely because this biographical perspective seems to be so informative and elucidating, however, that it threatens to circumscribe Kafka's fiction within limited interpretive confines. As I have argued in the essay "Biography as Criticism in Kafka Studies," there is good reason not to immobilize Kafka's texts in this hermeneutical straitjacket. Especially for undergraduate students, biographical explanation provides an easy way of circumventing and repressing the often threatening openness and interpretive uncertainty produced by the intrinsic polyvalence of Kafka's texts. Teachers should keep this caveat in mind when applying biographical approaches to Kafka in the classroom.

Kafka was his own first (auto)biographer; hence the most intimate introduction to his life is afforded by his own diaries and letters, all of which are readily available in German and English in relatively inexpensive paperback volumes. Most instructive for an understanding of Kafka's sociopsychological situation is *Letter to His Father*, easily accessible in the Schocken dual-language edition. Heinz Politzer's *Das Kafka-Buch* assembles in a convenient and inexpensive collection many of Kafka's most insightful self-reflections and observations from letters and diaries, juxtaposing them with some of his shorter fictional works. For example, Politzer places "Das Urteil" adjacent to Kafka's first epistolary contacts with Felice Bauer and the author's own critical commentaries on this story recorded in his diary. For English readers, Nahum Glatzer's collection *I Am a Memory Come Alive* provides similar excerpts from Kafka's life documents. Those interested in Kafka's relationship with Felice Bauer, documented in his *Letters to Felice*, will find a sensitive analysis of this correspondence in Elias Canetti's *Kafka's Other Trial*. Kafka's aphorisms, available in English in the Schocken volume *"The Great Wall of China,"* also provide insights into his themes and the mechanisms of his literary imagination; the aphorisms may also be applied as productive pedagogical tools when examined in conjunction with particular stories. When employing Kafka's autobiographical reflections, however, it is important to recognize, as Walter Sokel has pointed out, that Kafka was by no means a confessionalist poet in the traditional sense and that, consequently, the life he portrays in his letters and diaries is subject to calculated literary self-stylization (*Tragik und Ironie* 10).

The biography by Max Brod, Kafka's intimate companion and literary executor, is still cited by the survey respondents as an authoritative source for knowledge about Kafka as man and artist (and it is available in English as well as German). At the same time, there is good reason to approach some aspects of Brod's Kafka, especially his sketch of Kafka's so-called religious personality, with some skepticism. Further testimony by friends and contemporaries of Kafka is obtainable in English translation in the section entitled "Recollections" of Angel Flores's *The Kafka Problem*. While Gustav Janouch's *Conversations with Kafka* is also often cited as a source of fascinating memoirs that capture reflections on and by Kafka, here too one should exercise a certain amount of caution. According to the noted Czech Germanist Eduard Goldstücker, although Janouch's impressions of Kafka may be accurate, those statements that Janouch attributes to him are probably either vague approximations or wholly apocryphal (238). Wagenbach's monograph on Kafka in the Rowohlt series, which is structured around Kafka's self-reflections and profusely supplemented by photographs, is the standard biographical study in German. Binder's somewhat academic, occasionally pedantic biography, which forms the bulk of the first volume of his *Kafka-Handbuch*, has been republished as a separate paperback under the title *Franz Kafka: Leben und Persönlichkeit*.

It is ample testimony to the fascination Kafka has held for English-speaking audiences that several major biographical studies have been written in English. Among the best known, Ernst Pawel's sensible and sympathetic biography finds more resonance among teachers than does Ronald Hayman's, which one respondent describes as "reliable, although not perspicacious." Moreover, Pawel's work is more comprehensive, shedding light not only on Kafka's religious background but also on his sociopolitical environment. Frederick Karl's lengthy biography, the most recent to appear in English, is the closest approximation to Binder's dry thoroughness available in English. *A Hesitation before Birth*, Peter Mailloux's biography, tends to stylize Kafka's life (as the title would indicate). The substantial Kafka biography by the Italian Pietro Citati has also recently appeared in English translation.

Critical Studies

Three major investigations of Kafka's entire oeuvre have remained the "standard" scholarly works for several decades, and they are consequently named almost unanimously by survey participants as central to the study of Kafka: Wilhelm Emrich's *Franz Kafka*, Politzer's *Franz Kafka: Parable and Paradox*, and Sokel's *Franz Kafka: Tragik und Ironie*. Emrich's study orients Kafka's literature at the rupture between classicism and modernism, and he finds in Kafka's protagonists the prototype of "modern" human beings who exist in a world that lacks all binding universalities. Politzer argues that paradox, as the symptom of an absurd, wholly secularized world, is the principal theme of Kafka's texts; in articulating this idea, Politzer helped introduce into Kafka studies the now widely held view that it is precisely the lack of any unitary, conclusive message in Kafka's stories which in fact constitutes their primary message. Sokel relies heavily on psychological perspectives, arguing that the struggle for power, prefigured in the conflict between Kafka and his father, forms the prototype for all Kafka's texts. Sokel perceives a gradual shift in the treatment of this theme over the course of Kafka's life, moving from tragic portrayal in stories such as "The Judgment" and *The Metamorphosis* to a more distant, ironical stance in the late, parabolic stories. The primary strength of Sokel's investigation is its ability to link developments in Kafka's characteristic thematics to changes in literary structure and form. Unfortunately, unlike the other two seminal studies, Sokel's monograph is not available in English. To acquaint students with his ideas, teachers not fluent in German must therefore rely on *Franz Kafka*, his brief monograph in the Columbia Essays on Modern Writers series, or turn to any of his numerous scholarly articles written in English (some of the most important are documented in the list of works cited). Readers of German will also profit greatly from Dieter Hasselblatt's and Jürgen Kobs's books on Kafka's fiction, as well as from Dietrich Krusche's succinct study *Kafka und Kafka-Deutung*, which concentrates on the communicative function of Kafka's fictional structures and their relation to the scope of his critical reception. Gerhard Kurz's *Traumschrecken* offers an existential examination of Kafka's fiction. Henry Sussman's *Franz Kafka: Geometrician of Metaphor* affords insightful and highly accessible deconstructive readings of Kafka's texts. Also informed by recent developments in literary theory—for teachers who seek to pursue contemporary directions in Kafka criticism—are two noteworthy critical studies of Kafka written in English: Corngold's *Franz Kafka: The Necessity of Form* and Clayton Koelb's *Kafka's Rhetoric*. Survey participants also cited James Rolleston's and Erich Heller's book-length studies as especially helpful to undergraduate teachers using English-language sources.

While the above-cited works tend to have a scholarly, academic orientation, a number of more-general critical studies also may serve as introductions to Kafka's work. Ronald Gray's monograph was named often by survey respondents, one of whom singled out Gray's opening chapter as a succinct survey of critical approaches to Kafka. While Martin Greenberg's book on Kafka and modern literature is somewhat dated, his discussion of the dream texture of Kafka's fiction is still quite relevant and revealing. Kurt Fickert's study provides a useful introduction to Kafka's life and art, as does Sokel's Columbia monograph. For readers of German, Ludwig Dietz's introduction to Kafka's fiction affords a convenient and compact critical summary.

Many survey participants cited various collections of critical essays on Kafka as good practical introductions to the problems of his fiction and the principal questions that have concerned Kafka scholars. The essays assembled in *The Kafka Debate*, edited by Angel Flores, and in *Franz Kafka Today*, edited by Flores and Homer Swander, not only provide an excellent cross section of critical views but also open up perspectives on the historical evolution of Kafka scholarship over a period of nearly three decades. Numerous respondents stressed the breadth of J. P. Stern's anthology *The World of Franz Kafka*, and one maintained that it is "the best conceived anthology for beginning teachers." Leo Hamalian's collection also deserves mention, although some respondents compared it unfavorably with the compilation of essays edited by Ronald Gray. Of interest as well is the special Franz Kafka double issue of *Modern Austrian Literature*, which gathers a series of very diverse essays on Kafka written in both German and English; the Kafka centenary issue of the *Literary Review*; and Franz Kuna's semicentenary anthology. The most recent publications of this nature in English are

Harold Bloom's volume of Kafka scholarship in the Modern Critical Views series and the Critical Essays on World Literature volume edited by Ruth Gross, both of which offer excellent overviews of the myriad critical perspectives on Kafka's fiction. Bloom's anthology, in particular, assembles in English some of the most important essays on Kafka published in the last forty years, including Walter Benjamin's "Some Reflections on Kafka" and Theodor Adorno's "Notes on Kafka." Two essays highly recommended for a thorough understanding of Kafka's short fiction are likewise reissued here: Dorrit Cohn's "Kafka's Eternal Present" and Alwin Baum's "Parable as Paradox in Kafka's *Erzählungen*." Those interested in examining the perspectives on Kafka revealed by the various directions of contemporary critical theory will want to consult Alan Udoff's collection of essays. The most significant assemblage of critical essays in German is the Kafka volume in the Wege der Forschung series, edited by Politzer.

Certain critical works afford guidance tailored generally to Kafka's short fiction or specifically to one of the five stories that take center stage in this volume. Above all, teachers will want to consult Allen Thiher's monograph on Kafka's short fiction, the only critical work in English that treats Kafka's short stories as a whole. Peter Heller's essay "Kafka as Story-teller" provides a brief and useful introduction to Kafka's position in the history of Western fiction. Martin Walser's and Friedrich Beissner's essays on narrative form in Kafka, while they have been superseded in part by more recent investigations, still supply important insights into the peculiarities of Kafka's fiction. Roy Pascal's study *Kafka's Narrators: A Study of His Stories and Sketches* represents the most detailed English-language account of narrative form in Kafka. Those who read German will also want to consult Clemens Heselhaus's early typology of Kafka's fictional modes, as well as Heinz Hillmann's monograph on this subject. The relevant sections of Binder's *Kafka-Handbuch* also give good summaries of the issues of narrative form and structure in Kafka's stories.

Regarding scholarly essays on individual stories, one will find ample critical material in English on "The Judgment" in Angel Flores's collection *The Problem of "The Judgment."* The innovative narrative structure of this "breakthrough" story is treated in detail by John Ellis, and Kate Flores explicates the autobiographical dimensions. Those teaching *The Metamorphosis* should consult Corngold's essay "The Structure of Kafka's *Metamorphosis*," as well as his extensive bibliography, both found in his book *The Commentators' Despair*. In addition, his Bantam edition of this text includes a selection of excerpts from the most important critical essays on *Metamorphosis*. Of the numerous critical essays that treat this text, two standouts are David Eggenschwiler's " 'Die Verwandlung,' Freud, and the Chains of Odysseus" and Sokel's "From Marx to Myth," the former of which is reprinted in Bloom's anthology. Another excellent source of critical readings of this story is the collection entitled *The Metamorphosis* in the Chelsea House Modern Critical Interpretations series. Teachers of "In the Penal Colony" should consult the documentation supplied by Wagenbach in his edition of the text (Kafka, *In der Strafkolonie*). The essays on this story by E. R. Davey, Dale Kramer, and Arnold Weinstein provide good general introductions in English. Those interested in pursuing the psychological issues broached by this story and "A Hunger Artist" will profit from Margot Norris's essay on sadism and masochism. An indispensable tool for those teaching "A Country Doctor" is Hans Hiebel's critical commentary, which details the literary, biographical, and social contexts relevant for the story; provides an analysis of structure and symbols as well as a detailed textual commentary; and gives a complete biography of criticism. Gregory Triffitt's examination of the entire group of tales Kafka published under the collective title *Ein Landarzt* offers further insight by investigating the cotextuality of the stories joined together in this collection. Cohn's essay on "A Country Doctor" and Kafka's other first-person narratives is required reading for those concerned with questions of narrative stance. No collection of criticism on "A Hunger Artist" is yet available, so teachers should look to the essays by Richard Sheppard and Harry Steinhauer. Breon Mitchell's essay discussing Kafka's text in the context of the historical phenomenon of hunger artists is also strongly recommended.

Finally, readers should study the interpretations of each of these texts offered in the concluding section of this volume. Further references to secondary material for all these stories can be found in the bibliographies mentioned above.

Didactic Approaches

Because Kafka's fiction has become a standard part of the literature curriculum in German schools, a considerable body of didactically oriented materials has been developed; for North American undergraduate instructors who teach Kafka in German, these works often make good resource tools for pedagogical approaches and methodologies. Karlheinz Fingerhut's two-volume collection, which is divided into a student book and a teacher's guide, concentrates on documents providing a historical and cultural understanding of Kafka's stories. Martin Pfeifer's collection *Franz Kafka: Erzählungen mit Materialien* likewise supplies historical materials for the interpretive understanding of Kafka's stories. Richard Meurer provides a didactically oriented interpretation of selected stories, as do Albrecht Weber, Carsten Schlingmann, and Gert Kleinschmidt in their book. The latter volume, which includes discussions of "Urteil," *Verwandlung*, and "Landarzt," is particularly valuable. The recent volume by Rüdiger Scholz and Hans-Peter Hermann explores creative approaches to the use of literature in the classroom, based on examples drawn from Kafka. The authors emphasize stimulation of the students' imagination, urging teachers to help them expand on and recreate Kafka's literary visions in their own fantasies.

Student Readings

Background and Biographical Studies

For those teaching Kafka in literature courses taught in German, survey participants recommend three works that both provide adequate literary-historical and cultural background and are written at a level of German manageable for undergraduates: Hermann Glaser's *Wege der deutschen Literatur*; *Geschichte der deutschen Literatur*, by Willy Grabert, Arnot Mulot, and Helmuth Nürnberger; and Claude Hill's *2000 Jahre deutscher Kultur*. For those teaching Kafka in translation, survey participants generally recommend that one refer students to a general European cultural history or to a history of German literature, depending on the context and aims of the course. One may also employ literary memoirs such as Stefan Zweig's memorable *The World of Yesterday* to evoke for students the cultural and political atmosphere in which Kafka and his fiction evolved. Teachers may approach Kafka's place in literary and intellectual history by examining the perspectives on his work held by other modern writers. In this context essays by Auden, Borges, Camus, Nabokov, Roth, and Updike, for example, can make for stimulating reading and provide a provocative basis for classroom discussions. One respondent reports considerable success teaching Kafka against the backdrop of Max Horkheimer's sociocultural essay "Art and Mass Culture," which gives an insightful analysis of particular reflexes of modern civilization that also manifest themselves in Kafka's fiction. Those who wish to emphasize the patriarchal family and the power structures of bourgeois society will profit from reading Kafka's *Letter to His Father* and "The Judgment" in tandem with Horkheimer's essay "Authority and the Family."

Letter to His Father also serves as the best introduction to Kafka's biographical situation when used alongside the autobiographical reflections recorded in his diaries and letters. One teacher especially recommends requiring students to read Kafka's description of the creative process that produced "The Judgment," documented in the diary entry dated 23 September 1912 (*Diaries, 1910–1913* 275–76). Particularly since Kafka himself notes that while writing this story he had "thoughts of Freud," studying this passage in relation either to Freud's description of the creative process in "The Relation of the Poet to Day-dreaming" or to the mechanisms of the dream language examined in *The Interpretation of Dreams* may prove pedagogically rewarding. As for biographies, respondents most frequently name those by Brod, Hayman, and Pawel as the best available in English for undergraduates interested in a detailed examination of Kafka's life; Wagenbach's Rowohlt monograph is the most commonly cited German source appropriate for student reading.

Critical Studies

Many participants in the survey stress that undergraduates are in no way prepared to confront the subtleties and complexities of Kafka scholarship, so these teachers are reluctant to subject their students to the abstractions and intricacies common to critical studies of the author's work. Nevertheless, some of the secondary sources referred to above in "The Instructor's Library" are fit for student use. Some respondents cite Politzer's *Parable and Paradox* as appropriate for sophisticated undergraduates, and one believes that the "Discourse on Method" (1–22) contained in his initial chapter will supply students with a succinct introduction to the problems inherent in reading and interpreting Kafka. Sokel's Columbia monograph is also appropriate for sophisticated undergraduates. Of the general introductions to Kafka's work, the book by Ronald Gray is frequently assigned, especially the chapter reviewing interpretive directions of Kafka studies. Meno Spann's volume on Kafka in Twayne's World Authors Series is also geared to student readers, as are Thiher's book on Kafka's short fiction and Anthony Thorlby's guide to Kafka. Some teachers assign or recommend to their students selected essays from one or more of the anthologies of criticism listed above. The collections by Ronald Gray, Stern, and Bloom are often named as the most useful for students, but the Angel Flores anthologies deserve mention as well. With regard to critical essays on individual stories, Flores's volume specifically on "The Judgment" offers many readings suitable to undergraduates, as does the selection of excerpts from essays on *The Metamorphosis* compiled by Corngold and appended to his Bantam translation. John Hibberd's student guide to *Die Verwandlung* provides a close reading of the text but otherwise supplies no critical materials. Angel Flores's *Explain to Me Some Stories of Kafka* offers texts and interpretations appropriate for students studying "The Judgment," *The Metamorphosis*, and "A Hunger Artist." For the other texts, those essays listed in the "Critical Studies" section above are also generally accessible to student readers.

Aids to Teaching

As a rule, the survey respondents were skeptical about the usefulness of audiovisual aids when teaching Kafka's literature, and some even consider diverting students' attention away from Kafka's texts themselves pedagogically problematic. Some teachers, however, feel that such materials help make this author and his literature more readily approachable for students. Those who wish to invoke the atmosphere of Kafka's Prague can turn to a large number of illustrated books as well. Klaus Wagenbach deserves credit for having retrieved and published numerous photographs of Kafka, his family and friends, and the localities in Prague where he lived and worked. These pictures are published in Wagenbach's Kafka biographies as well as in his *Franz Kafka: Pictures of a Life*. Jirí Grusa's commendable *Franz Kafka aus Prag* similarly employs photographs to chronicle Kafka's life in Prague, as does Hartmut Binder and Jan Parik's *Kafka: Ein Leben in Prag*, which juxtaposes pictures of Kafka with Parik's photographs of contemporary Prague. Another instructional tool that can help one recreate the atmosphere in which Kafka's writing evolved is the film version of Gustav Meyrink's *Der Golem*, which not only was filmed in Prague but also, many feel, evokes that mysterious atmospheric quality characteristic of Kafka's fiction. Rotraut Hackermüller's pictorial study, which follows Kafka's life from the diagnosis of his tuberculosis in 1917 until his death at the sanatorium in Kierling in 1924, also is an excellent source of documentary material.

Some of the participants in the survey draw on reproductions of expressionist and surrealist paintings to fashion a broader aesthetic context in which to orient Kafka's fiction. The artistic visions of such painters as George Grosz, Wassily Kandinsky, Paul Klee, Oskar Kokoschka, Edvard Munch, and Picasso, for example, lend themselves well to comparisons with Kafka's fictional world. In this context it is important to recall that Kafka himself—in this respect similar to numerous other expressionist artists—was not only active as a creative writer but also had ambitions as a graphic artist. While most of Kafka's drawings have unfortunately not yet been published, some are reproduced in Brod's *Über Franz Kafka* (395–403), and teachers can fruitfully use these sketches to initiate classroom discussions of Kafka's aesthetic sensibilities and his view of modern human beings. Those interested in pursuing more closely this aspect of Kafka's artistry can consult Wolfgang Rothe's remarks on Kafka as a graphic artist, published in Binder's *Kafka-Handbuch* (2: 562–68).

That Kafka's literature has in turn inspired works by numerous graphic artists bears testimony to his seminal position in modernist aesthetics as a whole. Teachers may consider approaching Kafka through some of these artistic interpretations. For example, Kafka's stories have engendered numerous illustrations. Noteworthy here are Hans Fronius's many lithographs, especially those that accompany "A Country Doctor." Claire Van Vliet has also produced lithographs to this story, as well as to some of Kafka's short parables. Other striking illustrations to Kafka are Rolf Escher's etchings for *The Metamorphosis* and C. O. Bartning's lithographs for "The Judgment" and *The Metamorphosis*. Of interest as well are the numerous portraits of

Kafka himself that have been produced by various graphic artists. Rothe's *Kafka in der Kunst* and Richard Hiepe's volume *Bilder und Graphik zu Werken von Franz Kafka* are excellent resources for those who wish to employ such materials in the classroom. Binder's *Kafka-Handbuch* (2: 841–51) also includes a thorough section with bibliographical information, valuable for teachers who seek more information about the resonance of Kafka's literature in graphic art.

In the category of films, teachers may choose from a wide spectrum of possibilities. Documentaries such as *The Trials of Franz Kafka*, *Kafka and His Work*, *The World of Mr. K.*, and *In Search of "K,"* for example, are available from the German Information Service and the Goethe Institute. Several television documentaries have been produced in German and in English, and interested teachers may consult the *Kafka-Handbuch* for titles (2: 877–78). With regard to the historical and aesthetic context of Kafka's texts, one can turn to expressionist films by such directors as George Pabst and F. W. Murnau, even to the early films of Fritz Lang. An essay in this collection deals specifically with the use of Robert Wiene's *The Cabinet of Dr. Caligari* in conjunction with Kafka's short fiction. Of course, there are also numerous film versions of Kafka texts available for screening in the classroom, the most famous of which is without doubt Orson Welles's filming of *The Trial*. Of interest to those who wish to evoke the atmosphere of Kafka's texts in visual images are two films created by the Zweites Deutsches Fernsehen, one of *The Castle* and one of *The Metamorphosis*. *The Castle* is also available in English in a BBC production. Further references to film documentaries and screen versions of Kafka's texts may be found in the *Kafka-Handbuch* (2: 825–41). The film *Kafka*, starring Jeremy Irons, is available on video.

Finally, teachers may wish to explore using recordings of performers reading Kafka's texts. The most significant of numerous available recordings is certainly Lotte Lenya's reading of several Kafka stories in the Muir translations. "Ein Landarzt," read by Heinz Moog, is also available, and some teachers may like the radio version of *Der Prozess*, read by the famous German actor Gustav Grundgens (an interesting historical document in its own right).

NOTE

In the essays that follow, English-language quotations from Kafka's short fiction, unless otherwise credited, are from the Schocken edition of *The Complete Stories*, abbreviated as *CS*.

Part Two

APPROACHES

Kafka and Modernism

Walter H. Sokel

A review of a recent biography of Kafka carried this title: "He (Kafka) Found Himself Transformed to a Giant Modernist" (Hafrey)—the latest proof that critical discussion of literary modernism has generally included Kafka. He has been ranked among the "high" or "classical" modernists (Quinones 18), though any discussion of his relation to modernism must, of course, be preceded by the question, What was modernism?

The term *modernism* was first used in Anglo-American criticism in the late 1920s (Faulkner viii). By 1960, when Harry Levin's impassioned "necrologue" on modernism appeared, the use of the term was already well established. It denotes the wave of experimentation in the arts in general, and literature in particular, that agitated the first half of the twentieth century. With mock precision, Virginia Woolf set the date for its beginning: " [o]n or about December 1910' " (Bradbury and McFarlane 33).

The concept of "the modern," however, as the revolutionary and unprecedented in the arts, long antedates the term *modernism*. It goes back to the French poet Charles Baudelaire, who invoked it in the middle of the nineteenth century. With Baudelaire, who in turn was decisively influenced by Edgar Allan Poe in this regard, the term *modern* acquired a meaning quite different from the merely modish or contemporary, with which *modern* had hitherto been synonymous. Henceforth *modern*, as applied to art and literature, came to designate a deliberate and programmatic rupture with all preceding art, a revolutionary turn in aesthetics and poetics.

This break with tradition implied two somewhat different yet related tendencies. One was the inoculation of art with the bacillus of capitalist-industrial modernity, which serious art had until then tried to ignore. In this respect, modernism converged, to a significant extent, with the contemporary movement of realism. The two trends united in their thematic emphasis on modern urban life, highlighting not only its banality, sordidness, and hypocrisy but also the enormous broadening of experience and sensation its technological advances betokened. Furnishings and sceneries of realism and modernism were often indistinguishable, and the boundaries between the two movements were extremely porous. An outstanding example of their overlapping are the works of the novelist Gustave Flaubert. A pioneering figure in the development of consistent realism, he was also, together with Baudelaire, a fountainhead of modernism. Kafka took Flaubert as his model and, like the French author, placed his narratives in the locales of contemporary bourgeois and petty-bourgeois life, especially during his early and middle period, in works such as "The Judgment," *The Metamorphosis*, and *The Trial*.

In its purpose, however, modernism sharply diverged from realism. Realism extended the parameters of art toward contemporary life at its most banal and uninspiring, to record it, to present the "real truth" of life, free from the idealization inherent in traditional "high" art. Modernism performed the same movement but aimed to "create the sensation of the new" (Abrams 422). It sought a radical extension of the aesthetic dimension by exploring the possibilities of the ugly, the grotesque, the bizarre, to shake art loose from inherited restrictions.

A second tendency characterizing modernism involves the notion of the autonomy of art, whose roots go much farther back than Poe and Baudelaire. They lie in the eighteenth century: in Rousseau and Diderot, in Herder and Romanticism, and particularly in the philosophy of Kant. The theory of the autonomy of art is part of the general emancipatory movement, called the Enlightenment, that sought to free humankind from the unquestioned rule of authority and unreasoning obedience to tradition. Its aim was that self-government, that autonomy, by which human beings give themselves the laws according to which they wish to live, rather than uncritically accept what tradition and authority decree. Autonomous art is the extension into the aesthetic realm of the emancipatory idea of the Enlightenment. Kant, in his *Critique of Judgment* (1790), was the first to give systematic foundation to its theory (Sokel, *Writer* 9). The Romantics, with profound modifications, continued the call for an autonomous art, but Baudelaire was the artist who made it the foundation of the aesthetics that was to inform modernism. Baudelaire held that art has no purpose beyond itself (Abrams 130). It is autotelic. It has no obligation. It should consider itself free from the ancillary relation to nature and society to which it was consigned by traditional aesthetics, both in the Aristotelian doctrine of mimesis and the representation of nature and in the Horatian demand that art be morally useful as well as entertaining. In protest against both traditions, Baudelaire called teaching, truth, and morality the "heresies" of poetry (Abrams 130). Stéphane Mallarmé, following Baudelaire, claimed that only "reportage," not "literature" proper, aims to "narrate, instruct, even to describe" (Abrams 134). Literature should rid itself of the duty to represent reality or to deliver messages—moral, philosophical, or otherwise. It is beyond good and evil, as it is beyond true and false. The ultimate objective of autotelic art came to be called absolute, nonrepresentational, nonobjective, or abstract art. Flaubert's wish-dream was to write a book without content, "a book about nothing" (Bradbury and McFarlane 25).

Autotelic art rarely went to such extremes. Most essential in modernist aesthetics, as begun by Baudelaire, was the conviction that art is not primarily a representation but a presentation, not the imitation of the actual world but the composition of a created world. The work had to obey no logic other than that imposed by its own expressive process. An artist would use elements of mimetic referentiality to the actual world not to offer a recognizable portrait of that world but to play their part in the composition of the work.

This idea, of a created rather than a represented world, does not imply formlessness; rather, form springs entirely from the work. The modernist critic Herbert Read called this concept "organic form," which is "self-chosen, inherent in the work, not imported from outside" (Faulkner 19). Internal function rather than relation to external factors became the decisive criterion for the elements of the work. Many of them were referential, borrowed from external reality, which imparted to the work echoes of the natural world. For Baudelaire, however, the point was to utilize these echoes to create a "counterworld," an "antinature," a composition that would compete with and constitute a superior alternative to the existing world. For this purpose, the poetic imagination "decomposes all of [natural] creation; then it gathers and organizes the parts according to laws springing from the innermost ground of the soul, and produces with them a new world" (Friedrich 41).[1] Creation might more properly be called transformation or recomposition. In the distortion and deformation of elements of the natural world, Baudelaire saw the "power" of the creative imagination at work. That power manifested itself by its refusal to be bound by plausibility and habitual expectation.

This transformative operation of the imagination on elements of the empirical world closely parallels what Freud called "the work of the dream" ("Traumarbeit"). In dreams, too, the individual elements come from the empirical world but are deformed and transformed according to rules unknown to the dreamer's consciousness. Each dream element, even though taken from waking reality, functions according not to the rules of that reality but to the "thought" that the dream seeks to express. Independent of Freud's *Interpretation of Dreams*, the Swedish dramatist August Strindberg, under the spell of Nietzsche, applied the logic of the dream to the writing of his plays *To Damascus* (1898) and *A Dream Play* (1902), followed by others, and thus founded the line within modernism that came to be called expressionism. Kafka, by the time he wrote "The Judgment" (1912), the work of his "breakthrough," had become familiar with Freud's theory and was also extremely fond of Strindberg; "I read him not to read him—but to lie on his breast," he confided in his diary (*Diaries, 1914–1923* 126). Indeed, Kafka saw his "talent" as lying in his ability to portray his "dreamlike inner life" (*Diaries, 1914–1923* 77). His writing can best be approached in terms of an oneiric functionalism.

Such an approach is particularly relevant in addressing the notion of character in Kafka's fiction. The fullest account of Kafka's poetics is to be found in his comments on "The Judgment," in which he wrote that the figure of the friend "is hardly a real person; he is perhaps rather that which the father and Georg have in common. The story is perhaps a walk around father and son, and the changing figure of the friend is perhaps the change of perspective in the relationship between father and son" (*Letters to Felice* 267; trans. modified). According to this statement, Kafka conceived of the friend not as the fictional portrait of an empirically possible person but as the mere function of a relationship. According to a diary entry (*Diaries, 1910–1913* 278), the friend must be seen as a counter in the struggle between father and son, as an indicator of the relative standing of the two combatants at the various points of their contest, and as a weight on the scale that helps decide the outcome. In the beginning, Georg, according to Kafka, thinks he has the friend on his side. As the story develops, however, Georg must learn that it is the father who really has the friend, while Georg has nothing and consequently suffers defeat. Since the friend is, as Kafka also notes, the connection between Georg and his father—their "common bond"—he also functions as a part of each. He is a projection like a figure in a dream. What matters is not his empirical existence, which the father at one point seems to doubt, but his signifying role in the battle.

A closer look at the text shows that the father, too, is less a mimetically conceived person than he is a function in the self-inflicted decomposition of Georg's adult self, his regression to a child who obeys parental commands and, beyond that, to nonbeing. The father functions as a projection of Georg's psyche. He accuses Georg of having attempted to displace and suppress him. His charges originate, however, in Georg's own fleeting thoughts. Georg notes the terrible darkness of his father's room and the father's unclean underwear and reproaches himself for having relegated his old father to the dark back of the apartment while having reserved for himself the bright, spacious front room with its commanding view of the outside world.

Even earlier in the story, it occurs to Georg that "during his mother's lifetime his father's insistence on having everything his own way in the business had hindered him" (*CS* 78). Together with this acknowledgment

of past frustration by and resentment of his father, Georg's triumphant satisfaction at the reversal of their positions since his mother's death is strongly
implied, although not explicitly stated. The enormous physical strength of
his father still impresses itself on Georg's mind when he sees his father,
after a very long absence from his room, as "still a giant" (*CS* 81). This piece
of inner monologue could be a sign of admiration, resignation, fear, or all
three in one. It is an observation that could be made by a combatant evaluat-
ing his foe as well as by an admiring son proud of his father's undiminished
strength. By entering his father's room, an unaccustomed act lacking apparent motivation, Georg literally goes to get his father's judgment. Georg is
about to take a decisive step into full adulthood by sending off a letter in
which he has at last announced his impending marriage. The recipient of
the letter is to be Georg's distant friend, who is closely associated with
permanent bachelorhood as well as with childhood and youth. The German
word for bachelor, *Junggeselle*—literally meaning "young fellow"—emphasizes this association with a state preceding full adulthood. For Georg, who
had for so long neglected his father and hardly communicated with him,
there was no need to go into the father's room to tell him about this letter.
Georg's act is unmotivated. In the light of what happens next in his father's
room, however, this act is a literal, if unconscious, eliciting of his father's
response to and judgment of Georg's declaration of adulthood.

In the scene that follows, the father reveals himself to be functioning as
an emanation of, first, the son's guilt, anxiety, and murderous resentment
and, ultimately, of Georg's childlike submissiveness. In the voice of his
suddenly demonic father, what had been lurking in Georg's fleeting thoughts
now confronts him from outside, with drastic explicitness. What happens in
this story is thus the enactment of conflicting forces in the protagonist that
never cross the threshold of consciousness to become reflective articulation.
Instead, they are projected onto a seemingly autonomous antagonist, Georg's
father, who articulates, in extreme form, the feelings the protagonist hinted
at but never fully admitted.

The world presented in this text behaves analogously to the way dreams
function according to Freud. Thoughts and emotions not admitted to the
dreamer's conscious awareness appear disguised as external events, apparently independent of the dreamer's will but strange, surprising, grotesque,
and enigmatic. In some of Kafka's later texts, the parallels to dreams and
their implicit, indirect wish-fulfilling function is more obvious than in "The
Judgment" and *The Metamorphosis*. In "In the Penal Colony," the penal
apparatus collapses as if in response to the Explorer's unwillingness to support its continuance. In "A Country Doctor," the magic horses that appear
from the doctor's pigsty, carrying him to his destination in a second, answer
his urgent need to follow the call to his patient. Their emergence together
with the groom, who then rapes the doctor's maid, pictorializes, with some
obviousness, the division within the doctor between his calling—literally

signified by the "alarm" of the bell (CS 225)—and his erotic desire, which, allegorizing a fundamental problem of Kafka's life, tragically awakens only at the moment when it has to conflict with his mission.

When Herbert Read speaks of the organic form inherent in the modernist work, "without consideration of the given forms of traditional poetry" (Faulkner 19), he has in mind above all the emancipation of such art from the restrictions imposed by genre. One crucial effect of genre is satisfaction of the reader's expectation of finding the familiar in the new, an expectation that a text such as "The Judgment" shatters. In this story a violent, wrenching shift of focus tears the text apart into two radically discordant sections, producing a dissonance that severely upsets the reader's generic expectations.

The oneiric functionalism that I have traced so far is only one aspect of modernism. In Kafka, it combines with a quite different principle of modernist composition, one that Marjorie Perloff has called "the poetics of indeterminacy," or undecidability, of meaning and that she locates in a tradition of modernist poetry beginning with Rimbaud. In contrast to symbolism, this extreme branch of modernism eschews even hidden referential meaning and restricts itself to the "direct presentation" of the image, to pure description or evocation that discourages the reader's hermeneutical attempt to "understand" (Perloff 37). The search for referentiality, deeply built into habits of reading, is counteracted by the very luminosity of the images that language evokes. Nonreferentiality is helped by the withholding of contextuality. The artist presents images, narrates events, and makes statements outside any discernible context, such as the context supplied by causality.

The poetics of indeterminacy—or undecidability or, in the literal sense, meaninglessness—is consistent with a general modernist attitude toward the reader. Indeterminacy completes the alienation of the reader which the antimimetic, antididactic theory of autonomous art had initiated. The doctrine of autotelic art relates to society in two different ways. Seen in the context of the liberal view of history—extolling the progressive emancipation of the individual from authority at work—indeterminacy is a big step forward, extending to art the general principle of liberty. In a view of history such as that of Marxism, however, it is a leap in the growing alienation of the artist from society and is therefore seen as typical of bourgeois, capitalist modernity. And, indeed, a radical and deliberate alienation from the public characterizes important formal and thematic aspects of modernism. Alienation resides above all in the break of the "mimetic contract" (Barthes, "Introduction") between author and reader—a break fundamental for modernism. That familiarity between authorial narrator and reader, their "shared sense of reality" (Faulkner 1) so characteristic of Victorian novels, was shattered by modernism. The cozy chattiness of direct address of the reader by an interventionist narrator, typical of the older novel, was severely interdicted by Flaubert and Henry James.

Alienation accounts for two seemingly contradictory but in fact closely related elements of modernism: on the one hand, its aggressive provocativeness, which seeks to shock, outrage, and scandalize, and, on the other hand, its withdrawal from public comprehension into obscurity, difficulty, and hermeticism. Both tendencies are aspects of the same antagonism toward the bourgeois public. In the indeterminacy of meaning, which both angers and excludes the public, the two tendencies join. The undecidability of meaning frustrates readers in their most fundamental concern: the attempt to understand, to recognize, to empathize, and to translate the newly encountered into the familiar. The modernist work makes it extremely difficult for the reader to cross the chasm that separates a text from life. Modernism is the enemy of a hermeneutics that seeks to appropriate art to life.

Kafka's *Metamorphosis* conforms, in an almost exemplary manner, to both aspects of the modernist assault on the reader. The transformation of a human being into "a giant specimen of vermin" (the literal meaning of the form into which, as the text tells us, Gregor finds himself transformed) shocks and disgusts the reader, and it likewise baffles understanding. The initial event of the story could be, and has been, used as a textbook case of a modernist alienation effect. Above all, Gregor's metamorphosis contradicts the most basic premise of mimesis.

Mimesis has social foundations. It rests on the actual or imagined participation of work and public in a shared reality. Even if the reader does not believe in the mythology that forms the setting of Ovid's *Metamorphoses*, they are still mimetic in the Aristotelian sense because they describe sequences of causally connected, and thus explicable, events. Within the convention of belief in supernatural beings as causal agents, the transformations of human beings into animals and plants is perceived as natural. By sharp contrast, Gregor Samsa's metamorphosis occurs and remains unexplained. It thus breaks the mimetic contract. Samsa's metamorphosis falls outside even the context of what one might consider miraculous, if miracles are thought of as linked to supernatural agencies and so embedded in an order that, though transcending sensory and empirical nature, is an order nonetheless. Gregor's metamorphosis does not point to any cause at all, not even a supernatural one. Tzvetan Todorov ranks it in the genre of the fantastic. In that genre, readers can never know whether a natural or supernatural explanation applies. According to that definition, however, the fantastic applies only to the world of the reader. It does not apply to the world within Kafka's text. Within the text, no question arises as to the cause of Gregor's fate. Gregor himself seems to view his transformation as a misfortune that could befall anyone—for instance, the head clerk of his firm. He treats it as an accident, a sorry contingency, tough luck. No one within the represented world, including Gregor himself, ever speculates on possible causes.

Thus we find a remarkable discrepancy between the represented world and the world of the reader. The reader looks for a causality with which the characters are not concerned. No causality can be established on the basis of what the text explicitly communicates. In this way, Gregor's metamorphosis behaves according to the poetics of indeterminacy.

Yet Kafka's story follows this poetics only partway. A narrative of high realism succeeds the initial shock of alienation. *The Metamorphosis* presents a causally connected chain of events, a sequence of described thoughts, actions, and feelings that are made perfectly plausible, or at least empirically possible, in the milieu and the circumstances described. After the initial event, the plot stays consistently within the conventions of narrative realism. This singularity of the nonmimetic occurrence, which initiates the plot and gives the story its title, sharply distinguishes *The Metamorphosis* from a text of indeterminacy, such as Rimbaud's *Illuminations*, and from the tradition of surrealism that followed it. "A Country Doctor," comprising as it does a string of "magical" events, comes much closer to surrealism than does *The Metamorphosis*. The latter story has been compared to a fairy tale, and it has also been discussed as an "anti–fairy tale" (Heselhaus). The distinction here is a thematic one. That events for which no causes are given constitute a common structural denominator of Kafka's story and fairy tales is not at issue. What does prevent the generic expectations associated with fairy tales to maintain themselves for the reader of *The Metamorphosis*, however, is the radical consistency of the realistic style of representation following the initial event.

Here we come upon a bipolar tendency as typical of Kafka as it is of modernism in general. At one of the poles, we find hermetic nonreferentiality, a frustration of the quest for understanding. At the other pole, we encounter what Aristotle called mythos—that is, mimetic narrativity, a representation of human fate and action that elicits the reader's empathy with the represented world. Kafka is a storyteller as well as a modernist.

If we apply the principle of dreamlike functionalism, which we have observed in other texts of Kafka, to the initial event of *The Metamorphosis*, we find that it counteracts indeterminacy and meaninglessness and thus extends the reach of mythos. Gregor's transformation acquires a definite function in a plot that is mimetic in psychological and social terms, though not in physical ones. Near the beginning of the narrative, the text presents Gregor's memories and reflections about the onerous aspects of his job. The reader is informed that Gregor has been intensely dissatisfied with the dehumanizing conditions of his job and would have resigned with a rebellious flourish if his father's indebtedness to the firm had not forced him to delay this decision. His metamorphosis thus functions as a fulfillment of his wish to be rid of his job without his becoming responsible for deserting his financially dependent family. An inexplicable event has absolved him of deliberate revolt. It fulfills his wish while not only relieving him of responsibility but also punishing him, since it transforms him into a creature that elicits disgust.

By presenting us with Gregor's reflections and memories, the text offers us the possibility, and even plausibility, of such a construction. We can deduce a functional rationale for the incredible happening.

Yet nowhere does the connection between Gregor's rebellious desire and his fantastic fate become explicit. Nowhere within the text does it emerge into consciousness. It remains a construction by the reader. Gregor, who is the sole registering consciousness in the largest part of the story, does not show any awareness of such a connection. Neither do the narrator or any of the story's other characters. This silence makes the text hermetic, since it withholds any referential, or mimetically understandable, meaning for Gregor's metamorphosis. That hermetic quality stands at what we might call the modernist pole of the text. At the opposite pole, in its hints of a possible connection between Gregor's thoughts and his fate, the text allows the possibility of establishing a meaning for Gregor's metamorphosis. It allows the reader to construct a mimetic representation of a causal link between the narrated facts and thus a mythos in the Aristotelian sense, a "story." Such a reading cannot account for the empirical impossibility of the crucial event, the metamorphosis itself, but merely by establishing a psychologically motivated link between the character's fate and his preceding intentions, this reading reintroduces a substantial element of mimetic representation. The designation "magic realism" would literally apply. For a realistic representation of human alienation and repression, in the circumstances of exploitative capitalism and the patriarchal bourgeois family, is coupled with the magic intrusion of empirical impossibility into the realistically described milieu. According to Freud's definition of magic as the "omnipotence of thought"— that is, the projection of inner-psychic constellations onto the external world—we can view Gregor's self-transformation as an unacknowledged application of magic, suspending the laws of physical plausibility (Sokel, "Freud").

Kafka's text presents itself on two levels. The literal or writer's level—the level of indeterminacy—withholds referential meaning and causal coherence. The second level, however, empowers the reader to discern functional roles in the elements of narration, which combine into a mimetic sequence. On this level, the text enables the reader to fill in missing links in the representation of an action that, though empirically impossible, achieves psychological and sociological plausibility and thus a meaningful connection with the world outside the text. Without officially consenting to it, the text—unofficially, as it were—invites the reader to reestablish referentiality. Fredric Jameson points out that the recommitting to mimesis—the translation of the alienating text into a mimetically explanatory mythos—is an integral feature of modernist works. They are "simply canceled realistic ones." When, as Jameson goes on to say, one "make[s] sense of" one of Kafka's texts, one inserts into it "the flux of realistic narrative" ("Beyond the

Cave" 129). We must add, however, that at least in Kafka's case, the text itself suggests and directs the reader's procedure, provided the dreamlike functionalist structure is recognized as informing it.

Kafka himself set the example for such a reading of his texts. After he had written "The Judgment," he asked Felice Bauer, his future fiancée, whether she found "some straightforward, coherent meaning that one could follow" in "The Judgment" (*Letters to Felice* 265). He himself, he admitted, found no meaning and could not explain anything in it. Yet immediately upon this declaration of total indeterminacy, he reversed himself and began to interpret the story as an autobiographical allegory. He drew attention to the close relation of the names of the characters to his own and Felice's. He found much that he called "noteworthy" and thus potentially meaningful in the very story that he, in the preceding sentence, had declared devoid of sense. His initial impression of meaninglessness thus gave way at once to the attempt to find meaning, to translate the unknown code of his text into the codes of real life.

Kafka's strangely puzzled response to his own writing reflects a fundamental change of the traditional view concerning the relation between writing and reading. It was a change wrought by modernism and its antecedent, the theory of autonomous art. The theory of autonomous art runs counter to the sharp division between writer and reader that existed in traditional aesthetics. In particular, it militates against the idea that the relation between writing and reading is a one-way street on which all traffic flows from writing to reading, where the reader is the passive recipient of the writer's message. The theory of autonomous art changed that vision in two ways. First, it depersonalized the author, while functionalizing character and event within the work. Second, it made the reader the writer's collaborator in the creative process.

Since Diderot and Kant, the doctrine of the autonomy of art had held that the only law to be observed in a work was the law its creator, the genius, gives to it. Genius, however, came to be understood not as an empirical person but as the function that makes genius what it is—namely, the creative imagination. The symbolists increasingly came to see the creative imagination not as a personal property or quality of the empirical author but as a productive process; not as arbitrary personal planning but as the artist's opening and surrender to the powers inherent in the medium of the work. The poet, according to Mallarmé, disappears "in the poem," an insight Mallarmé calls "the discovery of our [the modern] time" (Abrams 134). The poet "cedes the initiative" in creation "to the words" (Abrams 120) and allows language to direct the production of the work. In one of the most important documents of modernism, Arthur Rimbaud's "Lettre du voyant" ("Letter of the Seer"), Rimbaud advocates the breakup of the conscious and deliberate self, the empirical ego, by a systematic "dérèglement de tous les sens" ("unhinging of all the senses") in order to let another, deeper self, a buried unconscious other, take over. The "I" speaking in his poetry is not the empirical I but "an other." His famous programmatic sentence "For I am an other" could serve as the motto of all modernism. Roland Barthes's structuralist diagnosis of "the death of the author" in the self-productive and self-perpetuating flow of language that is seen as the true agent of creation appears adumbrated in the poetics of the symbolists and even in the statement of their Romantic precursor Victor Hugo that "the word is a living being more powerful than the one who uses it" (Friedrich 22). At the same time Rimbaud published his "Lettre du voyant," Nietzsche proclaimed in *The Birth of Tragedy* (1872), "The subject—the striving individual . . . can be thought of only as an enemy of art, never as its source. . . . to the extent that the subject is an artist he is already delivered from individual will and has become a medium . . ." (41). What Nietzsche, the French symbolists, and the structuralist Roland Barthes hold in common is the conviction that it is not the conscious, planning, empirical person, the "subject," that is essential in the writing process. The process of creation emancipates itself from the personal author. This strong belief in depersonalization is an integral part of the "dehumanization" that the Spanish philosopher José Ortega y Gasset saw as the dominant tendency of modern art and literature, a tendency that lies at the foundation of modernism. In Rainer Maria Rilke's avant-garde novel *The Notebooks of Malte Laurids Brigge*, Malte, wrestling with the task of becoming a poet, identifies the moment of his (possible) breakthrough with the passive voice: "I shall be written" (52). His birth as a poet would be the reduction of his person to point zero, to a mere medium, a mere instrument.

Such a depersonalizing unification of the empirical self with the creative process is what, according to a diary entry, Kafka felt he had experienced in writing "The Judgment"—the only one of his works with which he was and remained fully satisfied. He had, he confides in his diary, composed the story in a trancelike state,

> at one sitting, during the night of the 22nd–23rd, from ten o'clock at night to six o'clock in the morning. I was hardly able to pull my legs from out under the desk, they had got so stiff from sitting. The fearful strain and joy, how the story developed before me, as if I were advancing in water. (*Diaries, 1910–1913* 275–76)

And, enlarging his report into a program, a poetics, he adds, "Only *in this way* can writing be done, only with such coherence, with such complete opening of the body and the soul" (*Diaries, 1910–1913* 276). Conscious planning and intention have nothing to do with such writing. Kafka reported that he had intended an entirely different plot when he started to write, "but then the whole thing turned in my hands" (*Letters to Felice* 265). The story that emerged was not the result of his intention. Emphasizing his role in its creation as that of a medium, he compared himself to a mother giving birth to her child (*Diaries, 1910–1913* 278). This absorption of the self in the writing process remained Kafka's ideal even though, after the writing of "The Judgment," he never again attained it to his satisfaction (Sokel, "Kafka's Poetics").

Kafka's ideal of depersonalized writing has an important bearing on the relation of writing to reading. Since writing is not the product of conscious plan and intention, writers cannot know the "meaning" of their own work. A writer thus occupies an interpreter's, a reader's, position in regard to the work produced. Using E. D. Hirsch's equation of meaning with authorial intention, we can see that there is indeed no meaning in a text written without intention (46–48). According to the aesthetics of autonomous art, literary language can have no meaning in the ordinary sense, since it is free of the intent to inform, which launches mimetic representation and description as well as didactic instruction. Its only purpose is to stimulate the mind's or soul's activity. At the time this vision was forming, Kant distinguished the language of aesthetic from that of logical ideas: The former "does not . . . represent what lies in our concepts . . . but rather something else—something that gives the imagination an incentive to spread its flight . . ." (Sokel, *Writer* 11). Lacking meaning, such language engenders a search for significance. Writing provides merely the opportunity for this search to come into being. It is literally a pre-text for reading.

In Kafka's later work, writing itself, having ceased to be the flow carrying the writer, becomes the search for significance that makes it a kind of reading. Writing and reading become interchangeable, a circular continuum, without a break between them. Kafka expressed this relation in his parable "Prometheus" (January 1918). Here Kafka tells four highly idiosyncratic variants of the Prometheus myth. Together they describe a development of the myth, which Kafka's text calls legend, from its traditional version to a last one in which all the actors of the original myth have grown weary and bring the "*meaningless* affair" (my italics) to an end. "There remained the inexplicable [shape of] the rocky mountain range," which had given rise to the original myth. The "legend" had been the attempt to explain the puzzling shape of the mountain. It "tried to explain the inexplicable. As it came out of a ground of truth, it had to return to the inexplicable" (*CS* 432; trans. modified).

Here the desire to narrate forms a continuum with the need to understand—that is, to read. Representation is inextricably enmeshed with interpretation. It is the wish to read meaning into enigmatic givenness that begets the myth (i.e., narration or "writing," which are the same prior to the bifurcation of telling and writing). In terms of the parable, "writing" is inseparable from reading. Together they form the attempt to understand what is simply there—the strangely shaped mountain range. The telling of tales is presented as an attempt to produce meaning.

As in *The Metamorphosis*, we see a movement from indeterminacy to the telling of a mythos, here in the literal form of a Greek myth. The puzzling mountains function not only like the enigmatic event of Gregor's metamorphosis but also like the enigmatic text that Kafka found his "Judgment" to be. All three stimulate a reading and interpreting process that seeks to give birth to understanding. In "Prometheus," however, the movement evident in *The Metamorphosis* is reversed, or at least made circular. *The Metamorphosis* begins with the inexplicable, then supplies hints of an explanation, and finally narrates a mimetic story, a mythos. In the last section, the mythos actually turns into a kind of myth. It tells the rebirth of hope in the Samsa family after Gregor's self-imposed death, by which he liberates his family from himself. In the light of this ending, Gregor's metamorphosis takes on the character of a redeeming self-sacrifice and thus becomes a version of the myth of the scapegoat-savior that James Frazer's *The Golden Bough* had made popular in turn-of-the-century Europe (Trilling 14). Kafka was thoroughly dissatisfied with this mythic ending of his story. He called it "unreadable . . . imperfect almost to its very marrow" (*Diaries, 1914–1923* 12).

In Kafka's legend, the text begins with the mythos, in its original formulation as an actual Greek myth, then moves toward its cancellation. Here mythos functions as a temporary detour around the inexplicable "ground of truth." Storytelling is a provisional attempt to explain what permanently bears no explanation. In the end, we must realize that the ground of truth returns us to the meaningless, the literally unmeaning. The unmeaning gives birth to the reader and, with the reader, to the writer. Their joined mythmaking search is a series of displacements in which one version follows another on the road to exhaustion. In the end, the mythopoeic process is wearisome and has to be given up. However, mimetic mythos, by which we seek to explain the inexplicable, is a need in human beings that forever seeks fulfillment. Literature is that search. Its road is circular—shades of Nietzsche's "eternal return"?—and the attempt to read, which is writing, might begin ever anew.

Presenting such relationships, Kafka reveals himself to be the "giant modernist" he was called in the book review title I began by quoting. He was linked to modernism mainly for two reasons—first, because modernism was the response to a fundamental rift between the notion of truth or reality and the notion of meaning. In late-nineteenth- and twentieth-century philosophy the view became increasingly prominent "that the very object of realism . . . objective reality no longer exists" (Jameson, "Beyond the Cave" 122) and that a thing can be considered to exist "only with reference to the act of seeing" it (Ryan 11). In accordance with this fundamental skepticism concerning the very ideas of truth and reality, modernist literature could no longer abide by the mimetic convention. Where an objective reality cannot be determined, it cannot be imitated or represented either. Modernist art thus adhered to a radical perspectivism that abolished the omniscient narrator. The "unimental" perspective, a narrative structure in which the reader does not receive more, but usually even less, information than is available to the protagonist—a distinctive element of Kafka's narratives—dovetails perfectly with the epistemological relativism or perspectivism that typifies modern thought.

This severe restriction of the reader's traditional cognitive privilege leads us to the second reason we may call Kafka a true modernist: namely, that the work confronts readers as a challenge forcing them to participate in and, in a sense, continue the writer's activity. Provocation of art's addressee was, as we have seen, a fundamental feature of modernist practice. Its antecedents lay in the very idea of autonomous art. In sharply distinguishing aesthetic from logical discourse, Kant and his immediate successors saw the aesthetic effect residing not in orientation and information about either the phenomenal or the moral world but in the stimulation of the imagination, in the production of the most multifarious and variegated emotional and mental activity. According to Kant, the "aesthetic attribute" broadens the range of thoughts and feelings, quickens their flow, accelerates psychic metabolism (Sokel, *Writer* 11–12). In modernist literature, the contact between reading and writing lies not in "understanding" but in a kind of "magic suggestion" (Fokkema 19). Respect for the reader's freedom, independence, and "idiosyncracies . . . became a Modernist convention," dictating "the very organization of [modernist] texts" (Fokkema 18). The text was not structured to provide authoritative meanings directing as well as binding the reader. Instead, the text was to serve merely as a springboard, a possibility for the play of interpretation. That situation did not make reading an easy task, for along with dependence on an "official" line of understanding, the reader lost the comfort of authorial guidance and the opportunity of easy identifications. Without the author's "author-itarian" steering, reading became a hazardous venture on which no certainty beckoned as a reward.

"To unsettle . . . that is my role." André Gide's definition of the authorial function, which sums up the modernist attitude toward the reader (Fokkema 24), leads straight to Kafka. "A book," he said, "must be the axe for the frozen sea inside us" (*Letters to Friends* 16). With this programmatic statement, made in 1904, at the very beginning of his literary life, Kafka showed that, for all his isolation, he firmly belonged in a tradition, stretching back to Diderot and to Kant—the tradition of autonomous or nonmimetic art, in which art is not a representation of the world but a tonic for the soul.

NOTE

[1] Unless otherwise indicated, all translations are mine.

Gender, Judaism, and Power:
A Jewish Feminist Approach to Kafka

Evelyn Torton Beck

> Fiction is like a spider's web, attached ever so lightly
> perhaps, but still attached to life at all four corners.
> —Virginia Woolf, *A Room of One's Own*

Long before I became aware of the significance of gender, my approach to the study of literature was both contextual and integrative. I took it as given that art is not separable from life and that establishing the cultural and biographical contexts of an artist's work is as essential to an understanding of a text as is the analysis of symbol, imagery, and language.

Such an integrated approach is especially essential to Franz Kafka, for the membrane separating the life of this writer from his work is particularly permeable. For this reason, I always begin teaching his texts by establishing his historic realities and the value system of the worlds in which he lived. Students must know from the start that Kafka was multiply a minority. He was a German-speaking Jew living in Prague when anti-Semitism was widespread and the German language associated (by Czech natives) with the hostile ruling class. He was a Jew who despised and rejected his father's superficial way of being Jewish but who could neither believe nor entirely give up belief. He was also a man who had difficulty being sexual with women; who feared the responsibility of marriage, which he associated with the bourgeois life he saw as inimical to the artist in him. But, ironically, he also believed, in accordance with Jewish custom, that a man who did not marry would never be more than half a man. In addition, contemporary social pressure and Jewish mores kept him from ever contemplating the meaning of his sexual revulsion for women (made explicit in his letters and diaries) and perhaps facing his homoerotic attractions, which are amply manifest in accounts of his dreams and fantasies as well as in the homosocial worlds of his fiction and fragments (see Beck, "Kafka's Traffic" and "Kafka's Triple Bind").

These multiple contexts provide a basic framework within which it becomes possible to begin to analyze the stories. Because most students find interpretation of Kafka's fiction so formidable, I first concentrate on demystifying his work by demonstrating the ways in which he transmuted significant elements from Jewish culture and religion and reworked them in his fiction in an abstract way, giving these elements an aura of mystery and terror. In this process I show how Kafka's own method of decontextualizing makes his work so richly layered and open to multiple interpretations.

Becoming more specific, I begin with the influence of Yiddish theater on his work and show the coincidence of Kafka's artistic "breakthrough" in 1912 with the reawakening of his interest in Judaism, brought about by an extended encounter with an eastern European wandering theater troupe that performed Yiddish plays in Prague from 1910 to 1911 (see Beck, *Yiddish Theater* and "Kafkas 'Durchbruch' "). Kafka believed that this impoverished, semiprofessional troupe's repertoire of tragicomic plays, dealing with ancient and contemporary Jewish life, represented a more authentic form of Judaism than he had ever encountered, and for a time they gave him some relief from the pressing existential and familial problems that so troubled him. Kafka also became infatuated with both the leading actor and actress of the troupe. In September 1912, directly following this theater experience, he wrote "The Judgment," the first story to show the characteristic dramatic style that typifies Kafka's mature writing and stands in stark contrast to all his writing before that time (see Beck, *Yiddish Theater* 31–48).

Having established this background, I demonstrate to students how I came to trace not only the style but also the essential themes of Kafka's entire oeuvre to these Yiddish plays. Specifically, these themes are the impossibility of obtaining justice within the machinery of the law, the struggle against authority (both divine and temporal), the relationship between the individual and the "absolute" as well as the community, the cleanliness toward which Kafka's characters strive, the elusive knowledge they seek, the hunger they cannot sate.

Moreover, the effect of power on the Jew (particularly the Jewish male) is central to the Yiddish plays and made concrete in battles of power between fathers and sons within the nuclear family, king and Jew in the nation-state, individual Jew and rabbinic leader in Jewish communal life, and God and subject in the Jewish religious sphere. While heterosexual marriage, procreation, and adherence to Jewish law are offered in these plays as ideals to all Jews, women are also expected to be subservient to men and to sacrifice themselves willingly for the benefit of men. Kafka saw as important the guilt and punishment associated with disobedience of Jewish law and disavowal of Jewish ethics and values; in these plays such defiance inevitably leads to apostasy and abandonment of the community.

Kafka's echo of these themes should make it evident that the influence of Yiddish theater was particularly strong on the short stories under discussion in this volume, stories in which such themes appear in transmuted form without specific reference to Jewish history. The stories also include entire scenes whose origins can be traced to the plays, which Kafka saw several times in the space of a few months just before he wrote "The Judgment."[1]

The Yiddish plays themselves were aesthetically uneven and produced on a limited budget in a tiny theater in one of the poorest sections of Prague. Kafka's parents, especially his father, strongly disapproved of his interest in this theater. The plays performed there were written between 1880 and 1907 but remained untouched by the spirit of modernism that was sweeping

Europe in those years; rather, they were composed of elements taken from the traditional five-act play, the melodrama, and the burlesque.[2] Because the plays were performed under poor conditions, even the tragic scenes sometimes became comic, as for example when during one performance the dying hero's wig slipped off in the middle of a tragic speech. Kafka recorded such details in his diaries and seemed actually to find such juxtapositions oddly effective.[3] The familiar figure of the wedding jester, whose stylized mocking declamations infused traditional Jewish weddings in the small towns of eastern Europe, also found his way into these plays and, through them, into Kafka's narratives.

To make the relation of Kafka's fiction to Yiddish theater more concrete, I focus on "The Judgment" (1912) and *The Metamorphosis* (1914), which show the direct influence of three of these plays with particular clarity. The plays in question are Jacob Gordin's *God, Man, and Devil* and *The Savage One* and Abraham Scharkansky's *Kol Nidre; or, The Secret Jews of Spain*. In *Kol Nidre* the overlap of the father-child and God-Jew conflicts is particularly prominent. In *God, Man, and Devil* the father is a retired wedding jester who (under the influence of wine) inappropriately reverts to his public role in the midst of a family gathering. In "The Judgment" Georg's father echoes this jester role in a grotesquely comic fashion that quickly becomes menacing when Georg cannot withstanding his father's psychological attack (see Beck, *Yiddish Theater* 70–121).

In both Kafka's story and Gordin's play, a son is at first embarrassed by his father's out-of-control behavior (leaping onto a chair, wild gesticulation, and verbal attacks) but then takes control by carrying the father off to bed, where the old and foolish belong; in both works, however, the father ultimately triumphs over his son. Although the stark simplicity of the action in "The Judgment" may seem far removed from the involved plot of *God, Man, and Devil*, many of the story's most bizarre elements, and all the theatrical ones, correspond strikingly to the details of Gordin's play. Both works build up to a scene of trial and judgment, followed by the self-inflicted death of the hero, whose demise marks a return to order. Both fathers accuse their sons of abandoning them in favor of business opportunities and financial success associated with taboo sexual activity.

In each work, however, the father's accusation bears a unique relation to the realities of its respective text, and for this reason a comparison of the two is extremely instructive. While in the Yiddish play the son is truly engaged in an inappropriate, if not outright incestuous, relationship with his niece, in Kafka's story the father's objection to the son's adult sexuality seems so inappropriate as to suggest that it is he and not the son who is off balance.

> "Because she lifted up her skirts!" his father began to flute, "because she lifted her skirts like this, the nasty creature," and mimicking her he lifted his shirt so high that one could see the scar on his thigh from

his war wound, "because she lifted her skirts like this and this you made up to her, and in order to make free with her undisturbed, you have disgraced your mother's memory, betrayed your friend and stuck your father into bed so he can't move. But he can move, or can't he?"

(CS 85)

Georg's acceptance of his father's inappropriate judgment suggests that he cannot sustain his newly won independence and has completely internalized the father's voice. A complementary reading suggests that Georg's feelings for the "friend in Russia" (who he posits will be "so upset" by the news of his forthcoming marriage) are homoerotic.[4] "Since your friends are like that, Georg, you shouldn't ever have got engaged at all," his fiancée tells him (CS 80). The very different use to which Kafka puts the play's dramatic scene shows that he has taken a theme that was comprehensible in the Yiddish play and deliberately made it less easy to interpret in the context of his fiction.[5]

The startling ending of "The Judgment," in which the son literally carries out his father's verdict—"I sentence you now to death by drowning" (CS 87)—originated in Scharkansky's Kol Nidre. In that play the head inquisitor is a convert from Judaism who is forced to condemn his own child to death because she is revealed to be living as a secret Jew and she refuses to renounce her Jewish identity when it is exposed. She dies saying the Shm'a— "Hear O Israel: the Lord is our God, the Lord is One"—the traditional avowal of allegiance to Judaism recited at least twice daily by Orthodox Jews as part of morning and evening prayers and always recited under life-threatening circumstances. In Kafka's "The Judgment," this speech provides an ironic parallel, for Georg dies vowing loyalty to the very father who has condemned him: "Dearest parents, I have always loved you, all the same" (CS 88).

What separates Kafka's fiction from the Yiddish theater is its ambiguity and its creation of a fictional world in which one cannot judge the characters' perception or the accuracy of any accusation. In contrast, the Yiddish play makes clear who is guilty (of what) and when those who accuse are out of control. The Yiddish plays usually offer the possibility of an alternative perspective that bears some relation to a more sane "reality" outside the family or social system. Kafka's narratives present worlds so self-enclosed with characters so self-absorbed that they preclude the possibility of any external commonsense perspective. In this difference lies both the power of Kafka's stories and their frustrating resistance to a single interpretation.

The Metamorphosis, Kafka's best-known story, illustrates with particular clarity not only the continuing influence of Yiddish theater but also his working method. In theme, characters, structure, and technique, this story reflects the influence of several Yiddish plays, especially The Savage One, by Jacob Gordin, whose work deeply impressed Kafka as the most complex in the repertoire. Like The Metamorphosis, this play also contains a son,

Lemekh, who, like Gregor, is in some serious way "defective." Born gentle but retarded, in the course of events Lemekh is taunted and abused by his family and thus becomes the savage of the play's title; his situation closely parallels that of Gregor Samsa (once Gregor's condition has been concretized in insect form). Like the defective son in the play, Gregor is barely tolerated and is looked upon with disgust as an outcast whose very existence shames his family. In different ways the two sons combine the qualities of "thing" and "person." Both are presented as essentially simple, meek, self-effacing persons who become animallike creatures because of a drastic transformation that ends in catastrophe. The two works are also parallel in the number and kinds of characters they portray, down to the family housekeeper, in each tale the only person who does not fear the strange son (see Beck, *Yiddish Theater* 135–46).

The Oedipal conflict and broader theme of incest, presented in blatant and highly exaggerated form in *The Savage One*, are also played out in *The Metamorphosis*. In both works a son's sexual desire becomes inappropriately lodged in family members and played out in father-son rivalry. Gregor faints when he sees his father and mother embrace, and later he imaginatively projects himself and his sister into his locked room, where he would not only protect her against all "intruders," but also "raise himself to her shoulder and kiss her on the neck" (CS 131). In Gordin's play, in a scene with similarly sexual overtones, the hero literally locks himself into a room with his sleeping stepmother and swears to keep her as his own. Gregor's final degradation, startlingly signaled by his crawling around on all fours, finds its parallel in the Yiddish play in Lemekh's loss of rational control, after which he, too, ends up crawling on the floor.

Structurally, Kafka's stories progress like dramas, building through a series of crises to a final denouement. In a given story, the various episodes relate to one another like the separate, self-contained acts in a play. In handling setting, Kafka also adapts the techniques of the stage, limiting the relatively few characters to a small, clearly defined area, accounting for physical details as if they were to be made concrete on a stage. The movements of the characters are recorded with the precision of stage directions, and the exaggerated action often culminates in a grouping of characters that recalls the tableaux of the Yiddish theater. Kafka's language evokes the economy of a stage performance in which words resonate to suggest meaning beyond the literal. While one would never claim that the Yiddish theater experience was solely responsible for the breakthrough to Kafka's mature style represented in "The Judgment" and *The Metamorphosis*, it clearly influenced not only his central themes but also his imagery, with which he emphasized gesture, costume, comic pantomime, and stark visual effects.

I completed my research on the impact of Yiddish theater on Kafka's work in the early 1970s and find that it is still valid in the 1990s, although I am now painfully aware that I, like all other Kafka scholars of that time (and most, even today), completely ignored the issue of gender in my analysis. Starting in the mid-1970s I began to reexamine Kafka's writings from a feminist perspective, and in 1978 I made a presentation called "Feminist Criticism and Franz Kafka"; by 1981 I had organized a session at the Modern Language Association convention titled "Kafka's Sexual Politics/at Work/in the Text."[6] Since then I have come to believe that any interpretation of Kafka is seriously impoverished if it does not take gender into account as a factor of analysis.

It is not difficult to show that the question of gender is the single most ignored aspect of Kafka's work yet, at the same time, one of its most outstanding issues. A few observations should suffice to lay the foundation for this conclusion. Kafka's fictional worlds are almost entirely male—homosocial and often homoerotic. Woman is literally absent from many of the texts, and when she is not absent, her presence is obliterated, obscured, or trivialized. Where she is not obscured, she is seen as purely instrumental, as a vehicle or conduit for male activity, specifically for the male quest and the essential power struggles between males that are at the center of Kafka's works. Even in the few stories that have a central female character (e.g., "Josephine, the Mouse"), the male narrator speaks for her. Nowhere in Kafka does a woman speak from her own perspective.

More significant, the male heroes organize the text's way of seeing, and as a result, the angle of vision in Kafka's texts is necessarily androcentric. This viewpoint is especially clear when the male eye looks out at women. The narrative eye sees not the "person" of a woman but always an other or the physical body or part of a body. It is therefore no accident that Kafka's heroes have been described in strictly male terms, as Fausts, schlemiels, or even little boys. Woman in Kafka's world is purely instrumental: she can help or hinder the hero, but never can she herself be an active participant in the quest. Moreover, as Kafka represents her, she is incapable of understanding even the impulse to act or its spiritual dimension.

In analyzing Kafka's perception of women's function as nurturers and servicers of men, it is helpful to place his viewpoint within the context of Jewish attitudes toward women. Such attitudes are not essentially different from those of other patriarchal societies but are perhaps experienced more intensely in Jewish communities (and by other oppressed minorities), for whom community survival has always been at risk. As a Jewish male, Kafka saw women as nourishers of men. Given his sexual difficulties with women and the explicit revulsion of heterosexuality repeatedly recorded in his diaries, it is likely that Kafka's own sexual proclivity was toward men. Since this attraction was taboo as an open choice and specifically prohibited by Jewish law, Kafka lived out his life in a self-loathing he did not fully comprehend. When his internalized anti-Semitism is paired with his internalized homophobia, neither of which was speakable or was mentioned by name in his fiction, these submerged themes press upon his texts and give them particular force and intensity.

While Kafka exposed the virtual powerlessness of women in a patriarchy and laid bare the structures that bind them, he nonetheless also perpetuated the patriarchal ideology itself. Even his most disempowered hero seeks domination over women and thinks of them in the language of ownership. Thus, for a woman to read Kafka in the way he pushes us to read him, through the eyes of a Georg or Gregor, Josef K. or K., she must forget that she is a woman, which is what polite society and traditional literary criticism also invite her to do. But such an act of "forgetting" seems contradictory to Kafka's own vision of what a book should be—"the axe for the frozen sea inside us" (*Letters to Friends* 16). Foregrounding the gender of the characters in Kafka's texts and similarly locating the readers of his texts result in a clarifying re-vision that can keep us from mystifying Kafka's works. Such re-vision also helps modify the hopelessness of his vision, for if we keep the specificity of our own (as well as Kafka's) situation in mind, we need not blindly accept the notion that he describes eternal, existential, universal life conditions. We can more easily see how his vision grows out of his own life experiences, rooted as they are in gender, sexuality, ethnicity, religion, history, and culture. And though his texts may speak to us, they need not speak for us, need not define a limit; his ambivalence need not become ours. If we also begin to recognize that "us" and "ours" are not homogeneous categories, if we can learn to read Kafka "against the grain," we will facilitate this process.[7] Such a reading in no way diminishes Kafka's power as an artist but may fruitfully diminish his hold over us, which often depresses and frightens students. Perhaps if we can help students understand that the origins of Kafka's tragicomic creations lie in the ways he experienced Jewish life at a certain moment in history, they will be able not only to appreciate his humor (as well as his use of it as a coping strategy) but also to understand why his own life so terrified him.

NOTES

[1] This influence is not limited to the short stories but is also evident in the novels, particularly *The Trial*, whose opening scene—the arrest of an apparently innocent man who has been falsely denounced—is lifted directly from Asher Zelig Faynman's *The Viceroy* (originally translated as *The Vice-King*), a Yiddish play set at the time of the Inquisition, in which a man who has hidden his Judaism is denounced and arrested for continuing the forbidden Jewish practices.

[2] For a list of the Yiddish plays and a detailed description of them, see the references in Beck, *Yiddish Theater*.

[3] See Kafka's *Diaries, 1910–1913*. Detailed descriptions of the plays and the theater performances are scattered throughout the entries for 1911 and 1912.

[4] This reading is substantiated by numerous diary entries, letters, dreams, and

fragments as well as other fictional texts in which the erotic male dance is fairly explicit. Among the early works, see, for example, "Description of a Struggle." Numerous examples are documented in Beck, "Kafka's Triple Bind."

[5]Another significant parallel in the two works is the father's accusation that his son has betrayed a friend and is therefore a "devilish" human being. In *God, Man, and Devil* this charge is accurate, since the play is a reworking of Goethe's *Faust*; in this version, the hero has literally betrayed his closest friend by striking a bargain with the devil, who takes human shape. In Kafka's story Georg's mysterious "friend in Russia" is modeled on Yitzkhok Levi, the leading actor of whom Kafka's father disapproved violently, perhaps sensing the attraction between the two men. "Whoever lies down with dogs gets up with fleas," Kafka's father reportedly said, referring to his actor friend (*Diaries, 1910–1913* 131).

[6]The 1978 session took place at the meeting of the American Association of Teachers of German; the 1981 MLA session also included presentations by Angelika Bammer and Helen Fehervary.

[7]The concept of reading against the grain is elaborated on as a strategy of feminist criticism by Judith Fetterley, who rereads Faulkner, Hemingway, and other male writers of the American canon.

Kafka's "An Imperial Message" in a Comparative Context

Judith Ryan

The student who approaches Kafka's "An Imperial Message" will be immediately struck by the sense of reading something quintessentially Kafkaesque. The story tells of a person waiting for a message that never comes and of a messenger struggling to burst out of the confines of a labyrinthine structure of palaces, courtyards, and vast imperial geography. The narrative follows the messenger as he overcomes obstacle after obstacle to deliver the dying emperor's message to his faithful but distant subject; yet at the very moment when he seems to have made some progress, we hear that none of what he has accomplished is in fact possible: "never, never can that happen" (CS 5). At first glance, the situation seems to resemble what we have come to call a catch-22, and almost any student who reads this story today is bound to read it in that light.

But Kafka's writing is much more than a study in futility. He has important and highly original things to tell us about knowledge, consciousness, cultural traditions, and fiction, and it is essential that we not reduce these insights to platitudes. For this reason, I suggest here what may seem to some readers—although not those familiar with reception theory—a perverse procedure: that one approach Kafka by way of two of his literary successors. I hope in this way to create a different framework for viewing Kafka's fiction and, by thus defamiliarizing his texts, to distinguish their particular genius.

I propose to compare and contrast with Kafka's "An Imperial Message" two separate texts: an excerpt from Italo Calvino's *Invisible Cities* (appendix 1) and Jorge Luis Borges's "The Wall and the Books" (appendix 2). I begin with the Calvino comparison, since it enables us to work out some presuppositions basic to Kafka's writings, in particular the epistemological principles on which all his fiction is based. Borges's text, by contrast, allows us to explore Kafka's conception of the individual's place in history. Both comparisons, finally, shed light on Kafka's understanding of literary texts and their relation to their readers.

My selection from Calvino's *Invisible Cities* is the opening frame of the second main section of the book (27–29). Before approaching this excerpt, students need to know a little about Calvino's text, a work of extraordinary beauty in no easily identifiable genre. The framework—of which this passage is a part—narrates how Marco Polo communicates the experiences of his many journeys to the emperor Kublai Khan. As he listens to the accounts of the young Venetian, the great ruler attempts to take the measure of his empire, to encompass it in his mind, and to know its nature and structure.

As the narrative proceeds, it becomes apparent not only that Marco Polo's descriptions are more imaginary than real but also that the Khan is not unaware of this. In some sense, indeed, each of the places Polo describes accords with the innermost desires of both himself and the Khan. To what extent, *Invisible Cities* asks, is reality a function of subjectivity?

The excerpt I have chosen bears a clear relation to Kafka's "An Imperial Message" and forms a good preparation for understanding that text. Like the person in Kafka's story who dreams the imperial message at his window when evening falls, Marco Polo seems to relate "only the thoughts that come to a man who sits on his doorstep at evening to enjoy the cool air." "You would do as well never moving from here," the Khan reproaches him. Polo himself, however, seems quite content to accept the idea that what we imagine is all we can really know. Gradually it becomes irrelevant whose mind is at work in the descriptions of distant places: "Marco Polo imagined answering (or Kublai Khan imagined his answer)." The difference between speaker and listener begins to collapse: "All this so that Marco Polo could explain or imagine explaining or be imagined explaining or succeed finally in explaining to himself. . . ." Is *Invisible Cities* the story of a mind apprehending a world, a mind imagining a world, two minds communicating with each other, or a single consciousness meditating within itself? In the last analysis, *Invisible Cities* suggests that the solipsistic mind may be all that exists; certainly it privileges the imaginary over the real, individual consciousness over shared knowledge. '

To grasp the essential subjectivism of this work by Calvino is to lay the groundwork for a more sophisticated understanding of subjectivism in Kafka. Whether he narrates in the first or the third person, Kafka confines himself strictly to the consciousness of his protagonists, most particularly to their range of visual perception. The rare exceptions to this rule are well known, such as the ending of *The Metamorphosis*, which moves abruptly into something like an omniscient viewpoint. Kafka's own insistence on the principle of restricting his presentation to a single consciousness, as exemplified by his refusal to permit illustrations of the transformed Gregor Samsa (who cannot see himself from the outside), is also well known. "An Imperial Message" is unique among Kafka's works in that it is cast in the second person; nonetheless, to the extent that it follows a particular train of thought, it can be seen as part of Kafka's larger enterprise, the exploration of consciousness. Indeed, by addressing the reader directly, "An Imperial Message" seems to presuppose that we all think and experience in the same way. At the same time, the opening sentence identifies the story as something that "is said" to be the case: is it really true or just something that is held to be true? Does this text—do all Kafka's texts—share the same philosophy as Calvino's *Invisible Cities*? Do they posit a world that is merely a construction of mind?

To answer this question, we need to follow more closely the development of the narrative in "An Imperial Message" (see *CS* 4–5). The text opens with what purports to be a fact (that the emperor has sent you a message), moves rapidly to conjecture (the description of the messenger's journey), and ends in the imagination (your dream of the message as you sit by the window waiting). The story describes the elaborate architectural and geographical structures through which the messenger must pass to bring you the emperor's message. At first all that separates you from the emperor seems abolished as if by magic: the walls around the imperial bedchamber, the circle of powerful advisers, the majestic steps of the palace, the thronging crowd outside. But no sooner has this collapse of hierarchy been described than its possibility is called into question: "But the multitudes are so vast; their dwelling-places have no end. If empty fields opened up, how he would fly, and soon doubtless you would hear the welcome hammering of his fists on your door" (*CS* 5).

After this imaginary evocation of the impossible, the narrative returns to a more sober, and above all a more negative, depiction of the messenger's unlikely trajectory through all the rooms of the innermost palace, the stairways, the courtyards, the second encircling palace, more stairways and courtyards, another palace, and so forth. Except for the opening clauses, this whole section is couched in the language of conjecture, repeatedly countermanded by assertions that the messenger's progress is impossible: "never, never can that happen." Like the crowd making way for the advancing messenger, the propositions set up in this text collapse one by one in the face of their own sheer impossibility. In this respect, "An Imperial Message" seems to present a view opposed to that of Calvino's *Invisible Cities*: we can imagine what we like, Kafka's text seems to say, but imagination is always at odds with actual reality, and the power it claims is ultimately illusory.

But there is another contrast between the two texts as well. Whereas Calvino's *Invisible Cities* proposes that all is subjective, it confirms traditional beliefs in the value of the aesthetic, which it regards as a product of subjectivity and apprehensible only through subjectivity. Kafka's philosophy is more unsettling. "An Imperial Message" disturbs us because its second-person narrative urges us to place ourselves in a situation riddled with contradictions. The narrative slides uneasily among three different presentations: a factual account of an event, hypotheses about how this event might take place, and denial that it is even possible. By making us part of the "you" it addresses, the story attributes to us an intellectual confusion we do not necessarily wish to share and throws us into uncertainty about the value of the "dream" it articulates.

What is the difference between the dream of "An Imperial Message" and the fantasy worlds of Marco Polo in Calvino's *Invisible Cities*? Without attempting to label the different philosophies that underlie the two texts, the teacher can elicit some discussion in response to this question. In Calvino, the emperor may wonder whether there is a connection between Polo's fantasies and the realities of his empire, but ultimately the Khan seems untroubled by the notion that his realm may be nothing more than a mental construct. By contrast, Kafka's "An Imperial Message" makes us acutely aware of the discrepancy between what can be imagined and what can actually occur. It raises questions about the status and value of stories, and even though its final image assumes that we will continue to indulge our desire for them, the text never quite dispels our suspicion that stories are disappointing and deceptive. Our culture does in fact have ambivalent feelings about the value of fiction, and Kafka's texts make us uncomfortably aware of that ambivalence. The responses Kafka describes in "An Imperial Message" are what we feel, in a less acute form, while reading almost any work of literature: this is actually happening; if only this were to happen; never, never can this happen.

Borges's text "The Wall and the Books" may be used to reveal yet another dimension of Kafka's "An Imperial Message." Although "The Wall" includes motifs we have also seen in Calvino's *Invisible Cities*—a strong dependence on conjecture, for example—it is less urgently concerned with epistemological questions. Rather, it explores the relation between texts and history and, by extension, between texts and power, asking both what power texts have over the individual and what power the individual has over texts. Much of Borges's text is relatively accessible and will provide a great deal of material for discussion, but the final paragraph may require some explanation from the teacher. I return to this problem shortly.

First, we need to establish what type of text we confront in "The Wall and the Books." Unlike Calvino's novel or Kafka's story, Borges's text is not clearly definable as fiction. Written in the first person, it is cast in the form of reflections on an apparent paradox concerning the Chinese emperor Shih Huang Ti. Is this an essay, or is it a form of story? If I sometimes call the speaker or writer of this text "the essayist," I do not mean to suggest that "The Wall" is unequivocally an essay. Perhaps what we have here is a narrator masquerading as an essayist. The ambiguity is not unimportant.

The paradox on which Borges's text is based takes the following form: how could the man who built an extensive wall to protect his empire from the barbarians have himself done something so barbarous as to order that all books be burned? Although the essayist claims to be disturbed by this paradox of an emperor who both preserves and destroys, he finds himself in some sense "inexplicably satisfied" by the story (186). The question for this narrator is thus not simply "What happened?" or even "How can this paradox be resolved?" but, more important, "Why does it have this effect on me?" This first-person form, as opposed to the second-person form of Kafka's "An Imperial Message," has some crucial consequences for our understanding of Borges's text, since it personalizes what in Kafka purports to be universal. Whereas Kafka's story buttonholes us, turning each reader (by means of the powerful second-person pronoun) into the pitifully cowering subject of the dying emperor, Borges's text claims to be nothing more than the personal reflections of a particular individual, whose meandering thoughts we may follow or not as we please. In Kafka's narrative, the interpolation "it is said" in the opening sentence identifies the story as part of an oral tradition, possibly one of long standing, and attributes the story to no one in particular. By contrast, Borges's text, opening with the words "I read, some days past," situates itself within the written tradition and within one person's recent experience. In other words, Borges personalizes an essentially historical question, whereas Kafka universalizes what would otherwise be the story of a single individual.

Students can test these distinctions between the two texts by recasting the opening paragraph of "The Wall and the Books" in the second person or, conversely, recasting the beginning and ending of "An Imperial Message" in the third person. To what extent can we enter into Borges's text, as we would have to do if it were narrated in the second person? Do we really share the feelings of the essayist in "The Wall and the Books"? What happens to the time frame when Kafka's story is converted into the third person? How would the person waiting for the message at the end of Kafka's text appear to us if presented in the third person?

To observe these differences between "The Wall and the Books" and "An Imperial Message," however, is not to exhaust the ways in which Borges's text responds to Kafka's. Both are also concerned with the power of words over people: Kafka's cowering individual desperately longs for a message he will never receive, and Borges's emperor burns books containing messages he wishes to conceal. Both texts address the way in which traditions, written or oral, actually function.

Insofar as universality is often claimed to be a characteristic of literature in general, "An Imperial Message" also questions the notion that literary texts transcend time and place. Hence the paradox of the single individual with whom any and all readers are expected to identify, the remote culture and period into which we are expected to transport ourselves in imagination. Kafka's text in fact makes each individual reader do that which can "never, never happen": become a citizen of imperialist China waiting for a message from a long-dead emperor. In so doing, it asks us to think about the nature of literary texts and their claim to timelessness and universality. "An Imperial Message" asks, in effect, how do literary texts actually affect us as they do?

Borges's text begins with the other side of this coin. If literary texts speak to all readers equally in a kind of timeless present, history books specify individuals, times, and places in such a way that they are not assimilable to anything else. But despite its opening posture of rationality and its claim to know what is what "historically speaking," "The Wall and the Books" rapidly departs from the firm ground of historical fact. Its lengthy third paragraph is, in fact, nothing other than an extravagant series of conjectures. Thinking about history, trying to understand history, is revealed as nothing other than an imaginative exercise—a fictional text, in other words.

This perspective explains the surprising, and at first seemingly irrelevant, way in which Borges's narrator concludes his reflections on Shih Huang Ti. The text ends with a reference to Walter Pater and a statement, heavily dependent on Pater, about the nature of the aesthetic experience: "Music, states of happiness, mythology, faces belabored by time, certain twilights and certain places try to tell us something, or have said something we should not have missed, or are about to say something; this imminence of a revelation which does not occur is, perhaps, the aesthetic phenomenon" (188). What does the aestheticist movement have to do with "The Wall and the Books"? Some explanation of the theory of artistic autonomy will be necessary before students can make connections between Pater's aestheticist ideal and the Chinese ruler who tries to eradicate history and to wall in his empire. Repressing historicity (viewing the work of art as somehow outside time) and walling in the realm (regarding the work of art as sufficient unto itself, needing no extraneous explanation) are characteristic features of the aestheticist position. In Pater's view, phenomena are always "transhistorical"; that is to say, the similarities between two historical periods generally outweigh their differences. The work of art is meaningful, in the aestheticist view, because it subsists in a "mythological," "twilight" realm that cuts it off from the march of time and gives it a universal aspect. In a final twist that moves away from Pater, however, Borges describes the revelation promised by the work of art as one that "does not occur."

If we look back from "The Wall and the Books" to "An Imperial Message," we can see that some of the same themes are engaged. Cast as part of an oral tradition, "An Imperial Message" evokes the mythological (indeed, in its original context as part of the longer story "The Great Wall of China," the narrator introduces it as a "legend"). In ending his tale "as evening falls," Kafka invokes a familiar topos of turn-of-the-century literature, the aestheticist twilights Borges mentions at the end of "The Wall and the Books." Kafka asks us, in other words, to test "An Imperial Message" against the aestheticist model of the timeless, universalizing, and pleasurable literary text. If we think of the work of art as autonomous, we see why the messenger can never leave the boundaries of the complex sets of courtyards within courtyards that constitute its form. If the work of art is autonomous, if it has no real links to outside reality—to time, history, and real individuals—it cannot logically reach beyond itself to a reader waiting to receive its message. And yet, as we all know, that which can "never, never happen" somehow also does happen: the work of art draws us into its circle, promising us its never-quite-completed revelation.

Taken together, the two comparisons help open up a number of questions crucial for an understanding of Kafka. Does reality exist, or is it all in the mind? What is the relation between history and fiction? Is fiction really universal and timeless? Does the aesthetic experience have an objective value, or is it merely a projection of our own dreams and desires?

Had we been Kafka's contemporaries, we would have been more aware of the twin themes of Kafka's "An Imperial Message": its exploration of the limitations of consciousness and its critique of aestheticist theory. Kafka was in fact well versed in contemporary philosophy and psychology, especially those schools of thought that viewed subjective experience as the only reality. By the same token, he was thoroughly familiar with turn-of-the-century aestheticism and its notion that art was essentially divorced from other aspects of life. These concerns emerge as guiding themes in "An Imperial Message." Kafka constructs his text to bring out the hidden paradoxes of contemporary philosophy and contemporary aesthetics alike. These issues have tended to be obscured by the "horizon of expectations" today's reader brings to Kafka's texts. Expecting to find in Kafka what has come to be called the Kafkaesque, our students generally have difficulty moving beyond this reductionist vision. The theoretical questions, philosophical and literary, that Calvino and Borges ask as they construct their own reworkings of Kafka create a new mind-set that enables a more differentiated understanding of the abstract and challenging issues Kafka's texts in fact explore.

Appendix I

Excerpt from *Invisible Cities*, by Italo Calvino

"The other ambassadors warn me of famines, extortions, conspiracies, or else they inform me of newly discovered turquoise mines, advantageous prices in marten furs, suggestions for supplying damascened blades. And you?" the Great Khan asked Polo, "you return from lands equally distant and you can tell me only the thoughts that come to a man who sits on his doorstep at evening to enjoy the cool air. What is the use, then, of all your traveling?"

"It is evening. We are seated on the steps of your palace. There is a slight breeze," Marco Polo answered. "Whatever country my words may evoke around you, you will see it from such a vantage point, even if instead of the palace there is a village on pilings and the breeze carries the stench of a muddy estuary."

"My gaze is that of a man meditating, lost in thought—I admit it. But yours? You cross archipelagoes, tundras, mountain ranges. You would do as well never moving from here."

The Venetian knew that when Kublai became vexed with him, the emperor wanted to follow more clearly a private train of thought; so Marco's answers and objections took their place in a discourse already proceeding on its own, in the Great Khan's head. That is to say, between the two of them it did not matter whether questions and solutions were uttered aloud or whether each of the two went on pondering in silence. In fact, they were silent, their eyes half-closed, reclining on cushions, swaying in hammocks, smoking long amber pipes.

Marco Polo imagined answering (or Kublai Khan imagined his answer) that the more one was lost in unfamiliar quarters of distant cities, the more one understood the other cities he had crossed to arrive there; and he retraced the stages of his journeys, and he came to know the port from which he had set sail, and the familiar places of his youth, and the surroundings of home, and a little square of Venice where he gamboled as a child.

At this point Kublai Khan interrupted him or imagined interrupting him, or Marco Polo imagined himself interrupted, with a question such as: "You advance always with your head turned back?" or "Is what you see always behind you?" or rather, "Does your journey take place only in the past?"

All this so that Marco Polo could explain or imagine explaining or be imagined explaining or succeed finally in explaining to himself that what he sought was always something lying ahead, and even if it was a matter of the past it was a past that changed gradually as he advanced on his journey, because the traveler's past changes according to the route he has followed: not the immediate past, that is, to which each day that goes by adds a day, but the more remote past. Arriving at each new city, the traveler finds again a past of his that he did not know he had: the foreignness of what you no longer are or no longer possess lies in wait for you in foreign, unpossessed places.

Marco enters a city; he sees someone in a square living a life or an instant that could be his; he could now be in that man's place, if he had stopped in time, long ago; or if, long ago, at a crossroads, instead of taking one road he had taken the opposite one, and after long wandering he had come to be in the place of that man in that square. By now, from that real or hypothetical past of his, he is excluded; he cannot stop; he must go on to another city, where another of his pasts awaits him, or something perhaps that had been a possible future of his and is now someone else's present. Futures not achieved are only branches of the past: dead branches.

"Journeys to relive your past?" was the Khan's question at this point, a question which could also have been formulated: "Journeys to recover your future?"

And Marco's answer was: "Elsewhere is a negative mirror. The traveler recognizes the little that is his, discovering the much he has not had and will never have."

Appendix II

"The Wall and the Books," by Jorge Luis Borges

> He, whose long wall the wand'ring
> Tartar bounds . . .
> —*Dunciad 2.76*

I read, some days past, that the man who ordered the erection of the almost infinite wall of China was that first Emperor, Shih Huang Ti, who also decreed that all books prior to him be burned. That these two vast operations—the five to six hundred leagues of stone opposing the barbarians, the rigorous abolition of history, that is, of the past—should originate in one person and be in some way his attributes inexplicably satisfied and, at the same time, disturbed me. To investigate the reasons for that emotion is the purpose of this note.

Historically speaking, there is no mystery in the two measures. A contemporary of the wars of Hannibal, Shih Huang Ti, king of Tsin, brought the Six Kingdoms under his rule and abolished the feudal system; he erected the wall, because walls were defenses; he burned the books, because his opposition invoked them to praise the emperors of olden times. Burning books and erecting fortifications is a common task of princes; the only thing singular in Shih Huang Ti was the scale on which he operated. Such is suggested by certain Sinologists, but I feel that the facts I have related are something more than an exaggeration or hyperbole of trivial dispositions. Walling in an orchard or a garden is ordinary, but not walling in an empire. Nor is it banal to pretend that the most traditional of races renounce the memory of its past, mythical or real. The Chinese had three thousand years of chronology (and during those years, the Yellow Emperor and Chuang Tsu and Confucius and Lao Tzu) when Shih Huang Ti ordered that history begin with him.

Shih Huang Ti had banished his mother for being a libertine; in his stern justice the orthodox saw nothing but an impiety; Shih Huang Ti, perhaps, wanted to obliterate the canonical books because they accused him; Shih Huang Ti, perhaps, tried to abolish the entire past in order to abolish one single memory: his mother's infamy. (Not in an unlike manner did a king of Judea have all male children killed in order to kill one.) This conjecture is worthy of attention, but tells us nothing about the wall, the second part of the myth. Shih Huang Ti, according to the historians, forbade that death be mentioned and sought the elixir of immortality and secluded himself in a figurative palace containing as many rooms as there are days in the year; these facts suggest that the wall in space and the fire in time were magic barriers designed to halt death. All things long to persist in their being,

Baruch Spinoza has written; perhaps the Emperor and his sorcerers believed that immortality is intrinsic and that decay cannot enter a closed orb. Perhaps the Emperor tried to recreate the beginning of time and called himself The First, so as to be really first, and called himself Huang Ti, so as to be in some way Huang Ti, the legendary emperor who invented writing and the compass. The latter, according to the *Book of Rites*, gave things their true name; in a parallel fashion, Shih Huang Ti boasted, in inscriptions which endure, that all things in his reign would have the name which was proper to them. He dreamt of founding an immortal dynasty; he ordered that his heirs be called Second Emperor, Third Emperor, Fourth Emperor, and so on to infinity . . . I have spoken of a magical purpose; it would also be fitting to suppose that erecting the wall and burning the books were not simultaneous acts. This (depending on the order we select) would give us the image of a king who began by destroying and then resigned himself to preserving, or that of a disillusioned king who destroyed what he had previously defended. Both conjectures are dramatic, but they lack, as far as I know, any basis in history. Herbert Allen Giles tells that those who hid books were branded with a red-hot iron and sentenced to labor until the day of their death on the construction of the outrageous wall. This information favors or tolerates another interpretation. Perhaps the wall was a metaphor, perhaps Shih Huang Ti sentenced those who worshiped the past to a task as immense, as gross and as useless as the past itself. Perhaps the wall was a challenge and Shih Huang Ti thought: "Men love the past and neither I nor my executioners can do anything against that love, but someday there will be a man who feels as I do and he will efface my memory and be my shadow and my mirror and not know it." Perhaps Shih Huang Ti walled in his empire because he knew that it was perishable and destroyed the books because he understood that they were sacred books, in other words, books that teach what the entire universe or the mind of every man teaches. Perhaps the burning of the libraries and the erection of the wall are operations which in some secret way cancel each other.

The tenacious wall which at this moment, and at all moments, casts its system of shadows over lands I shall never see, is the shadow of a Caesar who ordered the most reverent of nations to burn its past; it is plausible that this idea moves us in itself, aside from the conjectures it allows. (Its virtue may lie in the opposition of constructing and destroying on an enormous scale.) Generalizing from the preceding case, we could infer that *all* forms have their virtue in themselves and not in any conjectural "content." This would concord with the thesis of Benedetto Croce; already Pater in 1877 had affirmed that all arts aspire to the state of music, which is pure form. Music, states of happiness, mythology, faces belabored by time, certain twilights and certain places try to tell us something, or have said something we should not have missed, or are about to say something; this imminence of a revelation which does not occur is, perhaps, the aesthetic phenomenon.

From *Caligari* to Kafka: Expressionist Film and the Teaching of Kafka's Short Fiction

Richard T. Gray

The popular film *The Wizard of Oz* has, I believe it safe to say, entered the collective North American consciousness to such an extent that it represents a body of shared material with which most North American undergraduates are closely acquainted. My narrative about the applicability of expressionist film, specifically Robert Wiene's silent film classic *The Cabinet of Dr. Caligari* (1919), to the teaching of Kafka's fiction takes an episode from this popular American film as its point of departure.[1] All of us recall the moment when Dorothy, the Tin Man, the Scarecrow, the Lion, and Toto (yes, Toto too) stand awestruck and trembling before the magnificence and power of the great Oz, depicted as a huge head enveloped in smoke and light, from which emanates a grandiloquent voice and the sound of thunder. In this scene Toto, the central motivator of plot throughout the film, plays one of his most significant roles: unintimidated by the ostentatious spectacle projected in front of him, Toto draws back the curtain of the projection booth to reveal the friendly white-haired wizard who operates the mechanisms of this imposing representation. This scene clearly presents a commentary relevant both to the overall narrative that the film itself recounts and to the general nature of film as a narrative medium: it reminds the audience, first of all, that the trip to Oz is a dream representation transpiring in the head of Dorothy, lying on her bed in a farmhouse in Kansas; second, it discloses that this narratively framed dream representation is itself a representation, projected through the cinematic medium, that takes place in the imagination of each viewer.

On the most general level, what *Oz*, *Caligari*, and Kafka's fictional texts have in common is their character as narratives of the psyche: they all tend to project the subjective psychic states of a figural consciousness into an ostensibly objective fictional world. It is this congruity that determines the significance of this example from *Oz* for the pedagogical project I outline here. Insofar as Toto's revelatory act represents a disclosure of the internal mechanisms governing representation, his action sums up the pedagogical aims of my procedure: an unveiling of certain narratological deep structures characteristically at work in Kafka's fiction. To be sure, this analogy is not meant to suggest that Kafka's texts are merely mechanical constructs whose mysteries are neutralized once one understands how this narrative mechanism operates. In *The Wizard of Oz*, we must recall, the wizard retains the power to transform his guests even after his representation has been unmasked; indeed, the demystification of his wizardry becomes the prerequisite for a transformative interaction between him and the characters who sought him out. But the role of this scene in the film's narrative has more substantive implications for a comparative study of *The Cabinet of Dr. Caligari* and such short fictional texts by Kafka as *The Metamorphosis*, "The Judgment," and "A Country Doctor." The relations among viewer, narrative frame, and internal dream narrative that the unmasking episode in *Oz* throws into relief are structurally homologous to the interrelations of these three dimensions in *Caligari*, as well as to those between reader, narrating consciousness, and psychic text in Kafka's fiction.

Most undergraduates are conventional readers whose habits and strategies have been nourished either on the conventions of popular literature and film or on the premodernist literary "classics." These students are hence accustomed to relatively reliable narrators who possess a perfect, pseudo-divine consciousness that, like a transparent lens, permits them as readers to bring into focus certain "objective" facts about the fictional world, its characters, and their psychic constitutions. Kafka's narratives, in contradistinction, present readers with few such clear facts, and students commonly respond to this phenomenon with confusion, maintaining that Kafka's texts are nothing if not "absurd." The procedure I describe seeks to reveal to students the narratological method behind this textual madness that has come to be known as the Kafkaesque.

Cinema, as a medium with which contemporary students are amply acquainted, suggests itself immediately to those searching for nonliterary examples that might elucidate fundamental problems of literature (see Faber 200–05). The viewing of *The Cabinet of Dr. Caligari* in relation to classroom analysis of Kafka's short fiction, however, offers a variety of specific advantages that go beyond the mere openness of students to the cinematic medium and also beyond the exposition of the structural homology that can likewise be demonstrated by using a more popular film such as *The Wizard of Oz*. *Caligari* possesses a profounder elucidatory power vis-à-vis Kafka's fiction because, as an artistic product contemporaneous to Kafka's writing, it can help characterize both the macro level of historical context and the micro level of narrative technique. For classes concerned primarily with the historical environment in which Kafka's fiction evolves, *Caligari* provides a cinematic prototype for the problematics and techniques endemic to German literary expressionism, an aesthetic movement that forms a revealing historical backdrop to the understanding of Kafka's fictional techniques (see Sokel, *Writer* 46–51; *Tragik und Ironie* 12–13). Classes concerned primarily with narrative technique can exploit the film's narrative devices to illuminate the subtle and complex strategies constitutive of Kafka's texts.

Let me first sketch in a preliminary manner the stages of the pedagogical procedure I am proposing. As an introduction to this endeavor, the teacher reconstructs the revelatory scene from *The Wizard of Oz* described above. This exposition may be supported with a presentation of this clip on video. As an introduction to the problematics of expressionist art, I find it helpful to discuss with students a brief expository text that describes the aesthetic aims and artistic techniques of expressionist literature. A text I have found very useful at this stage is the following passage from August Strindberg's prologue to *A Dream Play* (1901–1906):

> I have in this present dream play sought to imitate the incoherent but ostensibly logical form of our dreams. Anything can happen; everything is possible and probable. Time and space do not exist. Working with some insignificant real events as a background, the imagination spins out its threads of thoughts and weaves them into new patterns—a mixture of memories, experiences, spontaneous ideas, impossibilities, and improbabilities.
>
> The characters split, double, multiply, dissolve, condense, float apart, coalesce. But one mind stands over and above them all, the mind of the dreamer; and for him there are no secrets, no inconsistencies, no scruples, no laws. He does not condemn, does not acquit; he only narrates the story. (Strindberg 33)

Next, I undertake a guided screening of *Caligari*. My experience has been that students find it difficult to pick up on the narrative hinges in the film in a single straightforward viewing. For this reason, it is best either to point out some of the important scenes and turning points as the screening takes place or to review them on video after the initial screening. During this review one can encourage the students to comment on the relations between the techniques Strindberg identifies in his *Dream Play* and the cinematic mechanisms at work in *Caligari*.

The stage is now set for a reading of Kafka. After the students have read the chosen text, we examine selected passages together in class, attempting to uncover the structural and technical similarities between Kafka's textual and Wiene's cinematic narratives. After arriving at a characterization of Kafka's narrative techniques—such as point of view, narrative framing, and narrative discourse—I ask students to formulate interpretations that account for these questions.

Having sketched the basic pedagogical procedure, I now want to fill out this outline with some of the relevant arguments. Numerous complexes touched on in the Strindberg excerpt are relevant to the guided screening of *Caligari* that follows: the emphasis on dream texture; the tensions between such opposing principles as incoherence and logic, reality and imagination, the trivial and the significant; splitting and doubling of characters (note that the figures in Francis's narrative have analogues in the narrative frame; all the "imagined" characters are projections based on Francis's "colleagues" in the asylum). Most significant, however, is Strindberg's assertion that the narrating consciousness controls his story, providing the sole basis for consistency and unity. In *Caligari* this controlling consciousness is not that of a mere dreamer, as in Strindberg, but rather, as the narrative frame of the film makes clear, a consciousness deranged by mental illness. Precisely this distinction defines the illustrative power of the film in the context of Kafka's fiction. Kafka's third-person narratives, such as "The Judgment" and *The Metamorphosis*, present undergraduates with especially pronounced difficulties because the transitions from objective narrative frame to the internal narrative of the psyche are not obviously tagged. *Caligari*, however, employs straightforward cinematic techniques to mark these crucial transition points. When the protagonist Francis, in the opening scene of the film, begins to tell his story, the cut to the internal narrative is marked by a closing iris shot (the frame darkens in the form of a circle from outside to inside) that focuses its narrowing circle on Francis's forehead, indicating to viewers that the next scenes transpire in his subjective consciousness. For the sake of reinforcement, the film cuts back to the narrative frame twice in the early segments of Francis's story, returning each time to his mental visualization of the tale he is telling by way of the iris shot encircling his head. One can confirm the narrative significance of this technique by examining the story within a story that occurs near the end of the film. While Dr. Caligari sleeps, Francis searches through the doctor's books and papers. When he comes across the book describing the historical Caligari's experiments with somnambulism, Francis narratively reconstructs in his own mind Dr. Caligari's past and his motivations. This narrative reconstruction is again introduced by an iris that focuses on Francis's head.

Teachers primarily concerned with characteristics of expressionist art can highlight here that the ostensibly objective narrative about the murders and the Holstenwall fair are in fact the imaginings—indeed, the delusions—of the narrator. One particular scene in the film underscores graphically that Francis is the imaginative center of this narrative and that the narrated events are his psychic projections. After following Caligari from the fairgrounds back to the asylum, Francis pauses in the courtyard. He is situated on a circle from which rays emanate and this scenic representation suggests concretely that the depicted situations and events "emanate" from Francis's psyche (Byrne 189–92). It is important to stress for the students that this scene demonstrates an identity between narrative point of view and figural perspective, an identity underscored by the fact that Francis is the only figure who inhabits both the narrative frame and the internal narrative as the selfsame individual—an observation applicable to Dorothy in *Oz* as well. Once it has been established that Francis's psychic projections constitute the point of view from which the internal narrative is recounted, one can easily explain as reflexes of this "abnormal" narrative perspective the odd geometric shapes and the perspectival distortions typical of the film's scenic backdrops. Here the instructor can emphasize how Francis's distortions enter into our perspective as viewers: only when we disentangle ourselves from his consciousness, which governs the narrative, do we attain a distortion-free view of the narrated events. *Caligari* thus supplies students with a tangible example of the so-called radiation of the ego typical both of expressionist art in general and of Kafka's fiction. But unlike Kafka's texts, the film discloses to its audience in the denouement that it has tricked us by imprisoning our consciousness and point of view in the figural perspective of the insane Francis. My experience has been that after analyzing this film, students become more profoundly aware of the significant influence that narrative point of view may exert on the narrated events of a story and on their reception. It thereby becomes easier for them to comprehend, for example, Gregor Samsa's metamorphosis as a wish-fulfillment dream distorted by his own sense of guilt, to see the country doctor's experiences as the imaginings of a psyche torn between erotic desires and the call of professional and societal duty. Once revealed to be narratives of the psyche rather than objective narrations of empirically determined events, Kafka's stories open themselves up to new interpretive perspectives. Students can more easily investigate characters as ciphers or manifestations of psychic complexes, rather than as flesh-and-blood individuals. Above all, they come away from their readings of Kafka with a heightened awareness of the story as text: they can more readily accept the notion of the text as texture; as a fabric composed of structural threads, to paraphrase the Strindberg passage cited above, woven together into particular patterns by a manipulative narrative consciousness.

One can also apply the recognitions drawn from *Caligari* to the analysis of Kafka's narrative techniques. The problem of narrative perspective in Kafka's fiction can perhaps best be examined through an investigation of *The Metamorphosis*, since the text gives relatively clear indications that the narrative point of view is located in the consciousness of its protagonist. In the following passage I have marked the transition points from external to internal perspective or vice versa with double bars, and I have italicized the segments that I take to be reflections of the figural consciousness rather than of an objective narrator.

> As Gregor Samsa awoke one morning from uneasy dreams ‖ *he found himself transformed in his bed into a gigantic insect.* ‖ He was lying on his hard, as it were armor-plated, back and when he lifted his head a little ‖ *he could see his domelike brown belly divided into stiff arched segments. . . . What has happened to me?* ‖ he thought. ‖ *It was no dream. His room, a regular human bedroom, only rather too small, lay quiet between the four familiar walls.*   (CS 89)

The first two figural passages are clearly marked as descriptions recounted from Gregor's point of view: it is Gregor who "finds himself" transformed into a bug, and we perceive the details of his metamorphosed body through his eyes. This reliance on Gregor's perspective manifests itself in two dominant narrative techniques: quoted monologue and narrated monologue (see Cohn, *Transparent Minds* 58–98, 99–123). I take the final passage highlighted in the quotation above to be narrated monologue (i.e., figural narration cloaked in the discursive language of an objective narrator). Application of this narrative technique, which formally replicates the language of omniscient narration, is what makes the alternating figural and objective narrative sequences of this text blend almost seamlessly into each other. The confusion this procedure calls forth may be witnessed in the final sentence of the quoted passage. The narrative status of this statement is fundamentally ambiguous, since it can be read equally well as objective and as figural narration, and this duality underscores the consonance with which these two techniques converge in Kafka's fiction.

The following quotation is but one of numerous passages from *The Metamorphosis* that may be fruitfully analyzed in terms of narrative technique:

> He looked at the alarm clock ticking on the chest. Heavenly Father! he thought. It was half-past six o'clock and the hands were quietly moving on, it was even past the half-hour, it was getting on toward a quarter to seven. Had the alarm clock not gone off? From the bed one could see that it had been properly set for four o'clock; of course it must have gone off.   (CS 90)

Once clued in to the problem of narrative perspective in Kafka, students can usually recognize the movement of this paragraph as typical for the story: from objective narration that describes Gregor's action ("He looked . . ."), the passage moves by means of a transitional sentence of quoted monologue ("Heavenly Father! he thought") into narrated monologue ("It was . . .").

What clearly marks these final reflections as narrated monologue is, first of all, the emphasis placed on Gregor's perspective ("From the bed one could see . . .") and, second, the speculative character of the questions and assertions they present. An omniscient narrator, of course, would have no need to guess whether the alarm clock had been set and in fact gone off. Instructors interested in exploring narrative technique with their students may go on to examine further examples of quoted and narrated monologue in the text, eliciting from the class descriptions of the character and function of these devices.

One may also highlight restriction of the narrative perspective to Gregor's point of view by emphasizing the spatial limitations of the narrated situation. Shut off from the events that occur outside the closed and locked door to his room, Gregor is forced to speculate solely on the basis of aural clues about what is happening:

> "Anna! Anna!" his father was *calling* through the hall to the kitchen, *clapping* his hands, "get a locksmith at once!" And the two girls were already running through the hall with *a swish of skirts*—how could his sister have got dressed so quickly?—and were tearing the front door open. There was *no sound* of its closing again; they had evidently left it open, as one does in houses where some great misfortune has happened.   (CS 98–99, emphasis added)

The almost total restriction of the narrative to those perceptions that reach Gregor's consciousness could scarcely be portrayed more lucidly than it is in this passage, whose aural elements I have italicized. What is most striking here, however, is the manner in which the limitations of Gregor's perspective—limitations that, because the text represents them scenically, beg comparison with cinematic portrayal—lead him to pose questions and formulate speculative interpretations about the events he overhears.[2] His speculation about the open front door, moreover, gives rise to a gnomic commentary that is obviously attributable only to Gregor himself, not to an objective narrator. This comment, which is steeped in Gregor's self-pity, elucidates the extent to which the protagonist's own sentiments condition not only his interpretations of the narrated events but also those we make as readers. Finally, based on the reading of this passage, one becomes cognizant of Gregor's obsession with doors and can move from here to an examination of the door as a central motif in the text. The cited passage thus serves both to underscore the severe restrictions placed on narrative point of view in this story and to provide a springboard into questions of textuality and motific structure.

Once cognizant that Gregor's prejudices and desires influence the narrative point of view, students are more ready to accept the possibility that recurring objects and motifs form a self-referential symbolic web that can best be understood as internal textual references to Gregor's psychic patterns, rather than as allegorical keys that refer to meaning complexes residing outside the text itself. Resistance to this allegorical impulse is fundamental to a circumspect reading of Kafka's fiction. In this regard one can once again productively exploit the narrative structure of *Caligari* as a paradigm for Kafka: by examining the self-referential interconnections that link the narrative frame and internal narrative of this film, one can help clarify the structure of Kafka's literary texts as fundamentally self-referential, intratextual systems of signification.

It should be clear from this discussion of *The Metamorphosis* that the methodology I advocate operates on a "preinterpretive" level: it does not (necessarily) lead to any one specific interpretation of the text but, rather, seeks to sketch the narratological parameters that establish the interpretive ground rules for its analysis. As in *Caligari*, deviations from "normal" reality or traditional textuality must be viewed as distortions enforced on the cinematic or literary narrative by the manipulating consciousness of the protagonist-narrator. The radical "unreliability" of the narratives is connected to their refraction by the distorting lenses of Francis's and Gregor's minds. This recognition forms the condition of possibility for a critically sophisticated interpretation of Kafka's text(s).

The rich and varied interconnections between *The Cabinet of Dr. Caligari* and Kafka's fiction allow for numerous analogies and analyses other than those I have emphasized here. Within the sphere of fictional technique, the relation between narrative frame and internal narrative in *Caligari* may be taken as a point of orientation for discussions of narrative framing in Kafka's stories. "The Judgment," for example, begins with an ostensibly objective empirical description before shifting into Georg Bendemann's internal perspective and relating (primarily in narrated monologue) the thoughts that pass through his head as he sits "dreamily" gazing out his window (*CS* 77). The narrative returns to this external perspective—similar to the perspective in the concluding pages of *The Metamorphosis*—when Georg lets himself fall from the bridge into the water below: "At this moment an unending stream of traffic [*Verkehr*] was just going over the bridge" (*CS* 88). This unending stream of traffic, with its implications of commerce and, in the German original, of social intercourse and sexuality as well, transports the reader back to the prominent motific structures of the internal narrative. Once one recognizes this reiterative pattern, the elements of the narrative frame begin to lose their empirical objectivity and take on a kind of symbolic luminosity that links them to the events of the internal narrative. The bridge, the traffic, the monotonous row of houses—all these ostensibly "objective" details themselves—are revealed as a part of the internal referential system of the text. In much the same way, the ironic reversal of the internal narrative in *Caligari*, which reveals the psychopathic murderer to be in fact the director of the asylum, is repeated in the narrative frame when the Caligari figure is revealed to be a projection modeled on the insane narrator's attendant physician. The narrative frames of both Wiene's and Kafka's "texts" thus replicate structural patterns and motific complexes established in their internal narratives.

One witnesses the same phenomenon in Kafka's "A Country Doctor," with the interesting variation that in this first-person tale the narrative frame is constructed by the protagonist's gnomic reflections rather than by objective description. The text thus concludes when the protagonist's melancholy summary of his own situation is expanded into an aphoristic utterance that generalizes his personal experience into a universal metaphysical condition: "Naked, exposed to the frost of this most unhappy of ages, with an earthly vehicle, unearthly horses, old man that I am, I wander astray. . . . Betrayed! Betrayed! A false alarm on the night bell once answered—it cannot be made good, not ever" (CS 225). Far from providing an interpretive key that elucidates the narrated events, however, this gnomic reflection merely compresses into the universalizing rhetoric of the aphorism a reiterative outline of the narrative events themselves, repeating their motific structure and elevating them—in the response to the call of the night bell—to a level of parabolic universality.[3]

Moving beyond matters of textual structure and narrative technique, one can also come to terms with certain central thematic issues in Kafka's fiction by comparing them with related themes in *Caligari*. One prominent example is the treatment of authority in Wiene's film and in Kafka's "The Judgment." In *Caligari* official authorities such as the Town Clerk and the police officers are represented in a domineering perspective, scenically portrayed as perched on exaggeratedly high stools. This same association of scenic height with authority appears in "The Judgment" when Georg's father stands up on the bed to condemn his son. In both instances tyrannical authority is associated with a commanding perspective. This association has the ultimate effect of setting up a conjunction between this thematic complex and the problems of narrative perspective. Kafka's narrative technique, one might speculate, is nonauthoritative and nonauthoritarian to the extent that it is grounded in a figural narrative perspective, one that lacks any commanding overview. One may support this hypothesis by referring to some of Kafka's numerous reflections on the problem of perspective. The following diary entry from 1913, for example, reads like a condensation of the plot structure of many Kafka narratives:

> The truly terrible paths between freedom and slavery cross each other with no guide to the way ahead and accompanied by an immediate obliterating of those paths already traversed. There are a countless number of such paths, or only one, it cannot be determined, for there is no vantage ground from which to observe.
>
> (*Diaries, 1910–1913* 324)

One can suggest to students that the collapse of an objective narrative standpoint and the textual polyvalence it produces are responsible for the increasing significance of the reader's input in the interpretation of Kafka's fiction, a condition that is paradigmatic for the hermeneutical challenge posed by modernist literature in general. The same may be said, with certain reservations, about *Caligari*, for it is only with the addition of the narrative frame, which is not a part of Hans Janowitz's and Carl Mayer's original screenplay, that an authoritative perspective is established in the film (Kracauer 61–76). The tension between tyranny and chaos, which according to Siegfried Kracauer dominates Wiene's film, may also be investigated in Kafka's "The Judgment" in the lifestyles represented by Georg and his friend in Saint Petersburg. Georg, like Dr. Caligari, approaches life with designs of mastery and control over others; the friend, by contrast, is exposed to the chaos and upheaval of the revolutionary events in Russia. Questions of authority, domination, control, and chaos thus figure centrally in both narratives, and this thematic complex may in both cases be studied with reference to questions of narrative stance and perspective. One can assist students in their interrogation of this connection between a domineering perspective and questions of mastery by discussing the relevance of the following aphoristic text by Kafka to the problems manifest in "The Judgment."

> The diversity of views which one can have, say, of an apple: the apple as it appears to the child who must stretch his neck so as barely to see it on the table, and the apple as it appears to the master of the house who picks it up and lordly hands it to his guest.
>
> (*Great Wall* 164; trans. modified)

The greater overview of the "master of the house" is portrayed here as a reflex of his ability to manipulate objects in his immediate environment. Viewed in this context, the relative perspectivelessness, the lack of overview characteristic of Kafka's protagonists, like that of the child in this aphorism, appears as a trait constitutive of their ultimate powerlessness, their inability to take decisive charge over themselves and their empirical life world.

The advantages of the pedagogical methodology advanced here for an understanding of Kafka's short fiction are twofold. Not only does a guided screening of *Caligari* provide students with a technical "key" that allows them to unlock some of the secrets of Kafka's narrative strategies, but it also helps to demonstrate the coherence of Kafka's techniques and themes within the broader scope of expressionism as an aesthetic phenomenon. Of course, when we deal with texts as complex as Kafka's, no pedagogical approach we choose will be an interpretive panacea. Indeed, while my experience has shown that the procedure outlined here can help students better understand the operations of Kafka's narratives, this approach alone is no guarantee that

they can move from this awareness to a coherent and consistent interpretation (supposing that such uniformity is possible or even desirable in reading
Kafka). Nonetheless, as teachers we can derive a certain satisfaction if, as
our students enter Kafka's textual labyrinths, we are able to put a thread
into their hands that at least reassures them they will find their way back
out again, even if they fail to return with the interpretive treasure they
seek. Surely this lack in itself marks one of the most important lessons
undergraduates can cull from Kafka's writing.

NOTES

[1]*Caligari* is readily and inexpensively available both as a feature film and on
videocassette. The film can be ordered through the film services of the German
Information Agency for a modest rental fee plus shipping costs. The video, in either
VHS or Beta format, can be purchased from the German Language Video Center,
7625 Pendleton Pike, Indianapolis, IN 46226 (tel. 317 547-1230), or can be obtained
through the Video Exchange Program of Tamarelle's International Films, 110 Cohas-
set Stage Rd., Chico, CA 95926 (tel. 916 895-3429).

[2]A further related consequence of the narrative's limitation to Gregor's perspective
is the portrayal of the inner thoughts of other characters in purely hypothetical
form, contained for the most part in what Dorrit Cohn calls "psycho-analogies"
(*Transparent Minds* 37)—that is, interpretations introduced by the qualifying phrase
as if. For examples in *The Metamorphosis*, see CS 100, 102, 103, 107, 113, 132.

[3]According to Sokel, it is characteristic of Kafka's later parabolic narratives that
they conclude with such aphoristic utterances (*Tragik und Ironie* 23).

Teaching Kafka in the
Second-Year German Course

Joseph L. Brockington

The discussion of a Kafka story in the second-year German course can be a source of anxiety for students and instructors alike. Kafka is a name most students recognize. Some may have read his works in English translation or in a high school German class. Kafka is a great and venerated German writer, and for students whose language skills are still recovering from a summer's nonuse, he is more than they want to take on. Thus they often approach the reading with trepidation and dread, fearful of Kafka's density, afraid of his depth, and leery of the psychological component. Likewise, the instructor may feel anxious when approaching a Kafka text, knowing its complexity, rejoicing in its density, yet fearful that the students will do little more than scratch the surface of all that Kafka has to offer. In a very real sense such instructors can easily become victims of their own training and expertise in literary interpretation, wanting their students to experience Kafka as literature yet knowing that, at least in the second-year language course, this connection seldom occurs.

The following approach to teaching Kafka in the second-year German course offers one solution to this dilemma. It is based on the premise that second-year students can be led to an adequate experience of the literariness of a short Kafka piece. That is, an instructor can take students beyond the mere reconstruction of what is said in the text into the variations, potentialities, and poetic texture of what is meant; this guidance can be accomplished entirely in the target language; neither the instructor nor the students need be Kafka experts; and together they can achieve this goal in one to two class hours. I have found this approach to be very effective for the teaching not only of Kafka but of other authors as well. It is also adaptable to a variety of interpretive modes and course aims.

The first step is to be sure that the students have mastered the surface presentations of the language of the text. Do they understand what is being said? To begin with, then, the students themselves pose questions about the story that concern words, phrases, sentences, even paragraphs about which they are unsure. Generally, when one student is troubled by a given section, another student can clear up the confusion. If not, we work on it as a group. We next summarize the action of the story, striving to do so in as few words as possible. This activity can be done in the students' journals, as a small group exercise (e.g., each group summarizes a paragraph in one sentence), or in a large group (each student contributes a sentence to the summary, or the group as a whole works out the action; the group also checks to make sure the chronology is correct). The purpose of such a summary is, of course, to ensure that everyone is talking about the same story. For the past few years my second-year students have read Kafka's "Vor dem Gesetz" ("Before the Law"). One recent summary was:

> Ein Mann (vom Lande) kommt vor das Gesetz, (das wahrscheinlich nicht auf dem Land ist). Er fragt, ob er hineingehen könnte. Der Türhüter sagt, jetzt nicht, vielleicht später. Der Mann wartet viele Jahre, bis er stirbt. Der Türhüter schliesst dann die Tür.
>
> A man (from the country) comes to the Law (which is probably not in the country). He asks if he might go in. The doorkeeper says, not now, maybe later. The man waits many years, until he dies. The doorkeeper then closes the door.

When everyone agrees on the facts, we turn our attention to interpretive questions about the story. Often such questions arise from our efforts to reconstruct the events of the story. Otherwise they may be generated by small groups. One class posed these questions: *Warum kann er nicht hineingehen? Warum wartet er? Was ist das Gesetz?* (Why can't he go inside? Why does he wait? What is the Law?) These questions serve both as an impetus to the literary analysis of the text and as a way of checking the results of our work; have we been able to answer all our questions satisfactorily? Three to five such questions are generally enough to serve this purpose. It is important that such questions come from the students. As such, they will be "real" questions, reflecting a real student's desire to know something about this piece of literature. Inevitably one of the questions about this Kafka story will concern the identity of the Law. Indeed, for most students, the obvious goal of reading this story is to establish the identity or the meaning of the Law. Although one may leave these interpretive questions unanswered until after completing the analysis, one may choose instead to answer them during the analytical process itself. With this particular story I find it interesting to let the students brainstorm a range of possible identities for the Law. My students have come up with a long list: for instance, symbol, leader, rules, knowledge, standard, religion, meaning of life, life in the city, king, door to heaven, order, and impossibility. I note all responses on the board without comment. The questions set the parameters of the discussion, in which the quest for the identity of the Law introduces an element of suspense: Which answer will be "right"?

We move then to the analysis of the various elements of the text, looking first at the time and place coordinates. By establishing the when and where of the setting, we begin to confront some of the story's Kafkaesqueness. There is no indication of time in "Before the Law" other than the years of waiting spent by the man from the country, followed by his death—naturally, an existential time. Nor is there any indication of place in the setting other than a vague reference to the man's origin: "the country." The entrance to the Law seems to be somewhere other than in the country, if only because the description of the doorkeeper has a vaguely foreign flavor (e.g., his Tartar beard). Space and time remain undefined, but nonetheless concrete. Likewise we learn some concrete yet incomplete details concerning the entrance to the Law and the halls beyond—each with a doorkeeper larger than the one preceding. Ideally the students themselves will glean these facts as they examine the text for indications of the setting. If necessary, the instructor can elicit such details through careful questioning or make them the subject of small-group or journal work. It is important that our second-year students learn to interact with the literature and that this experience be active and positive, especially if we want to see them in our upper-level literature courses.

The next step is to examine the two characters themselves. Who is the doorkeeper? Who is the man from the country? Again descriptions are assembled from the students' examination of the text and are noted on the board: for example, "the doorkeeper in his fur coat, with his big sharp nose and long, thin, black Tartar beard." Again we discover that we have not discovered much. The descriptions, although concrete and detailed as pertaining to the doorkeeper, are also incomplete and frankly not very helpful. Also, there is almost no description of the man from the country. Someone may raise a question concerning the identity of the two men. I deal with this issue by soliciting a number of possibilities from the students, as I did earlier when investigating the identity of the Law. I should stress that in my second-year course I do not discuss or even identify those characteristics of Kafka's descriptive language that Dieter Hasselblatt calls "progressive Verwicklung" 'progressive entanglement' and "konstruktive Destruktion" 'constructive destruction' (55, 127–29; see also Schild 189–213). It is enough that we have already met and come to terms with the effects of this technique in our efforts to establish the time-space coordinates of the setting and the descriptions of the characters. Regardless of how hard we try, we are not overly successful in either instance.

Finally, we consider two questions of causality. Ideally these questions will be among the first ones generated—as they have been in my class. The two causal questions are "Why can't the man go inside?" and "Why does he wait?" Consideration of the first question takes us back through the events of the story. In seeking to answer this question, the students must confront one of the major themes in Kafka's writing: the normal world of one of the characters is disturbed by an abnormal event, setting in motion a series of reactions from both the character and the world around him (see Schild 31, 87–89). In "Before the Law," this theme is triggered when the doorkeeper denies the man from the country entrance to the Law, a difficulty the man had not expected. The doorkeeper, however, invites him to try anyway but warns, "If you are so drawn to it, just try to go in despite my veto. But take note: I am powerful. And I am only the least of the doorkeepers. From hall to hall there is one doorkeeper after another, each more powerful than the last" (*CS* 3). The man from the country acquiesces. Although he repeatedly asks if the time is right for him to enter, he never wavers from his initial unquestioning acceptance of the doorkeeper's prohibition. The man from the country tries in every way imaginable to gain entrance to the Law (he attempts bribery, for instance, and even begs the fleas in the doorkeeper's fur collar)—every way save one.

From the recognition of the man's passivity follows easily the answer to the second causal question, Why does the man wait?—which is to say, Why does he die? He waits because he has been told to wait, and most important, after having been told to wait, the man then *chooses* to wait for the door-keeper to allow him entrance. He waits because he wants to. The doorkeeper gives the man from the country several opportunities to try to enter the Law; however, he does not make use of them. Instead he whiles away his life, using up his possessions in a futile attempt to bribe his way into the Law, all the while waiting for external permission to pursue his own goals and happiness. Having reached this conclusion, the students fully appreciate the irony of the final sentences of the story: "No one else could ever be admitted here, since this gate was made only for you. I am now going to shut it" (*CS* 4).

While it is possible from this point to give the story any one of a number of critical readings (e.g., psychological or Marxist), I prefer to reserve such activity for upper-level literature courses. For the second-year course, I stay within the text and ask the question "What should the man have done, so as not to die in this way?" Answers range from "go home" to "go on in." In short, if the man from the country had done *anything* else, he would not have died before the Law. Kafka's "A Little Fable" may be used to validate this point of view:

> "Alas," said the mouse, "the world is growing smaller every day. At the beginning it was so big that I was afraid, I kept running and running, and I was glad when at last I saw the walls far away to the right and left, but these long walls have narrowed so quickly that I am in the last chamber already, and there in the corner stands the trap that I must run into." "You only need to change your direction," said the cat, and ate it up.   (*CS* 445)

To conclude the class discussion of Kafka's "Before the Law," we return to the set of questions posed before the analysis, two of which have already been answered. Only the identity of the Law remains to be considered. When students examine this question in the context of the preceding analysis, they conclude that the Law, like the setting and the characters in the story, is an object of concrete uncertainty. We are never told exactly what the Law is or what it means (it could be any or all of the things suggested earlier), but we do know how it functions within the text. In this story the Law is a goal that is so meaningful to the man from the country that he is willing to wait and eventually to die, merely for the possibility of someday perhaps gaining entrance to it. The students are then confronted with an especially Kafkaesque question: Should one wait passively, and so definitely die, or do something else and take a risk? From this interpretation of the story emerges a topic for student essays: If you were the man from the country, what would you have done when the doorkeeper prohibited you from entering the Law?

The use of this text-centered approach to teaching Kafka in the second-year course has proved successful as a means of getting students to experience the literariness of the text in German. The discussion becomes more than merely another way in which the students are coerced into speaking German. It is a truly intellectual experience of the compacted potentials of a literary work of art by one of the greatest modern writers. I have also used this approach to "Before the Law" as a preface to discussion of Kafka's *The Metamorphosis* in my Introduction to German Literature course. Such preparation was very effective, giving students an opportunity to examine some of Kafka's narrative techniques in a smaller format before we tackled the long, metaphorically rich story of Gregor Samsa. If nothing else, the time spent analyzing "Before the Law" gives students of every level confidence in their abilities to read and understand Kafka in German.

Kafka and Women

Ruth V. Gross

The subject of Kafka and women is not one that naturally emerges in a literature class dealing with Kafka. Like the examination of women in relation to any particular male author, that of Kafka and women has found real interest only since the early eighties, when women's studies became a recognized discipline. In 1981 a session at the annual MLA convention on Kafka and women drew hundreds of listeners. A year later the *Newsletter of the Kafka Society of America* devoted an issue to the subject, and since then virtually every Kafka conference or collection has addressed some aspect of this topic. There are several avenues such discussions can take. One is psychologically biographical (or biographically psychological), examining Kafka's life and his relationship to women. Kafka's published diaries and letters reveal much about his relationships with Felice Bauer, Julie Wohryzek, Milena Jesenská, Dora Dymant, and the female members of his family. A second approach to this topic might be called the analytical and literary; it entails studying the female characters in his works and analyzing how they are portrayed. Yet another way to proceed on the topic might be to conduct what I term the feminist reading, which questions the universality of Kafka's discourse. Precisely what has been called universal in Kafka can be (and has been) seen as tendentiously masculine in perspective, as are many other elements of high modernism. To be sure, each of these approaches has its validity, and, not surprisingly, each has been applied to Kafka with greater or lesser success in the critical literature.

Biographical analysis reveals much about Kafka's attitudes toward women, but there always remains the question of how "truthful" his letters and diaries are. Kafka left behind a large body of personal writings in which his problems with women are well documented, but these writings, too, are part of a literary text created by a writer with an active imagination. All the women with whom Kafka had relationships have become a part not only of his biography but also of his oeuvre. So although the biographical method, interesting as it is, may bring to light certain facts about Kafka's life and the women in it, it may not be the best approach to the teaching of a Kafka story or novel.

Nevertheless, many critics have successfully applied Kafka the man to his texts. In *As Lonely as Franz Kafka*, Marthe Robert uses biographical information and Kafka's "autobiographical notations" to arrive at conclusions about his "identity." For example, she connects the years 1914 and 1920, the publication years of the novels *The Trial* and *The Castle*, with specific close relationships Kafka had with women at the time, understanding those relationships as crucial parts of the larger emotional and social factors that impelled Kafka to create these works. Robert also discusses Kafka as "a text-book example" of psychoanalytic theory with his "all-powerful father" and "passionate attachment to the mother" (22). Karl-Bernhard Bödeker has written an entire book devoted to women in Kafka's works and begins with a discussion of how women and family relations figured in Kafka's life. In his study, he keeps the two worlds of Kafka—the real and the fictional—quite separate; yet even so he makes certain conclusions about the fictional female characters on the basis of Kafka's attitudes toward women in his real life.

Other critics use the characters as the basis for an analysis of Kafka; that is, instead of using biography to analyze the literature, they use literature to create the biography. Understanding various characters as fictional dou-bles of Kafka, some critics extrapolate the meanings Kafka "intended" in his stories by using the comments in his diaries as factual statements about the various works and relate them back to his life. Of course, the female charac-ters in Kafka's novels and stories can provide the bases for character analyses. Women in the stories have been viewed as everything from traps and meta-physical principles to "reflectors" of Kafka's own writing. One study has called women in Kafka's works "connectors" who are "in contiguity with the essential" (Deleuze and Guattari 63–71; see also Carrouges 49). All these readings relegate women in Kafka to a secondary, if necessary, role—indeed, in one critic's view, to the "obstacle and the way" (Mykyta 628). In Kafka's world, the reader is always confronted first and foremost with the male protagonist, be he K., Josef K., Gregor Samsa, Georg Bendemann, or Karl Rossmann. Feminist readings that see Kafka's works as insidiously male-centered ask that we study Kafka with an awareness of his male perspective rather than be bullied or seduced into the acceptance of his stories as real representations of the world (see Beck, "Kafka's Traffic" 567–68). Such criticism, however, may fail to see that Kafka's male characters and constructs are no more real than his female characters. Kafka is no more the typical male than he is the typical Czech, Austrian, or Jew. Kafka is simply not typical.

So how might we, as teachers, better approach the subject of Kafka and women in a literature class? In my experience the best method is to stick firmly to the text at hand. Drawing on too much biographical material often confuses students and draws their attention away from the desired task, which is to learn how to be good critical readers. I also find that students believe an author's biography will ultimately uncover a single and unequivocal truth about his or her text; Kafka's texts consciously work against this kind of reading. Initially, students may find it irritating to consider a plurality of approaches to a single work (more-experienced critics face this same irritation every time they read a new article on Kafka), but this plurality is precisely part of the "Kafka problem" inherent in the act of interpreting his prose. Since I am partial to close readings of Kafka's prose that result from analyzing his language and his sense of linguistic play, I like to lead students into this kind of exercise. Using the text of *The Metamorphosis*, teachers can generate a good discussion on Kafka and women. One caveat: if we take this text or one like it, conclusions about Kafka's ideas on women should be drawn from studying the characters and the text without too much biographical intrusion. In this particular work Gregor's relationships—not Kafka's— are of prime concern.

There is no doubt that Gregor is the central character in the work. It is his story. The now famous first sentence establishes the plot. Quickly we learn that as a man Gregor had been a traveling salesman; the situation of the opening paragraph suggests not only Gregor's transformation from man to vermin but also his "unmanning." Kafka describes Gregor's new form with words indicating a roundness of form usually associated with things female: "vaulted . . . belly," "arch-shaped," "dome."[1] As if to accentuate his former masculine perspective, the second paragraph focuses on the only picture Gregor has in his room, "which he had recently cut out of a glossy magazine and lodged in a pretty gilt frame. It showed a lady done up in a fur hat and a fur boa, sitting upright and raising up against the viewer a heavy fur muff in which her whole forearm disappeared" (Corngold 3). The immediate narrative attention given this framed pinup provides a clue to the importance it will have later in the story. Like Chekhov's "gun on the wall," the lady in the fur boa, as an object, will have a dramatic effect and precipitate a catastrophe. The object here, however, has to be read as more than mere object, since it is a representation of the female, a fact hardly overlooked by critics.

The picture has been variously interpreted. For some it demonstrates the bachelor's "hidden desires," at the same time revealing "in its vulgarity how deeply the standardization and commercialization of modern life had penetrated the bachelor's unconcious." For others the picture is one of several clues "that Gregor's illness is sexual in nature." Still others have compared the picture with one of Felice Bauer that Kafka may have had and used as a model (Corngold 86). These interpretations are all interesting, but a strict textual reading would simply bring out the early introduction of the picture, its juxtaposition with the description of Gregor as a vermin, and the actual words that make us visualize the framed pinup. The female is a "lady" "done up" (*versehen*)—the German implies that someone else has *seen to it* that she has these props—perhaps to alter her appearance. The German prefix *ver-* literally translates to the English prefix *mis-*; in other words, the passage suggests a mis-seeing, an incorrect perception of the woman in the picture, as well as a "doing up" of her, as Corngold's translation reads. The possible double meaning is important, since the narrative often shifts perspective. It is unclear whether Gregor has "mis-seen" her from the time he cut out the picture or, now that his vision is impaired, is mistaking her for something she is not, but either reading is legitimate given the word *versehen* and Kafka's sense of linguistic play. Although I often teach Kafka to students who know little or no German, I feel it important to point out problems in translations and the difficulties of translation in general— especially of Kafka, whose prose is often so concise that one word can convey several alternative readings depending on its translation. A look at the German in such situations is always beneficial and enlightening to the students, heightening their awareness that the "commentators' despair" is matched by the translators' angst.

The woman's position is sitting "upright" (*aufrecht*). As Stanley Corngold points out, the gesture of raising her "bemuffed" arm "up against the viewer" suggests "the hostile stance of various idolized female figures in [Kafka's] novels" (Corngold 70). This lady in the fur boa who combines the passive and the aggressive, the civilized and the wild, the cultural and the tawdry, demonstrates the complex surrounding women in Kafka's fictive world. Although she is not a character in the usual sense of the word, she represents some aspects of the female in the story. For Gregor she is the desired object, the woman he can totally possess, unlike his sister or his mother. She is literally the "bird" in a gilded "frame."

In part 2 of the story Gregor's attempt to salvage this object—this representation of the female—for himself will precipitate his end. There is little doubt that Gregor's pressing himself against the glass of the picture of the "lady all dressed in furs" is an aggressive act, aggressive and hostile in two ways—to his sister and to the object itself: "He squatted on his picture and would not give it up. He would rather fly in Grete's face" (Corngold 36). When his mother faints at the sight of Gregor, "the gigantic brown blotch on the flowered wallpaper," Gregor wants to help but is at first held fast by the picture: "he was stuck to the glass and had to tear himself loose by force"

(Corngold 36). The dangerous female in furs holds him captive. The sight of Gregor pressed against the female representation, with all the sexual overtones of that scene, is what makes Mrs. Samsa faint. Gregor wants to advise Grete, who has run to another room to get smelling salts, but his condition makes him feel helpless. The incident culminates in Gregor's own fainting, after which he is trapped outside his room, his haven, "cut off from his mother" and every other female element—sister and desired object as well.

Gregor's relationship with his sister has often been commented on. According to Heinz Politzer and others, the similarity of their names—Gregor, Grete—illustrates a deeply rooted familiarity, almost an identity, between them. Clearly Gregor loves his sister dearly and attributes to her all kinds of cleverness and capability, deserved or not. In the first part of the story, when Gregor makes his appearance before his parents and the chief clerk, he realizes that the latter "must be detained, soothed, persuaded and finally won over. . . ." He realizes that no one but Grete is capable of accomplishing this goal, but to his dismay, she is not there. Gregor muses, "She was intelligent; she had begun to cry when Gregor was still lying quietly on his back . . ." (*CS* 102). Without his sister, Gregor cannot function effectively in his new form. This becomes clear in parts 2 and 3, when Grete begins to rule the family. She takes charge of Gregor's keep and guides the family in decisions about him. Slowly he comes to depend completely on her, just as, before the metamorphosis, the family had (at least apparently) depended completely on Gregor.

Even the narrative voice telling Gregor's story emphasizes Gregor's love for his sister. Grete brings her brother milk, which repels the changed Gregor. "Would she notice that he had left the milk standing . . . ? If she did not do it of her own accord, he would rather starve than draw her attention to the fact, although he felt a wild impulse to dart out from under the sofa, throw himself at her feet, and beg her for something to eat" (*CS* 107). Grete then brings Gregor a variety of foods "in the goodness of her heart" (*CS* 107). This solicitude reveals two aspects of Grete's character: on the one hand, it shows her good-heartedness, or at least Gregor's belief in it, as the narration tells us; on the other hand, it serves as a device to show that Grete believes Gregor to be an animal—her actions confirming Gregor's animal identity (see Corngold 86). By her gestures—touching his dish only with a rag and not bare-handed, spreading the food on a newspaper, leaving so as not to watch him eat, and giving him nourishment like bones, cheese "that Gregor would have called uneatable two days ago" (*CS* 108), and half-rotten vegetables—Grete has decreed Gregor to be no longer human. She becomes his keeper, feeding him only when the parents are asleep, and once again the narrative voice that speaks for Gregor attributes delicacy and decency to her: ". . . perhaps [his parents] could not have borne to know more about his feeding than from hearsay, perhaps too his sister wanted to spare them such little anxieties whenever possible, since they had quite enough to bear as it was" (CS 109). She keeps him alive by serving him, yet in her role as servant, she becomes dominant over him—so much so that Grete considers "herself an expert in Gregor's affairs as against her parents" (CS 117) and, according to the narrator, exaggerates Gregor's condition "in order that she might do all the more for him" (CS 117).

As the story progresses, however, Grete tires of her role as servant and takes less care in selecting his food and cleaning his room, which quickly becomes the dumping ground for all unwanted refuse from the apartment. Gilles Deleuze and Félix Guattari find female characters in Kafka's works often fulfilling a tripartite function as sister, maid, and whore (65). When the same character can embody all three elements, Kafka has created "the strange combination that [he] so dreams about" (66). Choosing not to extrapolate from the text to draw conclusions about Kafka himself, I try to show students how Grete incorporates those three realms of womanhood. At first she is simply Gregor's sister; then she becomes a clerk in a store while she takes on the role of his maid. Only at the moment when Gregor shows his attachment and attraction to the lady in the fur boa, at the end of the second part, does Grete turn on him, almost as a rival of that picture—the object of desire—and return to her position as sister, but with such authority that she becomes a kind of matriarch to the family.

When Gregor is suddenly moved by her performance on the violin and proceeds to seek the "unknown nourishment he craved," Grete suddenly takes on the third part of the complex laid out by Deleuze and Guattari.

> [Gregor] was determined to push forward till he reached his sister, to pull at her skirt and so let her know that she was to come into his room with her violin, for no one here appreciated her playing as he would appreciate it. He would never let her out of his room, at least, not so long as he lived. . . . she should sit beside him on the sofa, bend down her ear to him, and hear him confide that he had the firm intention of sending her to the Conservatorium. . . . After this confession his sister would be so touched that she would burst into tears, and Gregor would then raise himself to her shoulder and kiss her on the neck, which, now that she went to business, she kept free of any ribbon or collar.   (CS 131)

His desire for her at this point in the story, for whatever reason, is clear. After this event, which causes the three boarders in the Samsa house to give notice of their intention to depart, Grete seals Gregor's fate with the words "We must try to get rid of *it*," (CS 133; emphasis mine), and a page later gives her final dictum, which reads almost like Gregor's death sentence: "He must go, . . . that's the only solution, Father" (CS 134). Psychologically, Grete has undergone a great metamorphosis herself, changing from sister to servant to matriarch to desired object. As if to emphasize Grete's protean quality, the end of the novella focuses attention—her parents' as well as the reader's—on Grete's body, interpreting her stretching as a "confirmation of [the family's] new dreams . . ." (*CS* 139).

Clearly, Grete's function in *The Metamorphosis* is to grow and stretch as Gregor shrivels and dies. The tale reverses the romantic topos of woman as redeemer through love; Gregor's death redeems Grete and the family. It seems a necessary event; both could not flourish together. This tension between the masculine sense of responsibility, which Gregor feels at the beginning of the story, and the frustration of possibility felt by Grete (and Gregor, too) is resolved only when she assumes the mantle of responsibility, taking on the decision-making power in the household. The decision: to dispose of Gregor. The logic and horror of this transformation, its almost Nietzschean affirmation of life over death, health over illness, cannot be rejected out of hand, except by someone who can see and feel as Gregor does. That someone is precisely the reader. Kafka's women, whether they suffer or triumph, often have a sense of being beyond good and evil, beyond the moral shackles of the masculine sensibility. Therein lies not only their power but also their danger.

NOTE

[1] For certain descriptions I use Stanley Corngold's translation of *The Metamorphosis* because I find it closer to the German original in tone and nuance than the better-known translation by Willa Muir and Edwin Muir. When I use Corngold's translation or his editorial commentary, "Corngold" precedes the page reference.

The Language of Defamiliarization: Benjamin's Kafka

Carrie L. Asman

Confusion, nausea, disgust, and even distress are among the most pro-nounced mental and physical symptoms students have been known to experi-ence on their first encounter with a Kafka text. I don't wish to rob Kafka of this initial effect, as these anxiety-induced affective responses are a necessary step in the process of defamiliarization, which initiates students into an unfamiliar world that is most strikingly so precisely at moments when it feigns familiarity. The encounter with the unfamiliar is all the more unsettling since it blurs those freshly erected bounds separating the fantastic, the grotesque, and the everyday in a manner that draws the legitimacy of the boundaries themselves into question.

To gain a stronger foothold in Kafka's world, students should try to venture beyond their first reaction by exploring some of the various aspects of defami-liarization. To this end I have found that there are basically four types of defamiliarization represented to varying degrees throughout Kafka's texts. By defamiliarization, I refer to *Entstellung*, that is, to the various tangible manifestations (not the causes) of distortion and displacement that determine the spatial, the physical, the temporal, and the symbolic ground of Kafka's work. Defamiliarization is not unique to the work of Franz Kafka. Not only do elements of distortion and displacement appear in Brecht's "V-Effekt" and in the Russian formalist concept *ostranenije*, they also form the basis of Freud's theory of the unconscious and dreams, which function as complex systems of distortion and displacement. My point of reference here, how-ever, is to an even more literal use of the word *Entstellung*, first offered by Walter Benjamin in the early thirties, in his essay written on the occasion of the tenth anniversary of Kafka's death. It is this perspective, rather than method or approach, that I attempt to develop further here in a more pragmatic, if not systematic, fashion.[1]

After briefly outlining the four progressively complex aspects of defamiliar-ization listed above, I concentrate on isolated examples of physical distortion and displacement, since they are the most prominent aspects in the texts under consideration in this volume. Instead of showing how one or two aspects might apply to a number of texts, as I have done here, students may find it useful to create four separate lists as a guide for their readings of individual texts. Rather than limit this study to one text, I would like to demonstrate the general applicability of this typology to Kafka's work as a whole.

Most will agree that Kafka's tales present countless examples of disorienting spatial displacements, which we are invited to share if we wish to cohabit his compelling yet disturbing tectonic structures. On entering Kafka's texts, we find ourselves in a kaleidoscopic, slightly fantastic realm where everything seems to correspond to the world we know yet is at the same time distinctly different. There we encounter a group of disparate systematically recurring structures—rooms, halls, corridors, racetracks, and country roads that never end; labyrinthine passageways; landscapes studded with towers or lined by walls in which some vital element such as a beginning or end, entry or exit, window or adjoining door, is missing or askew. These architectural structures have one important common feature: their distinctly fragmentary nature seldom allows them to be reconstructed as a unified whole, although considerable narrative detail is devoted to a description of the parts. This feature is especially common in the short tales that focus on the construction of the tower of Babel and the Great Wall of China. Instead of moving toward structural completion, each part functions as a disjointed fragment that is superimposed against a labyrinthine whole which never offers a reliable sense of unity. Rooms and passageways are typically designed or situated in relation to one another in a manner that is disorienting to the reader and often even to the figures who move within them. This tendency toward fragmentation, in which the parts stand in a dysfunctional relation to any structural whole, applies not only to inanimate structures in Kafka's work but also to human body parts and to isolated gestural movements. Kafka's gestures may not be as pointedly didactic as Brecht's, yet they are nonetheless decisively dialectical.

Kafka's use of architectural structures could be understood as the spatial narratological translation or transformation of ancient mythological and metaphysical constructs back into a physical, concrete relationality among persons, objects, and buildings. Much of the material used in the texts about the building of walls, towers, and palaces is drawn from Greek, Hebrew, or Chinese myth and history, offering an exotic and distant backdrop for the dramatization of public and private events concerning individual and collective goals set within timeless situations of everyday work and communication. The contours and shadows of these archaic tectonic structures are not only central to the early short pieces but also firmly embedded in many of Kafka's other, larger narratives such as *The Castle* and *The Trial*, where their function has become abstract and ornamental through their separation from an original context.

In *The Trial* sociospatial distinctions between interior and exterior, public and private, are no longer discernible: K.'s middle-class boardinghouse is infiltrated and occupied by colleagues (whom he should know from work) posing as public investigators who carefully rearrange the furniture to stage K.'s first cross-examination. Later, the building where the secret yet public proceedings are held reveals itself to be a multistoried lower-class tenement that is periodically converted into a courtroom. Although access to the house and the rooms is at first confusing for K. and the reader, the organization of the different floors and rooms—connected by mysterious stairs, passageways, and openings—eventually presents itself as a one-to-one correspondence between the outer physical structure and the inner hierarchy of the judicial process.

While teaching *The Trial* in German to an upper-division literature class, struggling both with Kafka's language and with the concept of defamiliarization, I developed a small group exercise that enables students to discover for themselves the narrative as well as the dramatic significance of spatial displacement in Kafka's work. This exercise may be adapted to any number of texts. After reading the first chapters, four groups of five students each took on the challenging task of rendering a detailed floor plan of K.'s boardinghouse, the various dramatic arrangements of the furniture and objects in Fräulein Bürstener's room, or the courtroom-house. Assigning the groups the same space allows them to compare their floor plans afterwards.

Elements of distortion and disfigurement are prominent in Kafka's work not only on the spatial plane but also on the physical plane. His narratives offer a host of characters whose physiognomies are either shaped by or subjected to grotesque deformations. Gregor Samsa's experience of his unexpected metamorphosis from young man to vermin provides an example par excellence. On the level of physical distortion, Kafka's creatures may figure as humans, and people are often cast as creatures; the direction of transformation remains indeterminate. We see on this plane, too, how Kafka returns such metaphysical problems as guilt to the physical world of the concrete as a burden to be carried and illumined by hunchbacks, human beasts, and prisoners.

Distortion and displacement are created on the temporal plane through the interruption of actional and narrative sequences, which are fragmented in a manner that prevents them from developing along a linear continuum. Whereas literary narratives before Kafka were marked by a literal beginning and end, framing an action or idea that is in some sense brought to a conclusion, Kafka resists this convention by extending the principle of fragmentation from the spatial and physical planes to the temporal and the symbolic. Stripped of conventional notions of purpose and causality, his narratives rarely gratify readers' traditional expectations.

The disruption of this epic sense of linear unfolding is graphically underscored by Kafka's use of gesture, which is inherently both dialectical and asymbolic: as fragment, gesture suggests a forward complete motion that it simultaneously interrupts, not unlike the building of the wall whose finished parts give the individual worker the illusion of completion, although this cannot be so. The physiognomy of Kafka's narrative descriptions centers not on descriptive detail that would allow any one figure to be unique but on the gestural movement of body parts instead. Characteristic gestures in Kafka are figural posturings of the head (bowed, lowered), mouth (open, mute), and hand (clenched, flat, writing). Kafka's focus on the gesture represents a shift from the symbolic to a dynamic and dramatic tension created by the bodily movements of his characters.[2] This tendency toward desymbolization at the heart of the Kafkaesque gesture represents an alternative to language, a shift toward concrete things, away from static signs or symbols that stand in for abstract objects or ideas.

Undergraduates who have been trained to look for symbolic meanings behind or beyond the text should be invited from the onset to depart from this practice and encouraged to explore the possibility of viewing the text not as a series of words but as a series of gestures and displacements that do not point to a meaning outside themselves.

Reserving a more in-depth treatment of symbolic and temporal displacements for advanced students, let us return to examples of physical distortion and displacement abundantly supplied by the group of tales under scrutiny. A variety of Kafka's leading and peripheral figures reveal the back and the loin of the human body to be primary exterior sites of physical disfigurement where higher orders have left their mark. Gregor Samsa, Odradek, the many hunchbacks, and the prisoner of "In the Penal Colony" present numerous examples in which the back functions as the central target of disfiguration. In "A Country Doctor," "A Report to an Academy," and "The Judgment," loin and thigh figure prominently as locations for scars and open wounds. In "A Report to an Academy," the ape Red Peter tells the story of his assimilation to Western civilization, beginning with his first violent contact with the brutish colonizers who have forcefully taken him captive. The color of the scars disfiguring his loin and face gives him part of his name, and the scars themselves serve as a constant reminder, marking both his body and the historical moment when he was violently separated from a free and natural state. Western civilization is presented as a product of that separation since it is contrasted with a natural state, which Red Peter can no longer recollect.

In "A Country Doctor" and "The Judgment," scar and wound represent not only disfigurations but displacements of a pointedly erotic nature. In both tales, the scar of the father and the wound of the young boy entertain themes of castration and anxiety associated with repressed sexuality. Readers of "The Judgment" are prepared for a graphic disclosure that is systematically deferred three times to another region of the body. Their interest is piqued from the moment of Georg's ambiguous response to what he has seen behind his father's dressing gown, which accidentally parted as the father walked by. Georg's comment "My father is still a giant of a man" (*CS* 81) reveals that what he saw left a lasting impression. Invited to wonder what Georg could have seen that would have caused him to make such a statement, the reader engages in a voyeuristic quest to uncover what it is that makes the father such a "giant" in his son's eyes. Kafka fans this interest by manipulating the dramatic fluctuation between concealment and disclosure. Paragraphs later, the roles are reversed as the father, playing the son-child who is to be tucked into bed, draws the bedclothes even "farther than usual over the shoulders" (CS 84), only to rip them aside a few seconds later. Finally, Kafka alludes to a third gesture of disclosure. In this "showing" the father raises his nightshirt, childishly mimicking the seductive gestures of his son's fiancée, provocatively displaying not his sexual organ, which the increasing explicit context leads the reader to expect, but an old war scar instead. The reader's compulsion gives way to embarrassment and repulsion, which are amplified by Georg's response as he shrinks into a corner "as far away from his father as possible" (CS 85). Frustrated by the unfulfilled expectation, the reader is further irritated at having fallen prey to the seductive gestures that gave rise to such an expectation in the first place.

Kafka takes our gaze to places we have been told it should not go, and by consistently withholding and substituting the forbidden object with a harmless one, he holds our attention by maintaining a tension entirely created by displacement. Kafka reinforces a taboo by first defamiliarizing it, yet he does so in a manner that draws attention to the very mechanisms at work, thus constituting a critical self-reflexive moment in which the reader is actively encouraged to participate.

The gaping maggot-infested "open" wound in "A Country Doctor" actively contrasts with the mildly disfiguring traces of the "closed" ones presented by the scars in "The Judgment" and in "A Report to an Academy." The gruesomely detailed description of the wound—not suggested reading for those with squeamish stomachs—gives a recognizably accurate description of a female sexual orifice that mysteriously appears on the side of the young male patient only after the doctor has examined him twice. The wound is to be healed when the doctor lies next to the boy's open side. Kafka's description of the "rose-red" (CS 223) coloration of the boy's wound corresponds to the name of the servant girl, Rose, whom the doctor has reluctantly sacrificed to a lusty suitor in exchange for the unruly team of horses that replace his dead mare, thereby enabling him to carry out his house call in the middle of the stormy night. So, already having felt torn between home and work, between duty and desire, the doctor reexperiences this conflict in the family before him: the parents wish to save the life of the son, who, wishing to die, longs for an illness that will put an end to his suffering. Finding nothing concrete, the doctor manages to satisfy both parties by creating a wound as camouflage for the blasphemous desires of the son, who is thus given a tangible cause that no longer implicates the failure of the parents or of their parenting. The country doctor, who cleverly manages to fulfill the conflicting expectations of parents and patient, remains a savior to both by succumbing to ancient ritual and beliefs, sacrificing his medical authority before no one but the reader, who is confronted squarely with the mythic nature of our belief in science and in the doctor-patient relationship.

The contours of this dreamlike narrative are shaped at every turn by a twisted spiral of physical, spatial, and symbolic-erotic displacements. Rose's "defloration" is left to the doctor's wild imagination as he rides home naked, exposed, and betrayed by the false alarm set off by Rose's cunning and disgusting suitor, who had sent the doctor on his way in order to take advantage of his absence. Replacing the doctor, the suitor does with the servant girl what the doctor will not even allow himself to imagine, though the doctor has taken the boy instead as his unsuspecting object.

On the asymbolic plane, meaning (*sema*) is returned to its body (*soma*)— not through signification but through juxtaposition. When the naked doctor lies down on the bed next to the boy's "open" wound, the description of it as "rose"-colored is now no more accidental or symbolic than Rose's name, since Kafka physically brings the two together on a fictional plane where they can meet. The doctor fulfills his medical duty through the body of the boy, while carefully displacing his erotic interest in the servant girl.

"In the Penal Colony" is a story in which the physical collides with abstract meaning in a much more violent fashion. Unlike in other stories, where the cumbersome physical protuberances and misshapen bowed forms of the many hunchbacks are the concrete expression of guilt that is presented to the guilty and to the outside world, here we are introduced to the very instruments of its internalization. This interiorization process reunites the body with its alienated sign and meaning, which becomes an originary and immediate sensuous experience, a knowledge that is transmitted through the body without the abstract differentiation created by the written or spoken word. Separated from the body and the world of natural objects, the word returns to its point of origin as barely legible ornamental script that is painfully reinscribed on the body as the disfiguring judgment leveled by a higher order. This process reverses the conventional order of signification, in which words point to an abstract meaning outside themselves. Ordinarily directed to the eye or the ear as written or spoken word, meaning returns to the body as judgment veiled in an ornamental script that is applied to the body, thus returning the violence of abstraction to its concrete and perceptible form, whereby the understanding of content no longer privileges the abstract over the concrete.

In this story the act of writing on the back of the unwitting victim repeats in reverse order—using language as the common tool—the disfiguring violence that is done by humankind to nature. Here, language is revealed to be the instrument of "harrowing" pain, which, unlike other instruments of torture, does not force its victim to admit to a guilt that he struggles to conceal. Guilt is not something one confesses but a form of knowledge to be embraced as a means to another end. Kafka designates the human back as the physical location to receive the moral-physical burden of guilt—hence the prevalence of the hunchback figure in his work. The back also marks the site of the guilty man's literal and figurative blindness. Just as the reading of the ornamental writing on his back with his own eyes constitutes a physical impossibility, so the prisoner cannot be expected to recognize his guilt rationally. At issue here is not the cause or the legitimacy of the pronouncement but the acceptance on the part of the victim, whose suffering is to be necessarily embraced as a precondition for the redemption that follows. The same holds true of Kafka's *The Trial*, in which the outcome (i.e., the final verdict of guilty) is not as important as the process (*der Prozess*) of its interiorization. The reader's customary focus on the outcome, a verdict that is pronounced on the basis of the judgment of a specific event, is shifted to the process by which the accused *becomes* guilty.

For Gregor Samsa in *The Metamorphosis*, the back again plays a leading role, this time as the center of Gregor's new horizontal existence, which is spent primarily looking for a comfortable prone position. This new *Rückenlage* ("prone position") determines the angle of Gregor's new perception and, further, describes the position of the heavy, unwieldy torso that requires so many legs for its mobilization. The focus of Gregor's efforts is shifted from the material welfare of his family—his central concern until then—to the transport of his objectified body, now largely constituted by his back. As newfound center of existence, the back presents a fitting Dantean punishment for his earlier "spineless" subjugation to the dependent interests of family and employer—an attribute for which he pointedly criticizes his colleague in the opening pages (CS 91). In *The Metamorphosis*, as in "In the Penal Colony," the human back is that place where the patriarchal structure can reinforce its order. But unlike the harrow, the apple thrown by Gregor's father remains in the wound it has created as an outward festering sign and a reminder of Gregor's impertinence and the suffering he has inflicted on his family (CS 122), a suffering for which he is forced to pay in kind. The father's gaze is troubled not only by the transformed figure of his unsightly son but also by the apple in the gangrenous wound, bearing witness to the violence of the father's own impulsive reaction toward the creature that drove his wife into a swoon. The apple and the festering wound surrounding it have a twofold function as optical nexus, reminding both father and son of their original transgression.

These examples are only a few of the many one could choose to bring students closer to the concept of defamiliarization central to Kafka's work. With the help of the typology presented here, students may become acquainted with the different spatial, physical, temporal, and symbolic forms this process may take, providing a new perspective, if not a method, for continuing their readings of Kafka.

NOTES

[1] For a more systematic treatment and detailed analysis of this and other examples of temporal and symbolic displacement, see the relevant chapters on Kafka in Asman-Schneider. For Benjamin's use of the concept of *Entstellung* (literally, "displacement"), which Harry Zohn consistently translates as "distortion," see Benjamin, "Tenth Anniversary" 133–35. In "Some Reflections on Franz Kafka," Benjamin explicitly places the notion of distortion (*Entstellung*) in a spatial context illustrated by the spatial distortion of Arthur Eddington's *The Nature of the Physical World.*

[2] One of the largest parodistic compendiums of these bodily gestures is presented in vivid detail in "A Report to an Academy," in which the ape Red Peter demonstrates the difficulties in learning to smoke, spit, and drink like a man.

A Psychoanalytic Approach to "The Judgment"

Kenneth Hughes

By definition, the psychoanalytic approach to literature takes as its object some psyche involved at some point of the literary process. The most convenient objects to have offered themselves to date are the mind of the author, the mind of a text's narrator or of a character, and the mind of the reader. This sequence, which recapitulates the natural order of literary mediation (an idea occurs to the author's mind; the author "embodies" the idea in his narrator or in a character; the reader perceives the character's emotion and divines the author's intention as the motivating force behind it), also charts the three-stage historical course of psychoanalytic criticism.

Psychoanalytic theory was initially applied to the creative process by Freud and a number of his colleagues (such as Otto Rank and Karl Abraham), primarily in the decade following the publication in 1905 of Freud's *Wit and Its Relation to the Unconscious*. In the movement's first stage (dominating the 1920s), critics tended to scrutinize literature for clues concerning the personality and psychological profile of the author. Apart from such book-length studies as Axel Uppvall's *August Strindberg: A Psychoanalytic Study*, Katherine Anthony's *Margaret Fuller: A Psychological Biography*, and Edward Carpenter and George Barnefield's *The Psychology of the Poet Shelley*, the pages of the professional journals are full of articles with titles like "Psychopathological Glimpses of . . ." and "Psychoanalysis of . . ." (see Cassity; Dooley), many of which were written under the influence of Freud's chief American champion, G. Stanley Hall, at Clark University, who had sponsored Freud's famous American sojourn in 1909. Not without reason have such studies been called pathographies (see Schrey), and not without reason did they provoke the predictable reaction from defenders of formalism and aestheticism, who were intent on ensuring art a special realm above and beyond the processes of either normal or abnormal human psychology.

Generally superseding the pathography of the author was a second stage, which concentrated more intently than the first on the meanings of texts and did not so exclusively use them merely as tools in the analysis of the psyches of their creators; in this method—as in, for example, Marie Bonaparte's and Joseph Wood Krutch's studies of Poe—critics went beyond using the work as a tool to analyze the author, instead applying psychoanalytic understanding of the author toward a better understanding of the work. This is the manner of psychoanalytic criticism with which we are commonly most familiar, the manner that has dominated criticism of "The Judgment" from the beginning, since this story did not become widely known until the second stage had largely superseded the first.[1]

Clearly, however, there are problems with both methods. First, we can never know enough about an author to construct a convincing psychoanalytic profile: we cannot get that individual on the couch as analysand and allow the free association with the material of the dream work necessary for true analysis, and whatever insights we might think we have into the author's psychic life cannot be verified anyway—so why bother harrowing the text to begin with? Second, literary characters are, inescapably, fictional constructs, and even the most psychologically complex of them do not have, indeed cannot have, as roundly or fully profiled a psyche as that of even the flattest and most uninteresting real-life subject. How then, despite all the analogies that indisputably exist between literary character and real person, can the fictional psyche be profitably scrutinized with the aid of tools developed through analysis of the real minds of living people? And even if analysis were possible, could it be conducted by literary critics lacking the training and experience of the practicing analyst (Hughes, "Psychoanalytic Criticism" 163)?[2]

In the face of such practical impediments, the third stage of psychoanalytic criticism has tended to shift the focus of attention from the mind of an author or a character to the psyche of the reader, the one person in the literary process who is neither inaccessible to analysis (if only self-analysis) nor fictional in character. This manner of criticism is the third referred to by Norman N. Holland in his seminal 1962 essay "Shakespearean Tragedy and the Three Ways of Psychoanalytic Criticism," the manner that forms the basis of the psychoanalytically oriented reader-response criticism on which he elaborates in subsequent studies and that we may consider the third stage in a historical sense. In that essay, Holland appeals to a consideration of the literary work "as a total configuration or *Gestalt*, not as just a single character," as "the showplace of an interior drama in the minds of the playwright or his audience," and concludes that "in treating the work as an indivisible whole the critic assumes that the work of art is to be itself savored as a final reality, not as a filtered version of something else" (210, 211, 213). Holland alludes to (210) but does not cite a point that Freud made in his essay "The Relation of the Poet to Day-dreaming," a point that is of crucial importance in the psychoanalytic approach to "The Judgment." Freud wrote of

> the tendency of modern writers to split up their ego by self-observation into many component-egos, and in this way to personify the conflicting trends in their own mental life in many heroes. . . . in these [works] the person introduced as the hero plays the least active part of anyone, and seems instead to let the actions and sufferings of other people pass him by like a spectator. (51–52)

These two points, rather than the aspect of reader-response, are what I wish to examine here: the text is a total configuration, a gestalt, an "interior drama," and the apparent "hero" of a literary text may be no more than a passive spectator of a play enacted by the component parts of his own psyche. These two propositions provide us with an important key to understanding "The Judgment" as the staging of an oedipal drama in which all the requisite properties and actors (Georg's ego, id, and superego; son, father, and mother; present incidence and recalled memory) are present in some capacity in the text of the story.

Most of the psychoanalytic discussion of "The Judgment" has focused on objects and artifacts of the fictional texture (the so-called phallic symbols) and on its chief actors (Georg, the father, and the friend). The critics in question have rarely addressed other elements of fiction, such as metaphor, symbol, or image. But such intrinsic aspects of the text are essential to understanding what happens in the central scene of the story, the one in which Gregor puts his father to bed, and in the ensuing peripeteia, which leads to Georg's sentencing and death. Much of the ambiguity in this scene comes from the father's apparently unstable role: Is he a child, or is he a man? Is he helpless, or is he the dominant one? Heinz Politzer reframes this question in relation to the father's clinging to Georg's watch chain: does the gesture indicate childishness, contempt, weakness, or a firm grip? "The silent gesture . . . remains unexplained," he says (*Parable and Paradox* 57).

But let us recall significant passages of that scene to attempt an explanation. It begins when Georg evades his father's question about whether he "really" has a friend in Saint Petersburg (*CS* 82) and instead suggests making some changes in the father's living conditions:[3]

> ". . . I'll put you to bed now for a little, I'm sure you need to rest. Come, I'll help you take off your things, you'll see I can do it. . . ."
>
> . . . Georg [lifted] his father from the chair and [slipped] off his dressing gown. . . .
>
> Meanwhile Georg had succeeded in lowering his father down again and carefully taking off the woollen drawers he wore over his linen underpants and his socks. . . .
>
> He carried his father to bed in his arms. It gave him a dreadful feeling to notice that while he took the few steps toward the bed the old man on his breast was playing with his watch chain. . . .
>
> But as soon as he was laid in bed, all seemed well. He covered himself up and even drew the blankets farther than usual over his shoulders. He looked up at Georg with a not unfriendly eye. . . .
>
> "Am I well covered up now?" asked his father, as if he were not able to see whether his feet were properly tucked in or not.
>
> "So you like it in bed," said Georg, and arranged the blankets better around him.
>
> "Am I well covered up?" asked the father once more, and seemed to pay particular attention to the answer.

"Don't worry, you're well covered up."

"No!" cried his father . . .   (CS 83–84)

We must question who is being put to bed in this scene. On the most immediate plane of the narration, it is of course the father. All oedipal interpretations of "The Judgment" have naturally emphasized the symbolic aspect of Georg's putting his father to bed and "covering him up" as a representation of the son's replacement of the father as head of the household and of the business. And of course this interpretation parallels some biographical evidence in *Letter to His Father*, when Kafka commented, "My writing was all about you; all I did there, after all, was to bemoan what I could not bemoan upon your breast" (87). In this regard, Peter U. Beicken has noted that Kafka's work is "a continuation of the struggle against his father and the principles and values which he represented" (*Kritische Einführung* 206). Observing that before this scene Georg says to himself, "My father is still a giant of a man" (CS 81), and that immediately thereafter the father returns to his gigantic stature and sentences Georg, we can see the patriarchally superior and even "gigantic" (*Letter* 41) position of Hermann Kafka opposing the "slave" (29), of which Kafka also wrote in that letter.

But we must note that the father appears in both aspects that Politzer's query above suggests: he has Georg in his grip, yet he also appears in the guise of a child. Moreover, is he being child*ish* or child*like* when he plays with the chain? Walter Sokel ("Perspectives and Truth" 225) and Hartmut Binder (*Kafka-Kommentar* 150) refer this gesture to the father's supposed "senility" or "infantility," respectively, and Claude-Edmonde Magny has trivialized the point by claiming it to be a sign of "insanity" (84). But more important than a precise analysis of the father's mental state in this scene is the role reversal that takes place. According to the dynamics of the oedipal conflict, if the son displaces the father, then the father is automatically put into the position, vis-à-vis the woman, formerly occupied by the son. And since there is no evidence of the father's supposed senility, we must seek for another explanation of what is happening here. In fact, apparently the figure being put to bed is not only the father qua father but also, symbolically, a somewhat reluctant child, who, to prolong the process a bit and register whatever weak protest can be made, catches hold of Georg's watch chain and for a while refuses to let go. This event is completely within the experience of any adult wearing any chain, necklace, or (alas) eyeglasses who has ever tried to put an unwilling infant to bed, and Kafka's journals show us what an astute observer of children he was. Thus the image does not so much indicate the father's childishness or senility as it does his symbolic transformation to childlike behavior.

This interpretation, however, still does not explain why Georg should have witnessed this action with "a dreadful feeling." Here we must recall Freud's explanation of the artistic process. One of the most frequent failings of the

psychoanalytic approach to literature is that while it does apply Freud's categories to the work and the writer, it tends to overlook Freud's psychology of
creation and what that theory implies about the work itself. Freud states that
the work of art is a fulfillment of a wish "in which elements of the recent event
and the old memory should be discernible" (*Collected Papers* 181). It is to this
"old memory" that we can attribute Georg's "dreadful feeling": when his father
takes hold of his chain, Georg suddenly comprehends the role reversal this
gesture implies. In his father he recognizes the child he himself once was,
playing with his father's watch chain, and in himself he recognizes his father
putting him to bed. The oedipal conflict is for a moment jolted out of its
repression in Georg's subsconscious mind, and the old memory to which
Freud alludes enters the texture of the fiction along with the recent event.

Only this interpretation, it seems to me, can adequately explain Georg's
"dreadful feeling" ("schreckliches Gefühl") and the subsequent characterization of his father as a "dreadful apparition" ("Schreckbild") (CS 85). The
description of this feeling accords perfectly with Freud's definition of the
"uncanny" as "that genre of the *dreadful* which goes back to things long since
and intimately known" (*Gesammelte Werke* 231). "This uncanny," Freud tells
us, "is really nothing new or unknown, but rather something long familiar
to the psychic life but which has become estranged from it through the
process of repression" (254). It is particularly appropriate that Georg's uncanny feeling be evoked by his recognition of the role reversal, for precisely
in such situations does Freud locate the origin of this feeling: "The uncanny
in experience arises when repressed infantile complexes are revived through
an impression or when outlived primitive beliefs seem once again confirmed"
(263). We may thus conclude that the figure being put to bed here along
with the father is not just any representative of childhood but in fact Georg
himself as a child.

These two possibilities, however, do not even yet exhaust the purposeful
ambiguities of the action. Kafka pays unusually detailed attention to the act
of undressing, to the necessary physical motions of standing, seating, and
laying down—more attention than is necessary and more than can be justified
on the realistic plane of the fiction alone. In fact, the description of this
disrobing ritual seems more appropriate to a bedroom seduction scene than
to the symbolic undressing of even a reluctant child. Georg's provisionally
triumphant statement "So you like it in bed" is obviously not the least of these
ambiguities. Nor should we forget that this detailed attention to clothing is
charged also with the erotic associations that arise immediately after, when
for a moment the father actually plays the role of Georg's bride:

> "Because she lifted up her skirts," his father began to flute, "because
> she lifted her skirts like this, the nasty creature," and mimicking her
> he lifted his shirt so high that one could see the scar on his thigh from
> the war wound, "because she lifted her skirts like this and this you

made up to her, and in order to make free with her undisturbed you have disgraced your mother's memory. . . ." (*CS* 85)

To realize the sexual significance of this scar on the father's upper thigh, one need only recall the rose-colored "wound" on the side of the patient in "A Country Doctor," described in obvious genital association as "dark in the hollows, lighter at the edges, softly granulated, with irregular clots of blood, open as a surface mine to the daylight" (*CS* 223), and narrowly triangular in shape, "cut in an acute angle with two strokes of the hatchet" (*CS* 225).

Further evidence for the presence of a female component in Kafka's representation of the father is provided by his diary entry regarding "The Judgment": "Thoughts of Freud naturally . . . of Werfel's 'Giantess' " (*Diaries, 1910–1913* 276). The reference to Freud, so welcome to psychoanalytic critics, has obscured the even more useful reference to Werfel. What exactly Kafka had in mind we cannot know, but we can see that the entire passage is too sexually charged for the reference to a woman to have been irrelevant to him, and we cannot forget that Georg literally looks up to his father as to a "giant." It seems undeniable, then, that along with the father and the image of Georg as a child, there is yet a third person being put to bed in this scene: a woman, whom Georg's father also represents.

Kafka himself first pointed to the shadowy presence of Georg's bride in this scene. His diary entry of 11 February 1913 refers to "the bride, who lives in the story only through her relationship to the friend, in other words to what is mutual" (*Diaries, 1910–1913* 278–79). She is not merely a "catalyst" (Nagel, *Aspekte* 183); as Sokel has said, she plays a "decisive role" (*Tragik und Ironie* 48). In her absence from the scene as an actor and in the role she plays as an object of contention between Georg and his father, she neatly recapitulates the position of the deceased mother. We might go even farther and note that in accusing Georg of having dishonored his mother's memory through his alliance with Frieda, the father establishes an equivalence—in the sense of a substitution—between these two women. Georg first sees his father sitting in a corner "hung with various mementoes of Georg's dead mother" (*CS* 81), and the old Bendemann constantly reminds us that he and his wife have usually acted as a unit, not the least when he appeals to the mother's symbolic presence: "All by myself I might have had to give way, but your mother has given me so much of her strength . . ." (*CS* 86). But we do not have to dwell on any specific equivalence between mother and bride; in any oedipal situation the beloved reactivates the child's incestuous desire for the mother; the dynamics of the conflict itself create the association, so the image of the mother is always subsumed in the figure of the beloved.

The central scene in "The Judgment" thus appears to be a distillation of the oedipal drama, a reduction of the complex interactions of all the characters of the story to a symbolic nuclear familial constellation. Previous attempts to see the scene in the light of the oedipal conflict, concentrating on Georg's desire to do away with his father, have neglected the symbolic presence of the child and the mother and so have unwittingly slighted the aesthetic economy that Kafka achieved here. Naturally, this economy is purchased at the expense of strict psychoanalytic logic, but the "inner truth" of which Kafka spoke in reference to his story (*Letters to Felice* 87) is more important. It is not true, as he wrote to Felice Bauer, that "The Judgment" cannot be explained (265), for he himself had rendered a reasonable explanation in his diary (*Diaries, 1910–1913* 278–79) while reading the proofs. What counts is the quality of lyrical association, a suggestive juxtaposition of images: they are the chief ordering principles in this scene. Freud would of course object that to combine father, child, and mother in one person is a distortion of the oedipal situation. And so it is, but Kafka was not interested in a prosaic and unilinear development in his story. He was, rather, aware that an almost alchemical process had been at work in its composition, as he noted in his diary: "how for all, even for the strangest ideas a great fire is prepared, in which they perish and again arise" (*Diaries, 1910–1913* 276). This kaleido-scopic freedom of the images to combine and recombine in the reader's perception is undoubtedly what he had in mind when he insisted to his publisher that the story was "more poem than story . . . more lyric than epic" (*Letters to Friends* 125–26).

Nevertheless, all is not fluid, not even in terms of the oedipal representa-tion. For if we look at the cast of characters in the scene, we find that although they are symbolically telescoped (one is tempted to use Freud's term *condensed*) into one person, as well as being there in their own behalf, they nonetheless occupy a stage importance commensurate with their impor-tance in the real-life drama. The son is the person most palpably and immedi-ately present: the main perspective on the action is his, just as the oedipal conflict is in the first order a conflict within the son. Kafka seems to have had good reason for initially planning to include the story, along with "The Stoker" (from *America*) and *The Metamorphosis*, in a volume tentatively to be called *Sons* (*Letters to Friends* 96–97). Confronting the son here is a father who seems somewhat less real than the son himself but who in any case is real enough to be the rival and to emerge as victor and judge in the struggle. This relative unreality is also appropriate, for it is not only the real father who precipitates the oedipal conflict in the son but, equally, the son's image of the father as rival, potential victor, and judge. And the shadowy, symbolic presence of the mother in the text is equally suited to represent her situation in the actual conflict: she is the source of the struggle, the prize to be won, but she need not be physically present; it suffices that her "memory" is alive. Nor is an oedipal drama complete without the child himself. Again, in the conflict situation of the adult Georg Bendemann, the child can be present only symbolically, as representative of the original oedipal situation and, in the present case of an unresolved conflict, as "admin-istrator" of the adult situation.

"Do you know what the final sentence means?" the author asked of Max Brod. "I thought of a strong ejaculation" (Brod, *Biography* 129). Although there is reason to contrast the vital assertiveness of the world in that final sentence with Georg's sexual failure, Kafka probably meant not so much the double entendre of the word *Verkehr* (translated as "traffic" but meaning also "intercourse" in the sexual sense) as he did the precipitous relaxation of tension following on the extraordinary compactness of the preceding scene. That sentence, read as Georg is plunging to his death in the river and after his father has collapsed back onto the bed, is the only one in the story narrated from outside the torments of the oedipal struggle. It is orgasmic and centrifugal, its extreme decompression all the greater in contrast to the compression of the preceding pages. This view is borne out by Kafka's journal entry of the following day: "Only *this way* can one write, only . . . with such complete opening of the body and soul" (*Diaries, 1910–1913* 276). Charles Bernheimer connects Kafka's metaphor of the ejaculation with his later view of the story as having been born of him like an infant "covered with filth and slime" (*Diaries, 1910–1913* 278):

> [T]he ejaculation Kafka associated with the final sentence may have its genesis in the victory he felt his writing act had achieved over the spectre of hostile paternal narcissism that prevailed in the story's narrative. In the terms in which Kafka metaphorizes his creative process, the feminine experience of release through birth is prior to, and may even trigger, the masculine experience of release through ejaculation. Thus it would seem that, for Kafka, to mother a text is to triumph over that paternal threat of castration which structures the text's signifying function. (167)

It is gratifying to think of Kafka's resolution of the oedipal situation in this positive light. More immediate to the text, though, is a negative outcome: at the end of the story, there is no one left save the maid, the live woman frozen in fright on the stairs between the two dead oedipal contenders. For dead they both presumably are. Georg's execution of his father's sentence is so powerful that we easily forget the father's fate: "Now he'll lean forward, thought Georg, what if he topples and smashes himself!" (*CS* 86). It seems that precisely this event happens, for when Georg rushes as if pursued from the room, the last thing that he (and the reader) hears of Bendemann Senior is "the crash with which his father fell on the bed behind him" (*CS* 87).

In one painfully utopian passage in *Letter to His Father*, Kafka allows himself to imagine a situation in which both he and his father would overturn their real-life attitudes toward each other, a situation

> so beautiful because then I could be a free, grateful, guiltless, upright son, and you could be an untroubled, untyrannical, sympathetic,

contented father. But to this end everything that ever happened would have to be undone, that is, we ourselves should have to be cancelled out.   (115)

The extent to which Kafka's fiction of "The Judgment" enacts the sobering realization of that last sentence is truly astonishing: everything that "ever happened" has been, literally, "undone"; the actors themselves have been, literally, "cancelled out." The stage is clear; the set is struck; the house is dark. What remains is the fleetingly envisioned hope for a different play with a less tragic ending, a hope for the unending human movement, over the bridge, to the vernal green of the opposite bank.

Although not everyone agrees with Harold Bloom's appraisal of Sigmund Freud as "the principal writer and the principal thinker of our century," it is difficult to argue against his contention that "we live more than ever in the age of Freud" (*Freud* 1). Many literary critics, however, still object to the psychoanalytic approach as an "extrinsic" method, one essentially foreign to the behests of art and incapable of illuminating the artistic process or of contributing to our aesthetic appreciation of the text. One still hears comments like "[A]n emphasis on the oedipal conflict is virtually a psycholiterary cliché. . . . The reader and critic are seduced away from the rich subtleties and cognitive processes within the work" (Lindauer 21). But the latter statement need not be the result of the former, for it is clear from our analysis that by recognizing the oedipal drama underlying the text of "The Judgment," our appreciation of Kafka's enormous artistic economy is enlarged, not diminished. He has brought together all the requisite personnel in mature son, child (memory), father, and mother, and within the narrative he has assigned to each an immediacy and importance commensurate with his or her role in the actual conflict. Kafka has created an unparalleled ambiguity in which Georg's actions apply with equal credibility to child, father, and mother. This scene is aesthetic concentration at its most impressive: the desires for elimination of the father and possession of the mother are ultimately inseparable in the oedipal striving of the child. One can imagine how a lesser writer would have artificially bifurcated these desires by representing them in separate scenes or by putting more actors physically on stage. Thus it seems that our appreciation of the "rich subtleties" of the story is increased when we see it in an oedipal light.

Moreover, the psychoanalytic perspective enables us to recognize that this story, which seems so bizarre, so maverick, and so unique, has venerable literary ancestors all over the world—but especially in the German-language area of Europe. It emerges as nothing less than a variant of the "Godfather Death" tale (Aarne and Thompson, no. 59; see Belmont; Le Roy Ladurie, ch. 14), albeit a variant appropriately peculiar to Kafka, ending as it does not with the protagonist's marriage but with his death.

We gain such insights, it is true, when we bring psychoanalytic theory to bear on the text itself, not on the author or any of the author's fictional characters. In this way, these insights are particularly well suited to complement the perceptions gained through other methods of textual analysis, such as, for example, the application of rhetorical theory to Kafka's works. That perspective has demonstrated well that "the relationships among narrative elements in Kafka's fiction are intimately linked to relationships at the level of the verbal signifier" (Koelb 122). With respect specifically to "The Judgment," Stanley Corngold has argued persuasively that a fundamental aspect of the text is a kind of rhetorical alchemy with the words *Urteil* ("general judgment" *or* "judicial sentence") and *verurteilen* ("to sentence or condemn"): Georg seeks his father's judgment about the letter he has written to his friend, but instead his father sentences him ("ich verurteile dich") to death, so in fact Georg does get an *Urteil*, but it's a sentence instead of a judgment ("Kafka's 'The Judgment' "). Clayton Koelb has pointed to a specific incident in Kafka's life that may have prepared him for the rhetorical slippage in exactly these words (208–11). "Although it is certainly true that Kafka's pain could have existed in the utter absence of this rhetoric of *Urteile*," he writes, "it is also true that the particular sort of pain he suffered was formed according to the channels of possibility inherent in the German language" (210). This observation is completely convincing, and it is true that psychoanalysis has had very little to say about style, rhetoric, or the very rhetoricity—the sheer delight in linguistic possibilities—that Koelb has shown as basic to much of Kafka's writing, if not his very incentive and motivation to write. Rhetorical theory has nothing to say, however, about why Kafka's story chooses to exploit the rhetorical possibilities of the word *Urteil* expressly in a context that depends so signally on the properties and cast of the oedipal conflict: judgments and sentences can be about all sorts of things; they don't have to be about fathers, sons, mothers, marriages, and sex. Although the psychoanalytic perspective is not the only fruitful approach that one can adopt toward Kafka's writing, it is apparently capable of insights and explanations that are not within the province of other approaches.

NOTES

[1] The bibliography of criticism on "The Judgment" is far too extensive to be given even in part here. See Beicken's *Kritische Einführung*, Angel Flores's *Bibliography*, the occasional updates of the literature compiled by Marie Luise Caputo-Mayr and Julius Herz in the *Journal of the Kafka Society of America*.

[2] My analysis of the central scene presented here is adapted from that earlier study.

[3] I have somewhat emended the translations, here and throughout.

Georg Bendemann's Path to the Judgment

Elizabeth W. Trahan

"The Judgment" and *The Metamorphosis* are the two short works teachers most frequently select to introduce students to Kafka's world. The stories complement each other. *The Metamorphosis* immediately confronts the reader with the intrusion of a fantastic element on everyday reality, then shows how the various characters come to terms with the consequences and return to normalcy. "The Judgment," after a conventional beginning, accelerates toward a grotesque and highly irrational climax. Because the story begins so "normally," its strange ending tends to leave the reader puzzled and discomfited. The following approach has proved very successful with students who read "The Judgment" as an introduction to Kafka.

When asked for first impressions, my students tended to compare the story to a nightmare that follows its own dreamlike logic and therefore cannot be analyzed. Pressed further, they agreed that the story's main theme is a father-son relationship, but some saw it as the tragedy of a dutiful son who is destroyed by a tyrannical and half-crazed father, while others read it as the deserved punishment of a selfish son by his neglected procreator.

At that point I would state that all three readings make good sense, and, to buttress the students' confidence in their own critical opinion, I would point out the existence of an enormous body of diverse, often contradictory Kafka criticism. Thereupon I would propose that we subject the story to a close reading, with attention first to structure, then to style and significant detail, in order to search for evidence supporting any one of the three interpretations mentioned and to determine whether they coexist, overlap, or show one reading to be dominant.

Structurally, I would point out, "The Judgment" may be compared to a minidrama of four scenes with a cast of three—only two of whom appear onstage. The third—the friend in Russia—is written to and spoken of but does not turn into a persona in his own right. Instead, he functions as mirror, measure, link, catalyst, foil, and weapon for the other two. The action focuses on the relationship between a father and his son during an episode of personal interaction that at first seems trivial but then turns into a confrontation and eventually a life-or-death struggle. The struggle climaxes in the father's "judgment" and finds its denouement in the son's execution of the judgment. At first the confrontation seems a typical generational conflict, but it soon turns into a duel of wits between two idiosyncratic antagonists. Their weapons are primarily words but also gestures, postures, and facial expressions that impart to the confrontation elements of farce and melodrama. Despite strongly grotesque touches, the skirmish ends tragically, with one and possibly both protagonists' annihilation.

The action takes place during a short, "real-time" period of probably less than an hour, in a timeless present. There are two scene changes, and all scenes are visually interrelated. The first takes place in Georg's study, which fronts the river. It ends with Georg's leaving his room to go to that of his father. The two rooms not only are part of the same apartment or house but also are linked by some external similarities and contrasts. At the beginning of each scene, the room's owner sits on a chair by a window, but while Georg's room is bright and airy, with an open and cheerful view, his father's room is dark and cluttered and faces a wall. The letter that was the focus of scene 1 becomes a thrown gauntlet in scene 2. Scenes 2 and 3 form a spatial unit extending from Georg's entrance into his father's room to his exit from it. Here the transition is achieved through a climax—the father's "rising"— that introduces a shift in perspective and emphasis. Scene 4, in contrast to the preceding three scenes, is not static but resembles an accelerated film take in which the camera follows Georg's precipitous motion from his father's room to the river that was visible from Georg's window in scene 1.

Georg's outer journey corresponds to a journey inward. Scene 1, which functions as its prologue, contains a preliminary exposition of Georg's character and human environment, given at first by an apparently objective narrator, then as Georg's interior monologue. This "insider" perspective is seemingly straightforward, but a few details cast doubt on its reliability by suggesting slight ambivalences, perhaps even contradictions in Georg's character. Scenes 2 and 3 contain the main "action"—that is, the confrontation between son and father. Both scenes consist largely of dialogue. This dialogue, along with the narrator's brief descriptive interpolations, introduces further ambivalences, pertaining now to both father and son. The perspective in scene 2 is largely Georg's, in scene 3 increasingly that of the narrator. Scene 2 is dominated by the son, scene 3 by the father. Scene 2 ends with the father's stripping off the son's cover, literally and figuratively. Scene 3 culminates in the father's unexpected "judgment," which, in the fourth and final scene, the son carries out, equally surprisingly, with great alacrity, even joy. The short scene provides a structural counterpart to scene 1; it becomes an epilogue told by the eyewitness narrator.

This complex structural pattern, I would suggest to the students, indicates the presence of so elaborate a set of correspondences that an interpretation of the story as a dream or nightmare seems improbable.[1] We would therefore proceed to an examination of individual facets, especially the thoughts, feelings, actions, and reactions of the two protagonists, to establish what kind of men Georg and his father are; whether they remain the same, change, or reveal themselves gradually; and whether Georg emerges as victim or villain, a tragic or a pathetic figure. Taking our cue from Kafka's awareness, as a practicing lawyer, of the precise yet multiple denotations and connotations of individual words, we would focus primarily on the identification and interpretation—in the legal and literary senses—of any odd or ambiguous-sounding words and phrases. Spatial limitations preclude my giving here such a complete textual analysis, but I will present its main elements.

When Georg seals the letter to his friend, he does so with "playful lassitude" ("mit spielerischer Langsamkeit") (CS 77).[2] Does the phrase imply a relaxed relationship with the friend, or does it disguise hesitation and unresolved tensions? Likewise, is the fiancée's odd remark—"with such friends, you should not have become engaged" (CS 80)—merely facetious, or does it hide actual or potential tensions between her and Georg? These questions cannot yet be answered, but we should recall them if similar ambivalences or clues surface later.

Indeed, almost immediately there is another, more concrete cautionary sign: Georg's pride at his financial success is undercut by his admission that he was able to succeed only after his father's retirement, which, moreover, was at best semivoluntary. Though we do not have enough information to establish whether Georg's delayed success was caused by his insecurity or considerateness, by honesty, ambivalence, or duplicity, we begin to suspect that the surface calm of this sunny Sunday morning may be concealing turbulent waters beneath. And something else has now become obvious: the details Kafka gives us, no matter how factually presented, cannot always be taken at face value.

In scene 2, the ambivalences multiply. That Georg has not entered his father's room in many months casts suspicion on his manifest solicitousness. Likewise, Georg's surprise at finding the room so inhospitable and his father neglected (despite our having been told that Georg sees him for much of each day) shows Georg to be either less observant or less caring than he led us to believe. He makes the decision that his fiancée will simply have to accept his father's living with them·(*CS* 84) on the spur of the moment and without consulting either of the two. That it is either unconsidered or inconsiderate emerges clearly in retrospect, when his father's hostility toward Frieda surfaces. Whatever the impetus, tensions exist or are in the making, not only between Georg and his father but also between Georg and his fiancée.

Our sympathies for Georg erode further as his thoughts, words, and tone reveal that the image he presented of his father before was not accurate. In fact, when he discovers that his father is "still a giant of a man" who "in business hours . . . [is] quite different" (*CS* 81), we realize that he has not only misled us but deluded himself as well. All the more disconcerting is the exaggerated, almost ridiculous solicitousness with which he proceeds to undress "the giant," carry him to bed and cover him, as if he were a child. Equally suspect is Georg's admission that at least twice he concealed the friend's presence from his father: did he do so out of embarrassment? fear? jealousy? We will have to remain on the alert.

The father picks up Georg's clue and plays Georg's game, and he does so with a vengeance. Being treated as a child, he acts like one. Having been kept in the dark about the friend's presence, he now denies his existence. Since Georg fails to understand the implied reproach, the old man changes tactics. He rises, literally and figuratively, to the occasion. Thereby the balance between the two men shifts, and a new scene begins.

The father interprets Georg's solicitousness as an attempt to emasculate and dominate him, and we begin to wonder whether he might be right. But he does not stop there. He counterattacks on all fronts, drawing into his camp Georg's friend, mother, and customers, and—figuratively—annihilating Georg's fiancée. In the process, his vindictive and at times grotesque behavior shows that, no matter what Georg's weaknesses may be, the old man is clearly both evil and half-mad. Georg's memories of his father's past despotism and his uneasiness at his father's present strength seem borne out by reality.

Just as we are ready to side again with Georg, his behavior undergoes a strange transformation. Instead of treating his father as the half-senile tyrant he seems to be, Georg is totally unable to retain his equanimity or to justify himself. He responds with a strange dreaminess and absentmindedness and is unable to concentrate, even though he had "a long time ago . . . firmly made up his mind to watch everything very closely so that he should not be surprised by any indirect attack, a pounce from behind or above. At this moment he recalled this long-forgotten resolution and forgot it again . . ." (*CS* 85). The formulation is illuminating: though Georg has apparently mistrusted his father for a long time, he is still unable to face him. He not only lacks control of the situation but allows his thoughts to drift aimlessly or— when he tries to evoke the distant friend—seeks an escape from reality in another spatial and temporal dimension. Georg, the successful businessman, is totally unable to function, and the combination of his paralysis and his father's grotesque antics does indeed bestow on this scene the quality of a nightmare.

When Georg finally rallies, he adopts his father's tactics. When the old man calls him a "joker," Georg responds by calling his father a conniving clown (CS 86; the German word *Komödiant* is far more derogatory than its English cognate). Georg's word becomes a barometer that registers the rise in intensity of the verbal duel. It also indicates that even if Georg's "villainy" is trifling in comparison with that of his father, he is no match for the old man.

The moment the word *clown* has escaped Georg, "he realized at once the harm done and, with expressionless eyes, bit his tongue, unfortunately too late, till the pain made his knees give" (CS 86). That he immediately regrets his utterance suggests his awareness of having given himself away. Thus he has, it appears, committed a truly Freudian slip. The deep-seated guilt that it indicates is enhanced further when the long-suppressed feelings of animosity surface and find expression.

As Georg's ambivalence grows, his father becomes more reasonable. The old man admits that he has indeed been putting on a show, but what else could he do, relegated to a back room, plagued by disloyal staff and a son who, strutting about triumphantly and secretively, is reaping the fruits of his father's labor? He ends with a dramatic proclamation of love for his offspring that sounds genuine, though—or because—it reflects the father's solipsism: "Do you think I didn't love you, I, from whom you are sprung?" (CS 86).

In view of the old man's earlier behavior, we may well remain distrustful, all the more so since his speech contains a phrase that on first reading merely sounds odd but in retrospect seems truly ominous: "Tell me—and while you're answering be my living son still . . ." (CS 86). There is no clear indication that Georg has taken in the implied threat. His reaction, however, is even more revealing than the Freudian slip of a moment ago. If his real feelings for his father had forced their way out then despite Georg's attempt to suppress them, he now gives free rein to his hostility: "Now he will lean forward, Georg was thinking, what if he fell and broke his neck! The words hissed through his mind" (CS 86). The verbs Georg uses (*zerschmetterte, zischte*) leave little doubt: Absentmindedness and objectivity give way to outright hostility just when his father assures him of his love. Even if Georg is right in seeing his father's words as part of the same act that the old man put on before, it has by now become obvious that Georg's earlier display of solicitude has either yielded to or all along merely served to disguise a deep-seated hatred and that at least subconsciously Georg has been wishing his father dead.

The story illustrates immediately that this is indeed so. Though Georg is aware that his father might fall and kill himself, he does nothing to prevent or break his fall. Nor is Georg's behavior lost on his father. As one would expect, it provides new grist for his mill. "Stay where you are. I don't need you!" (*CS* 86). Once again the father seems to be testing Georg—and finds him wanting. And so he launches his final, all-out attack: If Georg thinks he is still free to come or go, he may be mistaken. He, the father, is by far the stronger man. Alone, he might not be able to confront Georg, but Georg's mother has given the old man her strength as well, he has joined forces with Georg's friend, and he has Georg's customers "here in my pocket" (*CS* 86).

Georg is unable to take in the full extent or the absurdity of these threats. His mind merely clutches at the word *pocket* and associates it, almost mechanically, with his father's nightshirt. But even that simple association is not retained for long—"since he kept forgetting everything" (*CS* 86). It is as if he were sinking ever more deeply into a dream, a trance, unable to act, unable to think, struggling vainly to regain his lucidity and detachment.

At this point the story takes on a slightly surreal dimension. When the father tells Georg that his main concern has been to keep the friend informed, he throws an old newspaper at Georg as proof that he has not even been reading the papers. The name of the paper is "entirely unknown to Georg" (*CS* 87), even though his father's withdrawal into the seclusion of his room dates only back to Georg's mother's death two years ago. Moreover, the two men have presumably been reading their newspapers together whenever Georg spent an evening at home. Not only is the "clown" again clowning, but he seems to have hypnotized Georg into accepting everything he says or implies, so that Georg's mind is increasingly estranged from reality. We are torn between the mixture of amusement, revulsion, and apprehension that a presumably funny but basically cruel trick film engenders. We also begin to realize that this situation cannot be viewed in the context of "everyday life," of a generation gap. Instead, it depicts a fateful moment in the lives of two men, an elemental struggle between a specific father and a specific son, springing from sub- or unconscious causes at which we can only guess and fought with weapons that are visible to us only in their effects.

The nightmarish interrogation ends with the father's monstrously exaggerated summation in which he accuses Georg of having taken so long to mature that his mother has died, the friend has almost perished, and he, the father, is in bad shape. His words imply that Georg has now reached maturity, but the ending of the story tells us otherwise. The father's statement was apparently meant as one more—the ultimate—test.

Georg does not pass it. Instead of justifying or asserting himself, he counterattacks—and once again does so by imitating his father's method. He accuses the old man of having lain in wait for him. No matter whether Georg is becoming increasingly irrational or whether he is right in suspecting his father of undermining him, one thing is clear: in this struggle to the death Georg, too, is now fighting with no holds barred.

With "offhanded compassion" the father counters that Georg must have meant to make this observation earlier, for now it no longer fits. He is clearly in full control of the situation, while Georg is unable to use his words effectively. And before Georg can parry, the old man delivers the fatal thrust. Accusing Georg of having been totally wrapped up in himself, of being both an innocent child and a truly devilish human being, the father pronounces his verdict: "And therefore take note: I sentence you now to death by drowning!" (CS 87).

Georg, instead of shrugging off the old man's ravings, seems hypnotized by them. He responds without a moment's hesitation, as if under a compulsion. The language in that final, compressed scene of only one paragraph, with its accelerated tempo and passive constructions, reflects both the nightmarish quality and the absolute finality of the judgment. Georg "felt himself urged from the room." He neither turns back nor hesitates, though "the crash with which his father fell on the bed behind him was still in his ears"— a crash that may well have fulfilled his wish to see his father dead. Like an automaton or maniac—the cleaning woman is horrified at the sight of him— he rushes down the staircase, "as if its steps were an inclined plane" (CS 87), runs out the gate, is "driven" across the road and toward the water. In the same frenzy he clasps the railing—"as a starving man clutches at food" (CS 88)—and swings himself over it.

Just then, there is one more brief shift in perspective. As Georg holds on to the railing "with weakening grip," he seems to become momentarily lucid. He reasons that the coming bus "would easily cover the noise of his fall." But instead of asking himself "Why would I want this?" or "What am I doing here?" and pulling back—he has always been athletic, we recall—or instead of calling out for help, his "reasoning" prepares the mind-set for his final words: "Dear parents, believe me, I have always loved you" (CS 88). With these words Georg indicates not only his voluntary submission to the verdict but also his acceptance of his father's assertion that he was speaking for himself as well as his wife.

In contrast to the three preceding, rather static scenes, that short final scene is one of precipitous and circular or, rather, spiraling movement. By leaving his father's room and heading toward the river, Georg completes the circle that led from his room with its view of the river through his father's room back to the river. But though he reemerges into daylight, into the sunny world of the story's beginning, he refuses—or is unable—to remain there and plunges into a darkness even deeper than that of his father's room, the darkness of the river, of death. Georg proceeds from the stability of his structured existence to a search for his origins and self and, when origins and self emerge as incompatible, to an affirmation of origins over self, to self-abandonment in the anonymity of nature.

At this point I would remind the students of the three initially posited interpretations and of our intention to establish which if any seem borne out by the text.

The dream metaphor seems to be applicable, but only to the last two scenes and even there only partially. As a key to the narrative, it is inadequate because the story has a definite and elaborate structure that, moreover, is closely linked to the thematic progression, and scenes 3 and 4 contain essential aspects of both. The dream metaphor can, however, attune us to the important insight that Kafka's world manifests itself in an unpredictable alternation between normal logic and illogical sequencing or transformations, such as we encounter in dreams. The link between the two states is supplied by ambivalence. Ambivalence may provide a happy hunting ground for the depth psychologist–biographer, but a legalistically inclined literary critic will prefer to see it as a signpost leading to the paradoxes that, according to Kafka, underlie all human existence. An even better comparison is now available, thanks to the new science of chaos theory: Kafka's world resembles the dynamic systems of fractal geometry, which contain an unpredictable factor and can therefore be mapped but not dissected, directed, or anticipated.[3]

It has become clear, however, that the theme of the struggle between father and son is indeed central to the story and that it is presented neither as a mere generational conflict nor as the exposure of a typical turn-of-the-century paterfamilias. Under the challenge of the confrontation, both men's true natures are revealed as far more complex and idiosyncratic than first impressions indicated.

When he is introduced to us, Georg seems a stable, "normal" character who is trying to adapt to the pressures of a difficult situation. But before our eyes he becomes more complex, then ambivalent, then a bundle of contradictions, finally losing, one after another, his willpower, free will, and individuality. While Georg's initially coherent figure thus deconstructs, the various facets of the older Bendemann's character gradually arrange themselves into a cogent entity. Despite its clear foreshadowing early in the story, his propensity for evil is couched throughout in ambiguities and paradoxes: he knows and does not know Georg's friend, he dislikes and loves his son, and he wants Georg to mature and to remain a child. At the same time, however, the threat he poses is stressed consistently, from the emphasis on his physique to the metaphoric images of the inscrutable idol, the malicious clown, and the threatening demon, finally to the full display of his omnipotence—as procreator, tempter, prosecutor, and judge.

The story's structure indicates the direction of Georg's disintegration. From the serene vista of the peaceful spring morning with its promise of regeneration, he moves into the turmoil of a dark, demonic cave with a monstrous guardian, then out into a tilted, shifting landscape, finally into the ceaselessly flowing water. In close parallel, Georg's conventional reasoning and traditional behavior yield to his guilt at not having been a good son to his father and at having usurped his father's place. When he fails in his attempt to defuse the accusation by becoming a "good father" to the child that his own father seems to have become, Georg tries to flee into absentmindedness but is unable to escape his father's domination. When he cannot cope verbally, he reacts emotionally, first with hatred, then with mockery, and finally with submission. Submission frees him from the burden of having to assert himself against his father; it returns him to the total irresponsibility and dependence of the child.

Thus Georg's outer journey fuses with his journey inward, into the dark depths of the paternal house and the equally dark depths of a Freudian world of neurotic responses, oedipal conflicts, and schizoid regressions.[4] The question, then, is not one of who is right and who is wrong, what is true and what is false. Georg is simply the wrong son for the wrong father, both too much and too little like him. The only way to deal with such a father would be to rebel, but from strength rather than from repression of guilt feelings (Georg's marriage might have become such a liberation), or to flee as far away as possible, to the friend in Russia.[5] Either solution could offer Georg an existence free from the father's dominating influence. Instead, he steps into his father's shoes, first by replacing him in the business, then by changing roles and "adopting" him as his child. Only as a last resort does he attempt rebellion. But whether because of his childhood under such a father (and with a mother who obviously did not provide a counterweight) or because of inherited genes, whether the fault lies with his inconstancy, his narcissism, his weakness, or a combination of all these factors, Georg is not man enough to assert himself, nor is he able to accept a helping hand. When the challenge is placed squarely on his shoulders, he can only capitulate.

Depending on the class's orientation and level, an instructor may wish to stop here or proceed to some extrinsic explorations, either through class discussion or in assigned papers.

Closest at hand, though most difficult, is the biographical or psychoanalytic dimension. When the story is linked to Kafka's *Letter to His Father*, to the pertinent diary entries and the first letters to Felice Bauer, its full impact as a personal catharsis may be traced.[6] Another approach that often intrigues students is an exploration of the story's biblical echoes, from the Christlike self-sacrifice and the conciliatory final words to the ascendance of a wrathful Old Testament God.[7]

In my experience the structural approach outlined above, whether used with or without these complements, invariably stimulates further interest in Kafka, especially if students learn that in 1913 Kafka wanted to publish

"The Stoker," *The Metamorphosis*, and "The Judgment" together in a volume called *Sons* (see *Letters to Friends* 96–97) and that in 1915 he suggested to his publisher a volume called *Punishments*, to consist of "The Judgment," *The Metamorphosis*, and "In the Penal Colony" (see *Letters to Friends* 113). Finally, it should be stressed that the paradoxes of guilt-innocence and rebellion-submission run through almost all Kafka's works.

NOTES

[1] Whenever the story served as an introduction to Kafka, I would refrain from references to its genesis and autobiographical aspects. If students wished to pursue these topics in their papers, I would caution them against oversimplification: I would explain that though all Kafka's works are somewhat autobiographical, the extremely complex metaphorical interaction between his life and art renders biographical, psychoanalytic, or metaphysical criticism too limiting for literary analysis. I would usually cite the following examples: On 4 May 1915 Kafka writes that to have someone who would fully understand him, perhaps a wife, "would mean to have a support from every side, to have God" (*Diaries, 1914–1923* 126). While anxiously awaiting a visit from Milena Jesenská, Kafka writes a letter to her in which he accepts the logical impossibility of a joint future—"we will not talk about the future ever again, only about the present"—but then uses the punishment machine from "In the Penal Colony" as an image of his precarious emotional state: "You know, when I try to write down something . . . [about my feelings], the swords whose points surround me in a circle begin slowly to approach the body, it's the most complete torture; when they begin to graze me it's already so terrible that I immediately at the first scream betray you, myself, everything" (*Letters to Milena* 177).

[2] The German text used is that of the third edition (1919–20), the last to be revised by Kafka. It can be found in Neumann, *Franz Kafka, "Das Urteil"* 7–19.

[3] Cf. the diary entry quoted in note 1: The total empathy that Kafka craves would overcome ambiguity.

[4] In his diary entry of 23 September 1912, Kafka describes the genesis of "The Judgment" the night before and lists, among "many emotions carried along in the writing, . . . thoughts about Freud, of course" (*Diaries, 1910–1913* 276).

[5] Cf. the diary entry of 14 February 1915, on "the infinite attraction of Russia" (*Diaries, 1914–1923* 115), and entries of 5 January 1912 (*Diaries, 1910–1913* 214) and 15 August 1914 ("Memoirs of the Kalda Railroad," *Diaries, 1914–1923* 79), on Russia as the epitome of distance and solitude.

[6] Neumann supplies all necessary leads, including the important and rarely made observation that the night of the writing of the story (22–23 Sept. 1912) was the night following the highest Jewish holiday, the Day of Atonement. The story is undoubtedly Kafka's stocktaking of his relationship with his father. By sacrificing Georg, it became possible for Kafka to survive his own struggle for identity and to accomplish his liberation through creativity.

[7] The story may be read as a parody on the crucifixion, its "taking back." Where Christ ascended, a widely visible symbol of redemption, Georg descends, dying unnoticed in the flowing waters of anonymity. Whereas Christ, an innocent, sacrificed

himself for humankind more or less willingly—the Gospels vary on that point—
Georg's ambivalence implies sinfulness or at least acceptance of an imagined guilt,
and his self-sacrifice, meaningless to all but himself, is a wasted gesture. Finally, if
Georg's father stands for the victory of a harsh and self-righteous Old Testament
God over Christ's message of love and mercy, "The Judgment" acquires an additional
ironic dimension for Kafka the Jew.

Kafka's *Metamorphosis* and the Search for Meaning in Twentieth-Century German Literature

Margit M. Sinka

Regardless of how often I lead discussions on Franz Kafka in my literature courses, I still find teaching Kafka a humbling experience. To "teach" Kafka seems, in fact, presumptuous. Even the Germanist Peter Heller says, in a wise article, that there is nothing in Kafka that he is sure of understanding sufficiently, since there are always possibilities of implications to lure him on and to dismiss him finally with a sense of failure. "This experience of incapacity to understand," adds Heller, "seems tantamount to understanding Kafka, at least in his essential and perennial message, the dramatization of a vast landscape of failures" ("On Not Understanding" 383).

Keeping in mind Heller's statement and my own failed attempts to attain conclusive meanings in Kafka, I find it presumptuous to state course objectives when Kafka appears on a class syllabus. Though Kafka insisted on the existence of a goal, he could never formulate it, and he stressed the absence of a way to reach it: "There is a goal but no way; what we call the way is mere wavering" (*Great Wall* 166). Instead of definite objectives that would seem hypocritical or, at best, highly inflated, this Kafka quote appears at the top of the syllabus for my third-year-level German course on modern literature.

There are, of course, both disadvantages and advantages to reading Kafka, as well as other authors, in German. Readily apparent disadvantages: some students have not yet bridged the gap between the different types of readings on the second- and third-year levels and thus have inadequate reading proficiency; others have only a slight interest in literature and sign up for the course mainly because of high oral proficiency in German attained while living abroad. Sometimes age differences become crucial, especially between the freshmen enrolled in the course because of high achievement on German placement tests and the juniors and seniors. The freshmen tend to balk at ambivalence; the older students are less threatened by it. Another disadvantage, perhaps not so apparent, is the shock some students who have been in my lower-level courses have to overcome: the shock at seeing their German professor, who once fussed about genders of nouns and stressed practical linguistic goals such as "oral proficiency," stray from language certainties on a functional level into ambivalent literary topics.

The most pronounced advantage, by contrast, is the possibility to spend more time on each work—and thus on its details—than would be justifiable in a survey course conducted in English. In the process of attempting to glean meaning, students concentrate more closely on language. Thus they frequently avoid facile solutions. Unfamiliar terrain seems, in addition, more acceptable to them if approached through a linguistic medium retaining foreign texture.

The Search for Meaning is the title and unifying theme of my third-year course on twentieth-century German prose before World War II. On the first day of the course, instead of starting with twentieth-century materials, we briefly step into the eighteenth and nineteenth centuries, discussing first Friedrich Schiller's "Ode to Joy" and then listening to Beethoven's rendition of the poem in his Ninth Symphony. Students thus sense the former belief in an anchored world—in short, the belief in meaning and the certainty in the values that provide meaning—so they are at least somewhat prepared to grasp the enormity of the changes that occur later.

Throughout most of the course, students read various chapters or excerpts from Stefan Zweig's *Die Welt Von Gestern* (*The World of Yesterday*), for Zweig demonstrates especially well how an age of certainty was transformed into an age of uncertainty. For additional background material, I lecture on Kant's and Schopenhauer's challenges to accepted ways of understanding the world. We then proceed to Gerhart Hauptmann's "Fasching," an example of naturalism, and afterward to Arthur Schnitzler's "Der Witwer," an illustration of impressionism. In conjunction with Schnitzler, we spend considerable time on the entire Viennese fin-de-siècle period and especially on artists and musicians (e.g., Gustav Klimt and Arnold Schönberg) who were accused of attacking the cherished ideals of rationalism and progress. At this stage, we also discuss Klimt's murals on "The Ode to Joy."

A unit on Sigmund Freud precedes Stefan Zweig's "Der Amokläufer," a tale in which the Freudian id can no longer be controlled. On subsequent discussions of Hugo von Hofmannsthal's and Rainer Maria Rilke's poetry, we proceed to Hofmannsthal's "Letter of Lord Chandos" and to an excerpt from Robert Musil's *Der Mann ohne Eigenschaften* (*The Man without Qualities*). Emphasis on the loss of belief in transmitted values and on the ensuing relativism leads to excerpts from Friedrich Nietzsche's *Also sprach Zarathustra* (*Thus Spoke Zarathustra*). In the next stage of the course we focus in detail on Hermann Hesse's *Demian*, which interweaves influences from Nietzsche and Carl Jung, and on Thomas Mann's *Tonio Kröger*. Kafka's *The Metamorphosis* then concludes the course.

At the outset of the three-week Kafka period, I assign the first chapter of Heinz Politzer's *Parable and Paradox*, a chapter providing numerous interpretations prompted by Kafka's ten-line parable "Give It Up." This selection not only enables students to read concrete examples of critical orientations such as the Freudian, the Jungian, the religious, and the Marxist but also demonstrates how previous background and subjective viewpoints determine the nature of the commentaries. Assured of student interest, I then discuss the whole problematic area of meaning in Kafka. Is it justifiable to think in reductionist fashion, to find only a single meaning in Kafka—one excluding all other interpretations? Or are all the many interpretations equally valid? Do they represent the accumulation of perspectives that Kafka once called the only possible truth? Or do all of the varied meanings cancel each other out and show that there is no meaning at all? Is it possible that Kafka's purpose was to demonstrate the absence of any meaning? Should one not stress instead that Kafka doggedly searched for a truth he sensed, even though he found its adequate expression impossible? At the end of this discussion, I tend to affirm Kafka's untiring quest for meaning. Because he cannot, he does not supply the "truth." But he always intimates its existence.

In the class period following the session on Politzer's chapter and possible ways of interpreting Kafka, I give students individual copies of many supplementary materials, most of them in English. While they include a long, excellent biographical article disseminated by the Austrian Embassy in New York, they consist mainly of book reviews or interpretive articles from major American magazines and newspapers directed at the general literate reading public (e.g., Auster, "Pages" and "Letters"; Roth; V. S. Pritchett; Steiner; Updike). The articles are not required reading, but they provide welcome aids for the particularly inquisitive.

Since I believe that no single Kafka work should be treated in entire isolation from the others, I pass out a list of Kafka quotes (mainly in German) gleaned from the entire spectrum of his writings. Examples: "A cage went in search of a bird" (*Dearest Father* 36); "What is laid upon us is to accomplish the negative; the positive is already given" (*Dearest Father* 36–37); "Theoretically there exists a perfect possibility of happiness: to believe in the indestructible element in oneself and not strive after it" (*Dearest Father* 41); "To reach clarity, it is necessary to exaggerate" ("Der Nachbar," in *Erzählungen* 346; my trans.); "I have no literary interest but am made of literature" (*Letters to Felice* 304). Individual students read some of the quotes out loud, and short discussions ensue. Sometimes I give only half of a quote, and students hypothesize about the rest of it.

Next, I spend two to three minutes reading titles of articles and books written on Kafka (e.g., "Moment of Torment"; "Kafka's Fantasy of Punishment"; "The Reality of the Absurd and the Absurdity of the Real"; "The Tragic Protest"; "The Alienated Self"). Then I provide students with a typed sheet of Kafka motifs (walls, doors, keys, food, the number three) and typical Kafkaesque developments (accelerated and terminated motion, decreasing appetite, frequent hiding and shrinking). To ascertain recurring patterns in Kafka, students refer to this sheet while they are reading.

During the last few minutes of the class, I mention Kafka's sentence "A book must be the axe for the frozen sea inside us" (*Letters to Friends* 16) and suggest that *The Metamorphosis* has become exactly the axe he was talking about. I then read its first sentence, probably the most famous beginning in all of twentieth-century prose. Rarely does a person hearing this sentence remain unaffected. In quick brainstorming, after a minute of appropriate silence, class members supply questions engendered by the sentence: Did Gregor truly become a beetle, or is he only dreaming? What could his "troubled dream" during the night have been? ("Troubled dream" is Vladimir Nabokov's translation of "unruhigen Träumen," generally rendered as "uneasy dreams" [256].) If Gregor has indeed turned into a beetle, how will he react? How will others react? What human traits, if any, is he likely to retain? Who turned him into a beetle? Does his beetle-self reflect his own feelings about himself? If so, how does he feel about himself? Will he be changed back into a human being? How will he have to change his manner of living as a result of being a beetle? How long can he live as a beetle? How will he change his perspectives on his spatial surroundings and on time? Not every class asks all these questions, and some classes ask other questions as well. In all classes, however, the first questions release a flood of others, especially since the students know that they are not yet expected to attempt responses.

With all reading assignments, students continue to formulate questions. At the beginning of the class hour, each student anonymously places a slip of paper with a question into a box. Either as a single group or in pairs, class members choose two or three of the questions at random and evaluate them, using criteria such as whether the answer is worth knowing and whether attempting to answer the question calls for genuine reflection. Later, students also provide possible answers. Through this process of producing questions and attempting answers, students become acquainted with *how* Kafka lures readers into his world of countless labyrinthine paths leading nowhere, least of all to explicit meaning.

Because students need help and time to accustom themselves to Kafka's style, I make the first reading assignment very short, not more than four pages. This brief text enables us to concentrate in class on how Gregor Samsa tends to follow, or be distracted by, most thoughts that occur to him. We scrutinize Gregor's rhetorical questions and quick self-justifications. We note how he avoids unpleasant thoughts by exaggerating the inessential and how the excessive details pertaining to inessentials hinder grasp of the essential. Students observe, moreover, how the prominent use of the subjunctive, the tense of conjecture and uncertainty, contributes to creating a world of ambivalence.

At this point I also find it necessary to inform the students of Friedrich Beissner's groundbreaking thesis, offered in 1952. There is no controlling authorial voice, says Beissner. We experience everything only from the viewpoint of the main character. Thus, instead of reaching conclusions about what is or is not real, we are doomed to floundering in the same indecisions and uncertainties as the main character does. To be sure, critics have contested the extent to which Beissner's thesis remains valid. In *The Metamorphosis*, for instance, the authorial voice enters not only in the conclusion (after Gregor's death) but also occasionally before then. Still, these episodes remain isolated instances, and I do not find it necessary to stress them to undergraduate students reading Kafka for the first time. It is more important, I think, to emphasize how Kafka's dominant narrative mode contributes just as much to creating the Kafkaesque as do the metaphors—for instance, the human entrapped in a repugnant animal—which refer to nothing beyond themselves.

For the remaining seven days spent on Kafka, I find Nabokov's university lectures on *The Metamorphosis* very useful, particularly his emphasis on visualizing. While I agree with Kafka that the beetle should never be drawn or appear as an illustration on a book jacket (see *Letters to Friends* 114–15), I think that readers do form an image of its appearance in their minds. Nabokov's observations, based entirely on Kafka's text, present a convincing case for the approximate size and shape of the beetle. Discussing students' perceptions of the beetle's appearance along with Nabokov's can lead to lively class encounters and to careful scrutiny of the text. Equally helpful are Nabokov's illustrations of rooms and doors and his comments about where the family members are situated at various times. Through Gregor's perspective, readers find out how the physical appearances of the family members change and what spaces they occupy in the apartment (e.g., sofa, table, living room, kitchen). To ascertain the family's reactions to Gregor, the readers must activate their own visualizing capacities to a far greater degree. Nabokov, to my knowledge, is the only person who has emphasized that Gregor is always in a different spot when family members see him. Though Nabokov does not develop this point further, students find it interesting to hypothesize on the effects that Gregor's changes of location, as well as the changes in his appearance, may have on the family members. Then they begin to realize that the constant shifting of perspectives so prevalent in Kafka's works occurs largely because of the interplay of mental and physical dislocations.

The emphasis on visualization also leads to greater appreciation of Kafka's grotesque humor, an aspect not sufficiently stressed by critics or, I suspect, by professors. Students who have already read *The Metamorphosis* for English assignments (generally not more than two in classes ranging from twelve to twenty participants) seem unaware of it. Thus I highlight the comical absurdity of Gregor the beetle's preoccupation with the alarm clock, the difficulties he has getting out of bed (our own difficulties magnified a thousand times), his doomed attempts to placate everyone with arguments uttered in a voice that cannot be understood, the hilarity of his looking at his mother eye to eye on the floor, she being on his level because she has swooned, and the ridiculous juxtaposition of his present self with his former self (the Gregor dressed in military uniform in a photograph). It is, in fact, this constant coupling of his two irreconcilable selves—the inner human self and the exterior animal self, neither allowing the other to gain control—that

conditions much of the grotesque humor of part 1 and consequently also the
reader's vacillations in considering Gregor mostly human one minute, mostly
animal the next. As Gregor behaves increasingly like an animal, even though
his thoughts seem to remain human, much of the humor disappears. This
development from a comically absurd world to a hopelessly bleak one should
not, I am convinced, be overlooked.

In general, I place considerable emphasis on structure by discussing the
development of certain motifs from part 1 through part 3. In the first part,
for example, Gregor awakens from a troubled sleep; in the second from a
deep, leaden sleep; but in the third part he barely falls asleep anymore,
either during the day or at night. At the beginning of the first part it is
morning; at the beginning of the second, dusk; but in the third part we find
Gregor awake in an utterly dark room, in a sense no longer needing sleep
to be plunged into darkness. Though this darkness starts to prepare us for
his death, Gregor actually dies at 3:00 a.m., able to experience the beginning
of dawn. Instead of waking up from "troubled sleep," Gregor sinks into
death from a "vacant and peaceful" state (*CS* 135). The light here is not "the
light on the flinching grimacing face" (*Great Wall* 174; trans. modified) that
Kafka elsewhere called the truth but, rather, a noncommittal light, a light
that makes it difficult for us to speculate about the possibility of an afterlife
for Gregor.

I also stress structural development when concentrating on the aspect of
motion. Part 1 shows us the difficulties encountered by Gregor (the traveling
salesman!) to move at all; in part 2 we find him crawling avidly all over the
walls and the ceiling, probably with the same senselessness characteristic of
his travels as a salesman but actually with a greater joy, since he does not
have to concoct any purpose for his constant movements other than their
salutary capacity to distract him from self-analysis and from formulating plans
of action for the future. In part 3 Gregor can no longer reach the walls and
ceilings, but he does crawl happily amid all the garbage in his room. Yet
these "wanderings," even more senseless and limited than his journeys on
the walls and the ceiling, cause him to become "deathly" tired (49).[1] He
moves constantly, to the point of exhaustion. His last trip outside his room
and then back into it does, in fact, result in the total exhaustion leading to
his death.

While time's restrictions on Gregor diminish (the alarm clock is not mentioned after part 1, and Gregor can't tell in part 3 whether Christmas has
already occurred), the space available to him becomes increasingly restricted. To a certain extent, Gregor himself limits his space—for instance,
when he squeezes into the darkness under the sofa and later arranges a
sheet over the sofa to hide himself completely. Though he can still position
himself at the window and crawl over walls and ceiling through most of part
2, toward the end of this section he does not even seriously consider escaping
onto the walls, especially since the cutting edges and sharp points of the

finely carved furniture provide only dangerous access to them. Whereas part 1 ends with Gregor kicked "far" into the room (19), part 2 ends with Gregor flattened on the floor, as if nailed down. In part 3 Gregor can no longer reach either the window or the walls, and he discovers—after his last return to his room from the family quarters—that he can neither see anything in the dark nor move anymore. With no space visible to him and his capacity for movement entirely gone, Gregor dies.

In the context of discussing structural development of movement and its termination, we also concentrate in detail on senseless circular movements and on the woundings that ultimately end all movement. Though not always (e.g., when Gregor is turning the key in the lock in part 1), to a large extent the circular movements are emphasized most when Gregor attempts to leave the family's quarters and return to his own room, and they are invariably connected with woundings. At the end of both parts 1 and 2, Gregor leaves his room in order to provide help: to detain the chief clerk, to help his mother. In each of these instances, the father chases him back into his room. In part 1, after Gregor slowly turns around, his flank becoming more and more bruised, his father shoves him back into his room. Gregor then bleeds heavily, but his wound heals quickly and leaves only a long scar by the beginning of part 2. At the end of part 2, though, the second apple thrown at Gregor by his father lands firmly in his back. This apple and the wound it causes remain, as stressed at the beginning of part 3.

Students hypothesize about why it is the apple in Gregor's body that causes his father to remember that Gregor is a member of the family and about why Gregor's wound starts to hurt whenever he hears his mother and sister crying. In contrast to medieval German epics, in which the hero's wounds are always cured by a physician, often the hero's beloved, no one dares touch Gregor to remove his apple and tend to his wound. To the others, Gregor is totally repulsive—entirely unlovable and untouchable. Inevitably, the more the apple rots in his body, the more quickly Gregor approaches death.

His deathly wound festering, Gregor no longer remains considerate of his family. Leaving his room in part 3, he does not seek to help others but, rather, pursues his own pleasure: listening to the music he did not appreciate in his human form but that now intimates the "unknown nourishment" he has been seeking (*CS* 131). Gregor's pursuit of this nourishment leads to his death. When his sister expresses her wish for his death, Gregor seems almost relieved. At this point we discuss in class the observation that his father no longer chases him back into his room. To turn around, Gregor frequently beats his head against the floor, thus inflicting his own deathly punishment. Surrounded by complete darkness, head and body completely wounded, entirely immobilized, his breathing failing him, and lacking any recourse for action, Gregor easily fulfills the sister's—and now his own—wish for his death.

Discussing the end, class members bring up on their own the two prevalent viewpoints stressed in Kafka criticism: Gregor dies at peace with himself and his family and enters a spiritual realm (suggested by his appreciation of music); with Gregor's death, the spiritual also dies and is supplanted by the physical vitality of Gregor's sister and the renewed energy of his parents. I remain bothered, however, by the exclusivity of each viewpoint and tend to stress Kafka's dissatisfaction with his ending. I cannot look positively at the family's vitality, nor can I really believe, on the basis of the text, that Gregor enters a more positive, spiritual world. Although Gregor claims to bear no grudges and appears to die peacefully, the end indicates to me the hopelessly trapped nature of some individual lives.

The number three, so often used in literature and art to suggest perfection and redemption, has an entirely different function in *The Metamorphosis*. Students note, of course, that Gregor leaves his room and returns to it three times, once in each chapter of the narrative. Pertaining to Gregor, the number three refers chiefly to actions leading to utter solitude and finally to annihilation. The number three suggests not perfection but merely completion. The role of the three lodgers, however, puzzles students the most. They remain unsatisfied by the explanation offered in Kafka criticism: the three lodgers reflect Gregor's parasitical behavior, and Gregor has to be removed just as the three lodgers are. Usually the students find my own conclusion more plausible (but perhaps only because I am their instructor): the three lodgers, who refuse to be intimidated by Gregor's father (unlike Gregor), function as a perfected entity of a threesome in the same sense that Gregor's father, mother, and sister act as a perfected threesome in no need of Gregor. As connected with the lodgers and Gregor's family, the number three is exclusionary: suggesting a complete solidarity impenetrable by others, it underscores Gregor's doomed isolation.

Gregor's isolation is far greater than the isolation of the protagonists in Hesse's *Demian* and Mann's *Tonio Kröger*, the two works discussed immediately before *The Metamorphosis*. Despite considerable self-doubt and pronounced alienation, Hesse's main character broadens his individual self until it contains aspects of the entire universe. While Mann's Tonio has a much more restricted self and remains alienated from society, he does affirm the love and the longing for normalcy that help condition his art. In Kafka's *Metamorphosis*, however, there are no redeeming ideas or redeeming love. Instead of representing the birth of a new man (*Demian*) or affirming his own self (*Tonio Kröger*), Kafka's Gregor Samsa dies and diminishes into nothing as he is swept out of the world. Kafka's *Metamorphosis* thus illustrates, at least in this course, the end of the so-called canon.

In their final essay for the course, generally ten pages long, students recognize this end by stressing the disappearance of values, both universal and self-created, that provide meaning in life. Though deeply affected by Kafka, most students envision a far more satisfactory life for themselves and continue to formulate specific goals related to future professions and to happiness with people. Still, Kafka's "landscape of failures," to use Peter Heller's words again, continues to haunt them.

NOTE

[1] I use the Norton edition of *Die Verwandlung* in my classes, and page references are to that edition.

Irony, Contingency, and Postmodernity: "In the Penal Colony"

Steven Taubeneck

> The landslides of recent history have done less damage
> to the model of the penal colony than to the ideal
> construction of [Brecht's] learning plays.
> —Heiner Müller

Kafka's "In the Penal Colony" is undoubtedly one of the most disturbing stories that students read. The bleakness of the colony, the cruelty of the machine, and the grotesque death of the officer often leave students alienated. For many, the text seems an anachronistic "emblem" of the "strangeness, cruelty, and duress of the modern world" (Neumann, "Nachwort" 67), a world from which there is little hope of escape. Often overlooked, however, are the irony and the contingency of the terrifying events described.[1] If students are shown this facet of the horror, they might see the text more analytically and more pertinently as emblematic of their own time and "the postmodern condition" (see Lyotard; Jameson, *Postmodernism*). Moreover, as Heiner Müller suggests in the epigraph to this essay, it is the openness to ironic contingency and the ambiguity of the text, in contrast to the pointed didacticism of Bertolt Brecht's learning plays, that helps Kafka's model of the penal colony to endure.

At first glance the plot structure of "In the Penal Colony" seems deterministic. As often in Kafka's writing, the opening sentence appears decisive for an interpretation of the text: " 'It's a remarkable piece of apparatus,' said the officer to the explorer and surveyed with a certain air of admiration the apparatus which was after all quite familiar to him" (*CS* 140). This sentence introduces the three major figures in the story, the apparatus, the officer, and the explorer, and establishes the narrative tendency to offer somewhat tangential observations. The basic structure of the ensuing conversation dominates the plot's unfolding: for nearly two thirds of the text, the officer explains the machine to the explorer, then puts it into operation.

All three figures—the apparatus, the officer, and the explorer—are types that play important roles in most of Kafka's work. As a pivotal object in the story, the apparatus functions as one of those fantastic entities that pervade Kafka's writing, apparently simple yet resonant with multiple associations. From the strange figure of Odradek in "The Cares of a Family Man" (*CS* 427–29) to Gregor Samsa as the "gigantic insect" in *The Metamorphosis*, objects and animals take on lives and character traits of their own. The recurring practice of giving familiar qualities to unfamiliar entities and placing them in unexpected situations demonstrates a sense that at any moment human experience may blur fantastically into other worlds. The nearly magical reversals in Kafka's texts open up a space for contingent events, giving chance the opportunity to take both characters and readers by surprise. Apparently so predictable at the outset, for example, technology in "In the Penal Colony" ultimately becomes the instrument of an unexpected general collapse.

The officer senses that something may go wrong and is "anxious to secure himself against all contingencies" (*CS* 141). Ironically, this very anxiety creates the space for contingency to emerge. Throughout his explanation, the officer tries to represent the machine with sufficient power to win the explorer's approval for his program. The officer dwells on the glory of the dead past—he describes himself as "the sole advocate of the old Commandant's tradition" (*CS* 153)—and on the efficacy of the punishment system, while relying on a slightly homoerotic play of seduction. Dressed in a uniform "too heavy for the tropics," the officer "looked uncommonly limp, breathed with his mouth wide open, and had tucked two fine ladies' handkerchiefs under the collar of his uniform" (*CS* 140). When the explorer comments on the uniforms, the officer stresses their association with "home": " 'Of course,' said the officer, washing his oily and greasy hands in a bucket of water that stood ready, 'but they mean home to us; we don't want to forget about home' " (*CS* 140–41). The officer is obsessed with keeping himself clean, explaining the machine, celebrating the validity of the old ways, and persuading the explorer. The combination of a compulsive obsession with cleanliness, a nearly fanatic devotion to order and tradition, and an ingratiating attitude bent on persuasion is central to several of Kafka's protagonists, from the opening narrator in one of his earliest stories, "Description of a Struggle" (*CS* 9–51), to, much later, the figures of Josef K. in *The Trial* and K. in *The Castle*.

In many of these texts, the obsessions of such characters ironically signal their collapse or death. Kafka frequently shows his characters overrationalizing themselves into destructive behaviors. This tendency seems to dramatize a psychological critique of the ascetic character type in general, an ironic subversion of obsessive asceticism that parallels the critiques of several contemporaries, including Nietzsche in *The Genealogy of Morals* and Freud in *The Interpretation of Dreams*. Kafka seems to enact an archaeology of the mind, in which the deepest layers of the psyche are shown in conflict with the surface layers of everyday consciousness. Gerhard Kurz, among many other Kafka interpreters, emphasizes these relations: "The archaeological impulse, the search for the 'city beneath the cities,' unites Nietzsche, Freud, and Kafka in a single configuration as modern excavators of the human psyche" ("Nietzsche" 128). Kurz describes Kafka as a prominent modernist seeking to unmask the facades of modernity.

But problems arise in this interpretation when the reader looks for layers of depth to appear in the texts. Students are among the first to point out that Kafka undertakes no depth analysis in his stories; on the contrary, he takes great pains to keep readers at the level of the surface behaviors and statements of the characters. Kafka, after all, was no Thomas Mann, a writer who in many texts gave extensive psychological analyses of characters. The "search for the 'city beneath the cities' " proceeds in Kafka's texts on the surface and avoids a conclusive assessment, except to suggest that such a search may lead to breakdown or death. The frequent unraveling of Kafka's figures—for no certain or explicitly stated reason—is a contingent process that often ironizes the characters in multiple ways. In terms of this emphasis on contingency, Kafka's writing illustrates Jean-François Lyotard's description of postmodernism. For Lyotard, postmodernism is characterized by an "incredulity" toward master or meta- narratives (26), a suspicion or hesitation in the face of any attempt to give all-encompassing explanations for human attitudes and behavior.

A further irony in the story appears in the characterization of the explorer, who seems at first indifferent to the entire situation: he "did not much care about the apparatus and walked up and down behind the prisoner with almost visible indifference" (CS 140). Soon he begins to admire the officer's fervor: "All the more did he admire the officer, who in spite of his tight-fitting full-dress uniform coat, amply befrogged and weighed down by epaulettes, was pursuing his subject with such enthusiasm and, besides talking, was still tightening a screw here and there" (CS 142). The explorer grows ambivalent toward the officer and his obsessions: repulsed by the harshness of the penal colony and the officer's devotion, he is also attracted by the officer's conviction. Simultaneously attracted to and repulsed by the officer, the machine, and the penal colony, the explorer resembles a figure with a "modern" mentality, superficially too educated and civilized to support such "primitive" methods, yet secretly drawn to the excesses of the system. In the end, the explorer's ambivalence turns to horror, flight, and repetition as he uses a threat of violence to escape the colony. An important postmodern element is this ironic transgression of the explorer's smugly modern thinking.

The final comment in the opening sentence—"which was after all quite familiar to him"—establishes the narrative tendency to add tangential bits of information. Such narrative asides, which occur frequently, range from evaluative to informative and complicate the description with another point of view. The irony of the comment lies in the uncertainty of its origin: although the aside seems to derive from the consciousness of the officer, it may also be seen as a commentary made by an omniscient narrator. A similar aside is made when the narrator describes the explorer's and the colony's attitudes: "The explorer seemed to have accepted merely out of politeness the Commandant's invitation to witness the execution of a soldier condemned to death for disobedience and insulting behavior to a superior. Nor did the colony itself betray much interest in this execution" (CS 140). With regard to the explorer, the colony, and the officer, the narrative fluctuates between internal and external perspectives. Above all, the verbs *to seem* and *to betray interest* represent a tendency to make partial judgments on the basis of appearances.

This wavering narrative stance, which veers from intimate knowledge to external appearances, relativizes assertions and multiplies points of view. Among the various perspectives, however, it is difficult to say which one reveals the truth. Certainty over the validity of assertions in the text is attenuated by the shifting narrative position. The indeterminacy of the narration, coupled with the ambiguous subversion of the major figures, links the text to more-recent literature: "Postmodern art similarly asserts and then deliberately undermines such principles as value, order, meaning, control, and identity that have been the basic premises of bourgeois liberalism" (Hutcheon 13).

To be sure, the officer's explanation seems to follow a strict narrative logic as it unfolds in three stages: first the machine is described in some detail, then the officer exhorts the explorer to support the colony's traditions, and finally the machine is set in motion. Since the machine is the most fascinating part of the story for many students, their interest can be sharpened by having them draw it. It would soon appear that the machine resembles a grotesque kind of typewriter. The machine consists of three parts: "The lower one is called the 'Bed,' the upper one the 'Designer,' and this one here in the middle that moves up and down is called the 'Harrow' " (*CS* 142). In general, the story is dominated by a triadic logic: as the machine has three parts, the story unfolds in three sections and concerns three primary figures. When the machine falls apart, however, the triadism dominating the text comes undone; the technology of the story itself disintegrates.

In the meantime, attention focuses on the machine:

> The Bed and the Designer were of the same size and looked like two dark wooden chests. The Designer hung about two meters above the Bed; each of them was bound at the corners with four rods of brass that almost flashed out rays in the sunlight. Between the chests shuttled the Harrow on a ribbon of steel. (*CS* 143)

The condemned man is laid on the bed, which is covered with a layer of cotton wool. The man is "quite naked," and there are straps for his hands, feet, and neck, "to bind him fast" (*CS* 143). The image of the condemned man, naked and bound fast in order to be penetrated by the needles of the machine, reiterates in more brutal terms the faintly homoerotic manner of the officer. As if in a grotesque fantasy of the Marquis de Sade, the machine becomes the site for a drama of sadomasochistic torture (see Norris, "Sadism").

Somewhat perversely, the explorer senses "a dawning interest in the apparatus," and as an eavesdropper the reader may also feel a growing interest. The economy of "interest" draws the reader into the conversation. Indeed, the reader may appear bound to a chain of imitation, along with the condemned man and the explorer: "The condemned man imitated the explorer; since he could not use a hand to shelter his eyes he gazed upwards without shade" (CS 143). The chain of imitation or mimetic desire implicitly binds the reader, explorer, and condemned man to the officer's explanation.

The reader's secret ties to the explorer become more unsettling as the machine's action is described; the reader may sense a loss of objective distance:

> As soon as the man is strapped down, the Bed is set in motion. It quivers in minute, very rapid vibrations . . . in our Bed the movements are all precisely calculated; you see, they have to correspond very exactly to the movements of the Harrow. And the Harrow is the instrument for the actual execution of the sentence.   (CS 143–44)

By this point, at the latest, many students begin to resist the description and to ask questions about it. Not coincidentally, this is also the moment when the explorer himself begins to ask questions more attentively. The rhetorical pattern of explanation-persuasion-seduction is interrupted, here and increasingly, which frustrates the officer and precipitates his self-sacrifice.

The officer is exasperated at the explorer's questioning, and hurriedly condenses his narrative around a single principle:

> My guiding principle is this: Guilt is never to be doubted. Other courts cannot follow that principle, for they consist of several opinions and have higher courts to scrutinize them. That is not the case here, or at least, it was not the case in the former Commandant's time. The new man has certainly shown some inclination to interfere with my judgments, but so far I have succeeded in fending him off and will go on succeeding.   (CS 145)

The "guiding principle," the assumption of universal guilt, seems paradigmatic for the colony during "the former Commandant's time." The paradigm of collective guilt has a strong impact on students, not to mention critics of the story, who tend to emphasize it in their interpretations of the text and of Kafka's writing overall. Yet it is important to note that the passage describes the system in the past and states that there has been a paradigm shift in the colony.

The explorer recognizes that a shift has taken place and feels "that some hope might be set on the new Commandant, who was apparently of a mind to bring in, although gradually, a new kind of procedure which the officer's narrow mind was incapable of understanding" (*CS* 146). Although the narrative highlights this view—again from a slightly external position—the officer is determined to proceed with "the essentials":

> When the man lies down on the Bed and it begins to vibrate, the Harrow is lowered onto his body. It regulates itself automatically so that the needles barely touch his skin; once contact is made the steel ribbon stiffens immediately into a rigid band. And then the performance begins. An ignorant onlooker would see no difference between one punishment and another. The Harrow appears to do its work with uniform regularity. As it quivers, its points pierce the skin of the body which is itself quivering from the vibration of the Bed. So that the actual progress of the sentence can be watched, the Harrow is made of glass. . . . anyone can look through the glass and watch the inscription taking form on the body. (*CS* 147)

The machine should literally "inscribe" a memory; the figure of the law should become material, producing writing or wounds on the body. Punishment and the demands of the law are to be fully mechanized and transformed by the machine into writing, a script related, for example, to the mosaics drawn on the bodies of various peoples in Africa and South America (see Hiebel, *Zeichen* 129–52). The machine embodies the machinery of the penal colony and of writing; it combines the aesthetic pleasures of writing with the pain of punishment and the fulfillment of the law. The mechanization of punishment extends beyond the machine: the entire colony seems devoted to punishment on a high level of machinelike specialization.

For the officer, in former times the punishment rituals were like a glorious festival:

> How different an execution was in the old days! A whole day before the ceremony the valley was packed with people; they all came only to look on; early in the morning the Commandant appeared with his ladies; fanfare roused the whole camp; I reported that everything was in readiness; the assembled company—no high official dared to absent himself—arranged itself around the machine; this pile of cane chairs is a miserable survival from that epoch. (*CS* 153)

The officer invests the execution spectacle with educational and moral value, but the spectacle also exhibits a scopophilic delight in cruelty. Because the harrow is made of glass, one can see and read the inscription being cut into the body. The officer gives special emphasis to the sight of the condemned man's face at the moment of his transcendence. For the officer, the pleasure of seeing torture is sublimated into the pleasure of knowing that torture is the "actual instrument" of enlightenment and justice: " 'Many did not care to watch it but lay with closed eyes in the sand; they all knew: Now Justice is being done' " (CS 154).

When the explorer resists this vision of the process and refuses the officer's attempts at persuasion-seduction, the officer strips off his uniform, handling "each garment with loving care," and stands "naked" by the machine (CS 162, 163). As if to prove its efficacy and to experience the promised enlightenment himself ("Enlightenment comes to the most dull-witted" [CS 150]), the officer prepares to enter the machine. It seems that he and the machine enjoy an almost symbiotic relationship: "It had been clear enough previously that he understood the machine well, but now it was almost staggering to see how he managed it and how it obeyed him" (CS 163). Even the explorer, who had been "touched" (CS 160) by the officer's explanation, finds the self-sacrifice appropriate: "If the judicial procedure which the officer cherished were really so near its end—possibly as a result of his own intervention, as to which he felt himself pledged—then the officer was doing the right thing; in his place the explorer would not have acted otherwise" (CS 163). By this point, the explorer endorses the officer's desire.

At the moment of requital, however, the machine breaks down, the officer is brutally executed, the explorer is driven away, and the entire system of justice in the penal colony falls to pieces. The triadic structure from the first sentence—two men and a machine—tumbles to its own destruction: like the machine, the rhetorical pattern of explanation-persuasion-seduction implodes and scatters the participants. In contrast to the expectations of the officer, the explorer, and presumably the reader, the structure that had seemed stable at the outset finally falls apart. This reversal of expectations, this implosion of structure, demonstrates clearly Kafka's expertise as an ironist, a contingency expert, and an analyst of postmodernity.

The machine's destruction harshly ironizes the officer's quest, and his body's torture signals the end of the old ways. Particularly important is the agency of destruction; some perceive the machine as undoing itself. According to this view, the machine is a self-defeating agent, an entity whose nature determined its own collapse. Kafka, in this reading, appears critical of the self-destructive tendency of rationalistic, legalistic technology, and such a position would parallel the analyses of science and technology by, for example, Nietzsche, Marx, Freud, and Heidegger.

Other critics, however, point out that the officer often states that the new Commandant and the women associated with him have contributed to the machine's downfall. Obsessively, the officer refers to the damage women have done to the machine and the system: they "stuff" the condemned men "with sugar candy," so that the officer asks, " 'because of this Commandant and the women who influence him, is such a piece of work, the work of a lifetime'—he pointed to the machine—'to perish?' " (CS 153). For the officer, the new Commandant and women were pivotal in ruining the machine.

But the agency of change is never made explicit. Instead, the machine simply comes apart:

> Slowly the lid of the Designer rose up and then clicked wide open. The teeth of a cogwheel showed themselves and rose higher, soon the whole wheel was visible, it was as if some enormous force were squeezing the Designer so that there was no longer room for the wheel, the wheel moved up till it came to the very edge of the Designer, fell down, rolled along the sand a little on its rim and lay flat. But a second wheel was already rising after it, followed by many others. . . .
>
> (CS 164–65)

The causal uncertainty marks the contingency of the event and discounts both the "self-destructive" and "feminist" interpretations. Even the explanatory metanarrative proposed here—"as if some enormous force were squeezing the Designer"—is uncertain at best.

The dispersed and uncertain qualities of the machine's disintegration and the officer's death are supplemented by the explorer's escape from the colony. After a brief visit to the teahouse and the old Commandant's grave, the explorer proceeds to the departing boats. The soldier and the condemned man try to follow him, but the explorer drives them away: "They could have jumped in the boat, but the explorer lifted a heavy knotted rope from the floor boards, threatened them with it, and so kept them from attempting the leap" (CS 167). The violence of the machine's collapse gives way to ambiguous and sinister flight. Though the explorer has been confronted with violence, he leaves the scene of the drama, threatens more violence, and floats away. A pattern of multiple transgression emerges in which the excesses of the colony spread to infect the explorer.

In the end, the text dissolves into a series of violent and ambiguous gestures. Students are confronted with worlds much like their own. Just as they deal with ambiguous choices on the way to potentially ironic conclusions, so the officer deals with the erosion of his ideal system, the explorer confronts a terrifying custom and a horrifying death, and the machine falls to pieces. Without direct explanations for the causes and effects of the disaster, the ending becomes ironically contingent, morally ambiguous, and aesthetically inconclusive.

The postmodernity of the text helps the story of the penal colony seem current. My contention is that contemporary students will respond to accessible, pertinent models. Kafka's model survives through its very indeterminacy. The postmodernity in this text does not exclude the modern but extends it through baffling and ironic uncertainties.

NOTE

[1] My sense of *irony* and *contingency* derives from Richard Rorty's use of the terms. On the relation of irony to postmodernity, see Behler 3–36.

The Text That Was Never a Story: Symmetry and Disaster in "A Country Doctor"

Henry Sussman

Although organized, perhaps, by an intense oedipal pain, Kafka's "A Country Doctor" never becomes what might be properly called a story. The results are so inconclusive, the characters so blurred as to deny any pretense to narrative cohesion on the part of this brief work. Twice the peasants who receive the doctor's judgments break out into incantations that, like the music throughout Kafka's writing, exemplified by Josephine's piping, are refrains of fugitive and unfulfilled desire. The doctor may indeed be stripped and placed beside the ailing young patient as the chants exhort, but he is "only a doctor, only a doctor" (*CS* 224). The peasant song, which lends the text the air of an anthropological encounter, declares the limits of its own expectations, as well as those of the patient.

But for all the tale's declared and dramatized inconclusiveness, it is a suggestive allegory of how texts configure themselves. There is no lack of structure here. The text begins and ends in the forbidding winter landscape to which an aging doctor no less harsh and forlorn has been summoned by his vastly inferior clients. The scenic and thematic symmetry of the two scenes constituting the narrative framework is duplicated within the dramatic core. The text dramatizes not one diagnostic scene but two. Only after an initially unsympathetic examination of the sick boy—on the basis of which the doctor concludes that "the boy was quite sound, something a little wrong with his circulation, saturated with coffee by his solicitous mother, but sound"—is the doctor persuaded to admit "that the boy might be ill after all" (*CS* 222, 223). A reexamination, which the doctor undertakes almost whimsically, reveals the extent and nature of the illness as it affects both patient and healer.

At the end of the narrative the doctor sits in the same coach that brought him to his appointment, no longer wearing his coat, perhaps, but facing the same climatic and personal bleakness with which the text began. If anything, the framework and organization of the narrative suggest structure: mirrored endpoints bracketing a doubled scene. And this structural symmetry, at least on the level of the text's widest components, is well suited to the doubling that takes place between characters and that is discussed more fully below. "A Country Doctor" is not reticent to admit the place of structure within its own encoding and decoding. Structure, however, does not so much account for or determine the allegory of the text as support or facilitate it. As I show, associations of a far more shifting nature disclose the qualities of this text but within the format that structure provides. The text gathers its resonance at the point where its structure embraces something other, something transformational and anomalous. And here, as throughout Kafka's fiction, the image bonding structure to theme, but precluding the narrative cohesion of a story, is nothing more than a metaphor.

The symmetry that so strikingly frames and colors this story places it in the nexus of Kafka's long-standing interest in doubling—as a narratological, psychological, and even phenomenological feature. Kafka's fascination with doubling, deriving from his most beloved literary sources, among them E. T. A. Hoffmann and Dostoyevsky, transcends the particular uses to which doubling can be put. Kafka began his exploration of this phenomenon in such brief works as "The Knock on the Manor Gate," in which the nearly undefinable guilt of the sister is displaced and irrationally magnified as it rebounds on the brother, and "A Crossbreed [A Sport]," in which an uncanny commiseration links the family son to his biologically and logically anomalous legacy. In stories even as late as "The Burrow," Kafka's artistic burrowing rodent projects the image of a predator, his semblable, who stalks him and deprives him of his supplies in the subterranean deep.

The title character in "A Country Doctor" finds unlikely doubles in the groom with whom he wages battle over Rose and in the twice-examined, twice-dismissed wounded little boy. The story thus reverberates off Kafka's brief masterpiece of doubling, "The Judgment," which Kafka believed to have been his breakthrough piece of fiction.[1] "The Judgment" records and dramatizes the undermining of a son's best-faith narrative of his own achievements, qualities, and prospects by a discourse of the other that turns out to emanate from his uncannily hostile father. The narrative voice is a willing conspirator in this confusion. It subliminally sides with and rationalizes the son's position until the father attacks him—not with heaved apples, as in *The Metamorphosis*, but with accusations: that the son tricked the friend in Russia (toward whom he feels condescendingly protective), allowed himself to be seduced by his fiancée, and violated the better interest of the family business.

"The Judgment" resides at a benchmark in the systematicness of the kinds of doubling it entertains. The excruciating dialectical tension between the discourse of the son and the father's debunking cynicism corresponds to the "split consciousness" that for Freud, at the time of Kafka's writing, constituted the very structure of repression (indeed, the vast majority of the manifestations Freud interpreted between 1893 and 1910 were conditions of repression, above all hysteria). In writing so penetratingly on ambivalence, whether Gregor's toward the family that takes his sacrifices so much for granted or the country doctor's toward the groom and the sick boy, Kafka performs Freudian acts of undermining the divisions that segment the divided consciousness. The systematic duplication structuring "The Judgment" is narratological and characterological as well. Georg Bendemann watches in horror as the friend in Russia, whom he regards as a subordinate, supplants him as his father's son; indeed, the letters by means of which Georg has attempted to control the relationship are duplicated and disqualified by the counter-correspondence that his father has maintained with his double. With regard to the relentless doubling that structures and informs "The Judgment," "A Country Doctor" may well be the countertext sharing the closest affinities.

In the very first episode of "A Country Doctor," we see already the major structural and thematic elements that will serve as a setting for the story's metaphoric transformation. When Rose, the maid who will become the source and object of the doctor's anxiety throughout the text, offers her comment on the scene—"You never know what you're going to find in your own house"—she touches on the narrative's key psychoanalytic and sociological concerns. The well-equipped and generally efficient country doctor—"I had a gig, a light gig with big wheels, exactly right for our country roads"—is in a frustrated rage. He cannot begin a house call to a neighboring village because his horse died the previous night: "Muffled in furs, my bag of instruments in my hand, I was in the courtyard all ready for the journey." The bleak weather in which he waits with impotent anger only reinforces the sense that he is a man without a horse, a man who has lost his horse, or his kingdom for a horse, a victim of his own horse: "but there was no horse to be had, no horse" (*CS* 220).

The motif of psychological repression in this text is reinforced by the dreamlike quality of its movements and transitions. The doctor arrives instantaneously at the remote hamlet he is visiting: "I was already there" (*CS* 221). Just as suddenly, the apparent solutions to his predicament emerge from an abandoned pigsty on his property that he kicks open in his desperation: a man whose open, blue-eyed face is reminiscent of other servants in Kafka's fiction (notably, Barnabas of *The Castle*), and two horses, whose steaming bodies and powerful buttocks evoke a power that contrasts sharply with the doctor's present frailty. The doctor is well conditioned to make optimal use of this unexpected man—and horsepower. He commands Rose to help the groom (*Knecht*) hitch the horses to his wagon (the groom has emerged from the pigsty ready to serve), and he threatens the *Knecht* with whipping when the latter inexorably turns his attentions to Rose. This pugnaciousness turns to anxious despair when it becomes clear to the doctor that Rose is fated to serve the groom's sexual whims, that his own home is to be the setting for the vigorous sexuality figured in the splitting and bursting of the door. The doctor's tormenting vision of the groom's sexual victory over Rose and himself haunts him throughout the text with the force of obsessional thought as Freud defined it.[2] Until the groom declares, "I'm not coming with you anyway, I'm staying with Rose," the doctor has treated her indifferently as "the pretty girl who had lived in [his] house for years almost without [his] noticing her" (*CS* 221, 223). In many senses, then, the narrative's first scene may be said to investigate repression as it operates in psychoanalytic theory. Distinctly sexual beings emerge from a repository on the property, a long-abandoned hiding place. Late-oedipal competition stimulates a previously stunted desire for the girl. The psychological locus of the pigsty is repression in the unconscious.

This first scene is reminiscent of another repression, the sociopolitical sort dramatized and subverted in the section of *Phenomenology of Spirit* that Hegel entitled "Herrschaft und Knechtschaft" ("Lordship and Bondage"; 104–19). The doctor is not oblivious to his bullying and threatening his *Knecht*, even though, as he acknowledges, the groom is "a stranger . . . I did not know where he came from, and . . . of his own free will he was helping me out when everyone else had failed me" (*CS* 221). The groom is described as the sibling of the two horses, which he calls Bruder (Brother) and Schwester (Sister). The groom's conquest of Rose thus completes a series of substitutions set into play by the upheaval of the doctor's authority. The groom's sexual displacement of the doctor results in a deflection of the threatened whipping from the horses to the groom. The ultimate victim in this sequence of powermongering is Rose, but the narrative, curiously, does not pursue that result.

The quick reversal of the doctor's mastery over his servants signals an ambiguity in characterization. Why does the doctor develop such a sudden, intense attachment to Rose? The contest over her may be between two distinct male characters or, as occurs at other points in Kafka's fiction, may represent a conflict within a single fictive subject, a conflict here between active heterosexual lust and repressive asexuality. More than any other major writer dealing in twentieth-century aesthetics, Kafka exploited the ambiguity between the intra- and intersubjective representations of dramatic interaction.[3] In the context of the intertwining and reversal of roles that will prevail between the doctor and the sick boy, it is perhaps not unreasonable to suggest that the doctor and the *Knecht* also exist as doubles in relation to each other. The doctor's doubling is doubled: he merges with his servants and patients. Doubling in characterization coincides with the doubling already observed in the scenic construction. "A Country Doctor" dispenses double medicine, but doubling, as Freud applies it to Hoffmann's tale "The Sandman," is a mark of the uncanny as well as of the familiar.[4] In Kafka's fiction, as in familial relations, it is sometimes difficult to ascertain where one identity begins and another ends. This soft border between fictive subjects becomes a major issue in the doctor's interaction with the peasant family.

For indeed, having arrived instantaneously at his patient's peasant cottage (this immediacy questioning again the status of distance and scale in the narrative), the doctor remains secure in the superiority and authority that have just been battered by the groom's conquest. In deference to the doctor, the patient's sister sets a chair out for his instruments and takes charge of his fur coat. No higher honor does the family pay the doctor than the precious glass of rum the father pours out for him.

Throughout Kafka's fiction siblings are implicated in one another's guilts and torments. The air in the Kafkan familial scene is stifling. Not only can the siblings exchange identities, but the horses get into the act as well, the same horses to which the groom referred as Brother and Sister: "each of them had stuck a head in at a window and, quite unmoved by the startled cries of the family, stood eyeing the patient" (CS 222). Throughout "A Country Doctor," but especially in the family setting, identities merge, making totemic distinctions useless. The highly visible horses in this text, at play in every aspect of the country doctor's interaction with the family, belong to a unique category of characters in Kafka's fiction: the mute and reactive figures who do not add to the action but comment on it with their silent gestures.[5] The horses' status as animals in no way impedes their serving this metacritical function. Their siblings in the world of Kafka's writing include K.'s servants, Arthur and Jeremias, in *The Castle*; the astonished villagers in "The Knock at the Manor Gate"; and the onlookers who witness Joseph K.'s arrest in *The Trial*.

Yet just as the doctor's mastery is undermined in the opening scene by the groom's (or his own) vibrant sexuality, so too does his encounter with the sick boy dissolve his air of superiority, his clinical detachment, his complacency, and his indifference. Intellectually, the doctor grasps the limits of his position when he thinks, "To write prescriptions is easy, but to come to an understanding with people is hard" (CS 223); this formulation, however, is only the weakest form of the lesson that the boy teaches him. During his initial examination of the boy, the doctor vacillates between two postures: contempt for the entire family, buttressed by a kind of self-aggrandizing rationalization, and a compulsive, morbid interest in Rose's current status:

> I am no world reformer and so I let him lie. I was the district doctor and did my duty to the uttermost, to the point where it became almost too much. I was badly paid and yet generous and helpful to the poor. I had still to see that Rose was all right, and then the boy might have his way and I wanted to die too. What was I doing there in that endless winter! My horse was dead, and nót a single person in the village would lend me another. I had to get my team out of the pigsty; if they hadn't chanced to be horses I should have had to travel with swine. That was how it was. (CS 222–23)

This passage intertwines the doctor's two roles as aggressor and victim. Having conceded his lack of philanthropic interest, the doctor dramatizes his self-sacrifices to himself in the way that a manipulative parent would attempt to induce guilt in his or her family. The climate is terrible, the pay is not good, he constantly makes concessions to his patients. The humor in the passage is that of uncontrollable self-indulgence. The doctor suggests that if he hadn't found horses to transport him, pigs would have had to do. The doctor thus places himself in the role of a temporary paterfamilias whose bad conscience spurs him on to increasingly outrageous assertions of benevolence. But the doctor's martyrdom would not be real unless he faced some immediate and dire threat. The loss of Rose is not only like death; it is death itself ("I wanted to die"). The form, if not nature, of the doctor's fear is hypochondriacal. What threatens him is not a condition but the self-representation of a condition. It is no accident that he ends up beside his patient. In all this posturing, Kafka does not allow the aggression, bad faith, guiltmongering, and hypochondriacal cries for help to remain implicit: "And I nodded to the family. They knew nothing about it, and, had they known, would not have believed it" (CS 223). The doctor protects his posturing by endowing it with the aura of superior knowledge.

Thus far, then, we have a story structured to favor its themes of jealousy, displacement, ambivalence, ambiguity of character, and social conflict. The most prominent themes also lend themselves to interpretation through two readily available models of repression: the psychoanalytic model and the Hegelian undermining of mastery through the more direct relation to material (including words) in labor. Yet only when the doctor, casually and almost by chance, condescends to review his diagnosis does the text crystallize an emblem for its own operation as a text. The text locates its image only as the practitioner concedes some small margin of error. And, just as important, the insignia that the text inscribes upon itself (as the punitive apparatus of "In the Penal Colony" writes its sentence on the human body) is the external manifestation of a disease:

> And this time I discovered that the boy was indeed ill. In his right side, near the hip, was an open wound as big as the palm of my hand. Rose-red, in many variations of shade, dark in the hollows, lighter at the edges, softly granulated, with irregular clots of blood, open as a surface mine to the daylight. That was how it looked from a distance. But on a closer inspection there was another complication. I could not help a low whistle of surprise. Worms, as thick and long as my little finger, themselves rose-red and blood-spotted as well, were wriggling from their fastness in the interior of the wound toward the light, with small white heads and many legs. Poor boy, you were past helping. I had discovered your great wound; this blossom in your side was destroying you.   (CS 223)

Unapparent during the initial examination, the wound opens itself like a hitherto undisclosed secret, like a groom hiding in a neglected part of one's estate, like the desire for a servant girl that has lain dormant under daily ceremony. The wound announces itself like a secret to the doctor, who discovers it and, as a competent practitioner, examines it both at a distance and in proximity.

Although located on the flank of a local boy, the wound is a metaphor for the secrets that have been disclosed to the doctor about himself. The festering wound, embellished with twisting parasitic worms, is an image of the doctor's own festering sexuality. These worms, for all the revulsion that they might inspire, consummate an intensity of narrative description rare in Kafka's work. Like certain tumors and growths encountered by practicing physicians, the boy's wound radiates a peculiar beauty—in this case, the beauty of vividness.

The wound is a displaced image for the doctor's sexual conflicts. While its color, "Rose," causes some syntactical ambiguity by virtue of its placement at the head of a sentence, the choice of hue relates the wound to the doctor's apparent competition with the groom over Rose. Kafka underscores the incorporation of the source of desire into the wound; he places in relief the inscription of desire as the wound's very nature. The wound is rosy. The doctor describes it explicitly as a flower in the boy's side. The bloody worms have white heads. They thrive on red fluid but are themselves consumptive. In different ways, the doctor and patient are both consumed.

The wound is the flower of desire. Desire here, as in Proust, is a disease. The boy, because he is affected with the festering wound of the doctor's desire, is the doctor's unlikely double. The bystanders are thus not being provincial when they place the two in the same bed, when they connect the doctor to his disease by means of metonymic contiguity. An aging man and an adolescent boy share a longing-sickness.

In the course of the story, then, the doctor is twice doubled, first in relation to the surprising groom, then with the sick boy. The image of the wound is both the mark and the agent of this doubling. It is that which connects the doubled framework to the doubled scene of medical speculation. The wound takes Rose out of the narrative's external shell, where she appears as a semiautonomous bone of contention, and internalizes her within a scene of subjective ambivalence. As Rose passes from exteriority to interiority, so too does the narrative as a linguistic wound fold on and consume itself. This text structures a desire for the resolution between its outside and inside, between its structure and its material. And the binding that it offers for its conflicts is the image of a wound. But a wound is traumatized tissue; it is the locus where the body capitulates to rather than resists dismemberment.

By virtue of its bruised texture, "A Country Doctor" may be taken as an instance of that weak cohesion that characterizes a literary work. It demonstrates that what binds texts need not be as tangible as themes, as abstract as ideas, or as systematic as logical schemes. The somewhat crumbly coherence of this text concentrates around the signifier rose, which functions simultaneously as the name of a character, the color of a wound, and the name and color of a flower. The character, wound, and color are depicted within the text's representational field, while the flower hovers beyond the textual margins as a metaphoric icon, insignia, caption, or shorthand for the narrative's "events." The boy's wound becomes allegorical of the text because of the shifting permitted, even solicited, by rose. Rose marks the spot, precisely, where the text's dramatic scenario, structure, semantics, and thematic underpinnings intertwine. By closely implicating a persona, Rose, within the metaphoric economy of a text, Kafka comes as close as any author has to admitting the semiological rather than substantive nature of fictive "characters." Characters do not exist (or even act) so much as play within an ultimately deranged exchange of positions demarcated by Hegel as the speculative limit of the notion of force. They gather and abandon meaning in texts as signifiers pursue chains of displacement in the Lacanian imaginary (see Lacan, *Ecrits* 146–78; *Fundamental Concepts* 42–52).

The overdetermination of the role of rose within the text helps account for the pronounced duplicity of the characterization and thematics. The self-referentiality dramatized by this signifier also serves as a precedent for the allegory of parasitism. A consumptive boy devoured by consumptive worms is a narrative representation of a metaphor that can both consume and fragment itself.

The boy is indeed correct, then, when he asserts, "A fine wound is all I brought into the world; that was my sole endowment" (*CS* 225). For this brief work as well as for the sick character, a wound constitutes the total equipment and production. The wound in the work as well as in the boy constitutes the fissure in the Möbius strip describing the text's configuration. Crowned by a rose, the wound is the site where the text endlessly folds and feeds on itself.

It is therefore no accident that any departure from this domain must be abrupt and arbitrary. If the narrative framework results in an unresolved conflict over a woman between the doctor and his double, then in the core of the text the doctor's link to his second double, the sick boy, is ultimately complicitous:

> "Do you know," said a voice in my ear, "I have very little confidence in you. Why, you were only blown in here, you didn't come on your feet. Instead of helping me, you're cramping me on my deathbed. What I'd like best is to scratch your eyes out." "Right," I said, "it is a shame. And yet I am a doctor. What am I to do? Believe me, it is not too easy for me either." "Am I supposed to be content with this apology?" . . . "My young friend," said I, "your mistake is: you have not a wide enough view . . . and I tell you: your wound is not so bad. Done in a tight corner with two strokes of the ax. Many a one proffers his side and can hardly hear the ax in the forest, far less that it is coming nearer to him." "Is that really so, or are you deluding me in

my fever?" "It is really so, take the word of honor of an official doctor." And he took it and lay still.   (CS 224–25)

As this consultation commences, the boy has no confidence in the doctor, and the latter shows no sign of deviating from his general contempt for the surroundings. By the end of the interchange, the practitioner has been roused out of his indifference and the patient is calm, reassured, and perhaps prepared for death. The motive for this double reversal of positions may well come from the potentials offered by the ax and its relation to the image of the wound. If the wound figures the ambiguous textual intertwining afforded by the movement of the shifter between structural, thematic, and semantic levels, the ax promises release from the uncertainty by the excision of the function that loosens while it binds. A wound is all the text brings into the world to hold itself together, yet precisely as a function of textuality, the wound marks the side of repression, desire, and internal and external conflict. It delimits the extent of life with surgical precision.

At the end of "A Crossbreed [A Sport]," both the marginal kitten-lamb and the narrator, the son for whom the creature and its intellectual conditions are an inescapable legacy, eye the butcher's knife as a possible escape from their despair. The execution of Joseph K. in *The Trial* may be described as the application of a penetrating instrument to the victim after it has playfully shuttled back and forth between the henchmen. In "A Country Doctor" as well, a sharp blade holds out the promise of resolution and acquires the thrust of a poignant wish. A double blow of the ax in a tight corner can free the patient from his inherited mark of Cain. Only in conceptually offering this instrument does the country doctor serve as a healer. The prescribed treatment involves, however, not a regeneration of tissue but an amputation. Two decisive strokes of an ax can release the prisoner from his double bind, can free him, perhaps, from the narrow path on which Oedipus meets his father. The ax strikes outward, beyond the confines of a constricting familial space, but, to complete its task, also strikes inward, penetrating the superficial layers of the flesh.

The image of the ax is the sum total of the country doctor's reassurance. The wound is not so severe ("übel"): done ("geschaffen") "with two strokes of the ax," both dispatched and created by the healing-incising ax. The ax is a messiah (or avenging angel) of resolution. Those who offer their sides to it, in reverence, may not hear it in the forest, but eventually its work is done, silently and implicitly ("geschweige"). The silent ax in the forest recalls the falling tree whose status is so crucial to ontology and to the hypothetical status of God. The ax, were there only an ax, would clarify, resolve, amputate, the duplicity and ambiguity whose locus is language and whose form is that of a congenital wound. But the closure provided by the ax may still be described only in terms of inscription: incision, marking, scarring. The poignant wish for a termination of involution and complexity is expressed by several of Kafka's characters; it hovers at the horizon in much of his fiction. This end-wish or wish to end wishes can be articulated only in writing, through the textual economy that writing both promises and renders bankrupt. The ax is only one moment of the wound that is both the flower and disease of writing.

The mere invocation of the ax is sufficient to release the patient from his tension. To terminate a text whose insignia assumes the form of a Möbius strip is, however, not so simple. The country doctor's exit from the narrative stage necessarily takes the form of a desperate escape. Only the fall of an ax can truncate this text. Like his arrival at the patient's house—"as if my patient's farmyard had opened out just before ["unmittelbar"] my courtyard gate, I was already there" (*CS* 221)—the doctor's departure is abrupt. These movements are as sudden as the shifts of location that Freud finds characteristic of dreams, but the doctor's concerns are hardly dreamlike. The narrative ends as the doctor helplessly reaches for his fur coat at the back of his gig. He remains naked, having been stripped by the peasants and placed in bed next to his patient. He despairs of ever reaching home, fears seeing his medical practice collapse as he is usurped by a successor—and, of course, he despairs at the sacrifice of Rose and at the groom's successful rage. "Betrayed! Betrayed!" moans the doctor as the text ends. "A false alarm on the night bell once answered—it cannot be made good, not ever" (*CS* 225). The betrayal that the country doctor suffers is systematic and not merely sexual. Events are simply out of control. The arbitrary truncation of this text is merely one further manifestation of the loss of control that it has embellished. The losses and concerns that the text dramatizes are not to be recuperated. Betrayal cannot be undone. The "false alarms" that will disturb the doctor's sleep forever are the tones of absence whose textual manifestation is the figure of a wound.

Related contrapuntally to the rhythm of the eruption and amputation of ambiguity that may in fact constitute this text's only story is the music that twice breaks forth from the peasants. Although the text provides some psychosocial context for this singing, its very outbreak in the text possesses a shock value that cannot be reduced or assimilated. The peasants' incantations shift the narrative's setting to a world of primitive, obsessive, and ritualistic thought.

> A school choir with the teacher at the head of it stood before the house and sang these words to an utterly simple tune:
>
>> "Strip his clothes off, then he'll heal us,
>> If he doesn't, kill him dead!
>> Only a doctor, only a doctor."   (*CS* 224)

The performative dimension of this chant consists of two imperatives and a judgment. The logic of the exhortations is the simple causality characteristic of infantile obsession. The stripping of the doctor is the initial phase of a sacrificial act. If we prepare the doctor for sacrifice, the logic runs, he will spare our martyr. If this effort fails, we will sacrifice him. The narrative rationalizes the singing in terms of the sociopolitical wish it expresses: to cut the doctor down to size, to strip him, literally, of his authority and paternalism. The song's prescriptions intertwine him with the boy. The doctor will suffer what he fails to cure. Because the doctor has been inscribed within the peasants' obsessive reasoning, the outcome of the boy's case is already fated to be his own condition. The peasant's final incantation celebrates the events that the initial one announces and, with inexorable logic, fulfills: "O be joyful, all you patients, / The doctor's laid in bed beside you" (*CS* 225).

The music in the text not only intensifies the arbitrariness of its events but also breaks free of the thematic networks that would seem to reinforce a sense of cohesion. The gestures celebrated by the music are precisely arbitrary: command, soothsaying, judgment, exaltation. The incantations become a counterpoint of arbitrariness arising from the text but then floating above it with impunity, only tangentially related. The music hovers above the text as the doorbell tone floats beyond the confining domestic setting of "A Fratricide," "right over the town and up to heaven" (*CS* 403). In Kafka's fiction music diacritically annotates the directional aspirations of his writing. Though of the text, the music hovers above it, uncommitted to the apparent trends in which the thematic level has invested. Music underscores the constitutive role played by the metaphor in Kafka's writing: a fleeting refrain that sings of the difference between texts and stories.

NOTES

[1] In *Diaries, 1910–1913* Kafka writes of "[t]he fearful strain and joy, how the story developed before me, as if I were advancing over water. . . . How everything can be said, how for everything, for the strangest fancies, there awaits a great fire in which they perish and rise up again" (276).

[2] A good general introduction to Freud's thought regarding obsessional ideas is to be found in the theoretical section of the "Rat Man" case history (*Standard Edition* 10: 221–49).

[3] This ambiguity in characterization may be said to structure such major works as "Description of a Struggle" and "A Hunger Artist." Kafka rehearses its potentials in "First Sorrow." For a full treatment of "Description of a Struggle" as an exercise in scenic construction based on a play between intersubjective and intrasubjective conflict, see Sussman 61–74.

[4] Freud develops his notion of the uncanny in a 1919 essay, "The 'Uncanny,' " whose major instance of this phenomenon derives from E. T. A. Hoffmann's "Sandman." Initially, Freud situates the uncanny at the end of primary narcissism, when a child's self-image of benevolent omnipotence is partially eclipsed by its opposite.

Freud realizes, however, the inadequacy of a developmental explanation in accounting for the full literary potentials of doubling (*Standard Edition* 17: 232–45).

[5] Of all critics, Walter Benjamin provides the best account of the allegorical gestic language in Kafka's fiction, an illustration of his broader notion of shock. For a discussion of Kafka's gestic language, see Benjamin, "Franz Kafka."

Purification unto Death: "A Hunger Artist" as Allegory of Modernism

James Rolleston

There really were hunger artists. My colleague Leland Phelps, on military duty in Frankfurt in 1952, witnessed a hunger artist's "show"—and fortunately preserved the publicity sheet for the event. Had he not done so, would we believe it? This hunger artist held the world record (fifty days' fasting)—so the notice claims—and was now aiming at seventy-five days; children, the unemployed, and those wounded in the war would be admitted at half price.[1] With a shudder we realize that Kafka has once again "invented" our contemporary world; we know so well the bureaucrats and lawyers of *The Trial*, we recognize the technologically obsessive death merchant of "In the Penal Colony," now we confront the "reality" of the hunger artist and his audience—and read the story's opening sentence in a new way: "During these last decades the interest in professional fasting has markedly diminished" (CS 268). Indeed, we think, such "interest" has surely vanished altogether; but if even one hunger artist demonstrably existed in this century, our Kafka reading is jolted in two specific directions. First, we ponder the other viewers of the Frankfurt show witnessed by Phelps: the unemployed and the war-wounded. As Kafka's story implies, the social circumstances of the audience are in some sense decisive for the impact (or lack of same) made by the hunger artist. Why would the desperately deprived populace of Germany before the "economic miracle" be especially interested in professional fasting? Such entertainment would seem unpromising as an avenue of escape. This symbiosis is enigmatic to us, the connection lost; the psychology of an everyday life confined within poverty, humiliation, dire memories, and material wreckage cannot easily be grasped from our (American) vantage point. And this realization prompts a second meditation, fully thematized in Kafka's text. The extreme experiences of the past, its cycles of prosperity and misery, are becoming ever harder to grasp imaginatively within the eternal present of consumer capitalism. A familiar paradox is that the more the past is visually documented, the more it loses its status as a past world with its own experiential rhythms: as the newsreel clips segue from bombed-out Berlin to its current glittering prosperity, the misery of the past becomes a mere ghostly backdrop, a reason to anchor ourselves all the more affirmingly in the present. The hunger artist means nothing at all to the "affable" overseer at the end: figuratively as well as literally obliterated by the panther's immediacy, the artist is forced into the realm of fable. What was obvious yesterday can be reconstructed only with difficulty today.

These preliminary thoughts remind us that two clearly defined sets of coordinates, spatial and temporal, are in place throughout Kafka's story: the artist is obviously separated from his audience (not only by the bars of his cage but also by the discipline of fasting as such) yet cannot be conceived (and never conceives of himself) apart from that audience. And the artist's project makes sense in certain historical circumstances (i.e., when he attracts an audience) but not in others. Again, there is an unsurmountable barrier between the artist and history understood as a coherent whole: he strives to be "the record hunger artist of all time" (CS 271), but, to adapt one of Kafka's aphorisms (see *Great Wall* 168), what if "all time" can be defined as "indifference to hunger artists"? This twofold relation, with society and with history, is precisely the scene of medieval allegory. In a morality play the rich man is portrayed both in his indifference to other emblematic figures in society, particularly the needy, and in his foolish denial of his own mortality, his accumulation of wealth that will be stripped from him at death. Kafka's work distances itself from this model in two respects: the narrative perspective is close to (although not identical with) the hunger artist's own, and the obliterative moment is not so much individual death (certainly not a timeless heavenly "judgment") as an enigmatic historical shift, reducing to nonexistence the values that defined the artist's identity.

That "A Hunger Artist" is allegorical has never been in doubt. But allegorical of what? Criticism of the story has undergone precisely the kind of cultural shift encoded in the text itself. Initially it seemed clear that the hunger artist was the emblem of artistic integrity, holding out against everyday triviality and uncomprehending fellow humans; this allegory is obviously related to the early understanding of Joseph K. in *The Trial* as the little man battling the impersonal regime of Big Brother. But in the early 1960s this reading was almost schematically inverted: the hunger artist was charged with being a fraud, his guilt placed beyond doubt by his own final confession. In this perspective, he is no artist at all, because he does not "shape" reality into something different but simply does what comes naturally. Moreover, his "art" has no constructive connection with human concerns; it simply denies their validity. This view receives perhaps its strongest statement in Richard Sheppard's 1973 article on the story:

> Because the Hunger Artist is unwilling to accept the limitations of his human existence, symbolized by his refusal to eat, he resolves to flee those limitations and the self which they define, in order willfully to pursue the ideal of absolute fasting which is vacuous because it is tantamount to death. . . . His task is to be a man among men, but he refuses this and turns his back upon men out of a deep-seated sense of pride. (228, 231)

Such an existentialist interpretation encounters obvious problems within the text itself: we are told near the end that the artist "was working honestly" and, after his confession, that "in his dimming eyes remained the firm though no longer proud persuasion that he was continuing to fast" (*CS* 276–77)—a phrasing that seems to maintain "fasting" as the artist's essence, beyond even his confessed fraud. As to his "honesty," Sheppard maintains that the narrator is an identifiably separate, bureaucratically obtuse witness who is simply wrong in his moral judgments. Whether or not this argument is convincing, there is something trivializing and reductive about the insistence on the artist's fraudulence. Why should it be everyone's "task to be a man among men"? And the whole historical dimension disappears if one harps exclusively on the artist's individual complexion as "a deeply unstable personality in which the will and self are disjunct" (Sheppard 230).

Clearly we need to extend the concept of allegory beyond the isolated figure of the hunger artist himself. One fruitful approach has been to link the motif of hunger to its frequent crucial appearances in Kafka's other fiction. Thus Gregor in *The Metamorphosis* is drawn to his sister's music as "to the unknown nourishment he craved" (*CS* 131); Georg Bendemann, at his moment of suicide in "The Judgment," grasps "at the railings as a starving man clutches food" (*CS* 88); and the hero of "Investigations of a Dog"—a story written, along with "A Hunger Artist," in spring 1922—is himself a kind of hunger artist: "I still hold fasting to be the final and most potent means of my research. The way goes through fasting; the highest, if it is attainable, is attainable only by the highest effort, and the highest effort among us is voluntary fasting" (*CS* 309). The dog is in search of knowledge (the meaning of his fellow canines' existence); the paradox of his quest, however, is that such "truth" appears to be outside the world and hence to mandate the discipline of fasting—whereas what he is supposedly investigating is the sheer ordinariness, the self-evidence of dogdom. Kafka's use of the hunger motif renders the very notion of the self allegorical: our opposing drives toward bodily satisfaction and spiritual enlightenment can be reconciled only through a process of elaborate self-deception, a process we call living, projecting a unitary self. As soon as we lay claim to such a self, the one hunger cancels out the other and, structurally speaking, we begin our death. Stanley Corngold sees this doubleness as defining Kafka's self-understanding: "Kafka's pride in his separateness equals his nostalgia for 'the music of the world' " (*Necessity* 71). When Kafka's heroes come into existence, they are defined by their separation from everyone else: to overcome that separateness is to begin the process of self-destruction, since the hunger for life and the hunger for spiritual uniqueness invariably coexist in perpetual mutual cancellation.

To think in these terms is to be protected against the temptation of viewing the hunger artist as a "self" who takes up fasting—that is, makes some sort of (fraudulent) existential decision. It is meaningless to assign to a Kafka hero a unitary existence supposedly already "containing" the irreconcilable hungers of body and spirit. The hero *is* those hungers. The hunger artist remains a special phenomenon, however, radically different even from the investigating dog. First, he is (as he tells us) unique in that he has only the one hunger; fasting brings him not privation but ease. Second, he is in quest not of truth but solely of new fasting records. He is perfectly self-contained, without longings or desires to be different. His one problem is that his self-containment is comprehensible only in its inverse relation to "the world." Fasting exists only if the world certifies its existence; without such certification (as at the story's end), it cannot be distinguished from dying. Kafka thus maintains the self's doubleness by locating one dimension of the artist's self—the actuality of his art—completely outside him. Another way of saying the same thing is that the world, that seemingly alien and uncontrollable force, is "internal" to the hunger artist in his full semantic being. Another story in this last collection published by Kafka himself is entitled "Josephine the Singer; or, The Mouse Folk," and Kafka stressed that the *or* connoted a kind of balance, an inseparability between the two halves of the title. It would be helpful, I think, to imagine some such title for our present story: "A Hunger Artist and His Public." For it is the very separateness of the two, the physical barrier and the mental alienation, that compels us to think of artist and public as ultimately a single entity. One could argue, of course, that the world exists independently of the artist; but such existence, Kafka suggests, amounts to little more than animallike impulses governed by perpetual amnesia. The onlookers at the end are utterly consumed by the panther's "freedom": they do not "want ever to move away" (*CS* 277).

The tight symbiosis between artist and public is illuminated by a passage that Kafka deleted from the final version and that J. M. S. Pasley printed for the first time in a 1966 article. Kafka often deleted sentences that skewed a text in the direction of a single "meaning." I translate a short part of this passage:

> [The hunger artist] himself sought out, among the large and vibrant crowd of spectators, gazes expressing the desire to sink deeply into his own. There followed a question-and-answer game played by the eyes. The spectator asked: "Have you really fasted so long?" The Hunger Artist responded: "Certainly, I've fasted exactly that long and will continue to fast for a long time. I understand that you can't comprehend this; it is incomprehensible." The spectator: "And you are supposed to be able to carry out the incomprehensible." The Hunger Artist: "Yes, I am."   (Pasley 104)

The exchange concludes with the artist's denial that he ever eats the smallest bite. This highly structured ocular dialogue clearly corresponds to the artist's ideal version of things. It *is* the work of art generated by his existence: a moment in time perfectly circumscribed by a "conversation" focused exclusively on the event of fasting yet at the same time a moment that opens onto an infinite repetition of identical moments in the future.

Both sets of coordinates are held in balance: the social realm is defined by an exclusive concentration on the purity of the fasting process, and the temporal dimension is defined as open-ended repetition of the same pure moment.

By deleting this passage, Kafka left us with a text in which such pure moments are not recorded. And indeed, they cannot exist in this imagined perfection, because fasting is in fact easy for the artist. There is nothing untrue in the dialogue, for the artist does find his own undertaking "incomprehensible"; nevertheless he knows he is falsely admired. He does not even try to conceal the truth: "He made no secret of [the ease of fasting], yet people did not believe him . . ." (*CS* 270). But the inescapable subjective reality ensures that the artist will be forever dissatisfied: either he strives to fast indefinitely—although there is no inner truth to that course either, just the prospect of fame—or he accepts the world's definition of a fast, which produces after the prescribed forty days a caricature of the perfect moment imagined in the deleted passage. And so the dream of controlling time and social intercourse dissolves into the rhythms of history and fashion.

Control returns only through the world's indifference at the limiting moment of death. But it does return, bringing the story to a haunting conclusion (in his testamentary letter to Max Brod, Kafka singled out this story as the one valid achievement among his not-yet-published writings [Glatzer 250]). What happens is that both possibilities open to the artist are lived through to their conclusion. On the one hand, his indefinite fast becomes sundered from "fame" altogether, since no one changes the number on his cage signifying days fasted. In driving him to actual death, fasting becomes his truth in a new sense: its "ease" loses meaning, entitling him finally to be described as "working honestly." On the other hand, his utter dependence on the world is figured in the final conversation with the overseer. The conversation is reminiscent of the deleted passage cited above in that it focuses wholly on the act of fasting (possible now only because of the overseer's indifference): indeed, the conversation evokes a crucial quality of repetition that certifies it as *the* aesthetic product of the artist's life and death. It is a set piece, not really giving new information (the artist's dislike of food is implicit in his earlier admissions) but spelling out the entirety of the truth without having to claim mastery over the future—the key claim of the deleted ocular dialogue. The artist controls his final exchange without semantic ambiguity: through it he is released from "pride" (*CS* 277), from the need to impose himself on the world. In this final reduction he really is fasting—that is, starving to death. Walter Sokel remarks that "it is in the dying of the self through which truth conquers and shines forth" (*Franz Kafka* 38). In the character of the hunger artist, truth and art are synonymous, and the last conversation constitutes an art-death analogous to the Wagnerian love-death, a language finally emancipated from compromise.

The question remains: Of what is this symbiosis between artist and public an allegory? The answer, I think, is that the text allegorizes the specific aspirations of modernist art, in a manner closely related to "Josephine," Kafka's last completed story. Josephine's claims upon her audience are explicit, while those of the hunger artist are implicit. But, as we have seen, the bars of his cage bind him to the world just as much as they separate him from it. And the force of the allegory derives from the transformative claim of modernist aesthetics. Grounded in a totalizing disgust at the bourgeois order of the nineteenth century, modernism pursues a variety of assault strategies, from the contemptuous realism of Gustave Flaubert to the ironic metaphysics of Thomas Mann. All the aestheticizing gestures of modernism involve an ostentatious withdrawal behind the "bars" of exoticism and dream (Baudelaire) or into a cultural-linguistic encyclopedia (Joyce). But it is usually an aggressive retreat: utopian visions presuppose a dystopian actuality and virtually propel the (modernist) dreamer into imagining a possible transformation of that actuality.

The hunger artist is a modernist in three distinct respects. First, in his refusal of all normal physical functions he symbolically rejects the claims of ordinary (bourgeois) living; his body becomes aesthetic material under the control of the spirit, purified of all independent impulses. Second, he imposes a coherent structure on the flux of time (time, according to Lukács's *Theory of the Novel*, is the substrate, the primary material of all modernist art). Time ceases to be the open-ended, unpredictable element of daily life and is organized into the minutes, the hours, and finally the biblical forty days of the fasting sequence. If we accept the fast, like a divinity, as the source of ultimate meaning, it will respond by filling the time of its adherents with meaning, structuring their days like those of medieval monks. Third, of course, the hunger artist seeks precisely such an infiltration into the daily lives of his spectators. If the deleted ocular exchange and the conversation with the overseer both have the quality of a catechism, it is no accident. If ordinary people can become fully focused on fasting, fasting as the incomprehensible that is yet occurring before their eyes, their lives (and, by extension, the world) will be transformed. Himself a modernist, Kafka understood very well the quasi-religious claims of modernism, advanced perhaps most unabashedly by his contemporary the poet Rainer Maria Rilke, whose *Letters to a Young Poet* (advising his correspondent how to live) became a bestseller. Kafka saw clearly the dubiousness of these claims, which opened vast new possibilities for charlatans and worse: the imagery describing the hunger artist's adherents in his heyday echoes closely the evocation of the throngs around the execution machine in "In the Penal Colony."

The question returns: Is the hunger artist a charlatan? A reluctant one perhaps. The "purity" of his enterprise lies in its transparency, its self-containment: the hunger artist requires nothing of his audience beyond unquestioning aesthetic contemplation. The transformative claim he advances does not, however, as in the modernist ideal, simply emanate from the utopian power of his undertaking. On the contrary, as we have seen, the hunger artist needs his adherents in order to compensate for his central weakness, the ease of fasting. This third dimension of the modernist enterprise (the transformative claim) is required, in other words, to disguise the flaws in the first two (aestheticization of space and time). The extended arguments about whether or not the artist sneaks some food are necessary for the artist, who welcomes the presence of his watchers. Without these arguments, the spiritual image that he projects would lose its meaning (since it does not actually derive from transformative struggle). The same is true of the aesthetic shaping of time: the artist is always unhappy at the forty-day termination, but if there were no such limit, there would be no value in his fast. He only appears to be an ascetic; hence his undertaking is dependent on his appearance, his reception by others. The question is not really one of fraud, since he does not conceal the truth. The issue is, rather, the implied transformative claims of modernism: as soon as the "value" of modernist art becomes inseparable from the reception of its transformative claims—Kafka saw this happening with many "activist" works of his contemporaries, the expressionists—the modernist aesthetic is sure to crumble from within. For, as all the greatest modernists knew, the indifference of the bourgeois world can be despised and ironized, but it cannot be denied.

As we have seen, the hunger artist ultimately not only accepts the indifference but endorses it; he actually gains the integrity that has eluded him, by purifying himself unto death. Was Kafka portraying himself in this story? At first glance his artistic problems seem wholly unlike those of the hunger artist; writing was never "easy" for him, and he never had any sense that a public even existed for his works. But in allegory extremes meet, and what separates (like the bars of the artist's cage) also binds. Kafka did suspect himself of charlatanry: his very addiction to writing, in particular the virtually orgasmic pleasure he felt at successful moments, seemed to him sinful, an offense against life. This valorization of ordinary life, however, is scarcely evident in Kafka's works, which express the contempt for the everyday that the hunger artist's perspective imparts to us (the supremely contemptuous Flaubert was the literary model Kafka admired most). Kafka and the hunger artist have in common that they are outside the "house of life" and cannot ultimately wish it otherwise. The artist lacks, however, a multitude of Kafka's well-known characteristics, such as irony, nostalgia, and humor. Basically, Kafka populated his late works with partial selves—and in fact originally imagined yet another one for this story. In a second, longer deleted passage, the artist converses with a cannibal ("Menschenfresser") who claims to be a friend from old times and likes to talk to the artist because there's nothing there to eat (Pasley 105–06). The cannibal is, of course, the opposite of the artist: he has a profusion of hair, a powerful head, "superhuman desires." But the cannibal "transforms" people by consuming them, just as the artist seeks to do so by refusing all consumption. Both characters body forth the modernist dream, its refusals, its ruptures, its aesthetic reinvention of the world.

Students are surprisingly interested in the aesthetic questions this story poses: Is something a work of art just because it is said to be one? Must something be shaped to qualify as art? How separate is the work of art from the artist's intentionality or "sincerity"? Can art exist as a stretch of time, or must it be an externalized object? My suggestion that the major claims of modernism resonate in the story's figures is not intended as key to its meaning. Rather, it seems to me a way of grounding the "return of the aesthetic" among our students, of helping them to understand why this text in particular fascinates them. Modernism is of course dead. But its products dominate our literary culture to such an extent that we have to come to grips with the meaning of aesthetic ideas and claims in a postmodern world. In one respect the hunger artist's own cyclical projection, "that new and better times might be coming" (CS 275), is confirmed by our students. But in another respect the receding of modernist ideology into the past opens its aesthetic premises and goals to misunderstanding and distortion. The circus of modernism is full of marvels, but if students are not to be confined (like the hunger artist's adherents) in a condition of passive wonderment, teachers must shed the roles of initiate and impresario and help them go behind the scenes, to examine the tent pegs and machinery that keep the circus in operation. Since he has become a marginal attraction, the hunger artist needs a second job: that of experienced guide to the whole show for later generations.

NOTE

[1]The English portion of the dual-language publicity sheet reads as follows:

> Big Sensation [*Weltsensation*]. Come and see the Starvation Artist [*Hunger-künstler*] Heros. World's Champion in 1950 at the Frankfurt Zoo with 50 days of starvation. He will establish a new World Championship: 75 days without taking any food in a sealed glass box. Münchener Strasse 56-58, opposite Maier Gustl's Oberbayern (near the Main Station). Medical care controlled by the Red Cross, Frankfurt-Main. The glass box is sealed in the presence of public, press, and police. During his time of starvation Heros will have only cigarettes and Hassia mineral water. Admission fee: DM 1.00. Unemployed, disabled, and children DM 0.50.

CONTRIBUTORS AND SURVEY PARTICIPANTS

Daniel Albright, *University of Virginia*
Salvatore F. Allosso, *University of California, Davis*
Carrie L. Asman, *University of California, Davis*
Manfred Bansleben, *University of Washington*
Evelyn Torton Beck, *University of Maryland, College Park*
Jeanine Blackwell, *University of Kentucky*
Joseph L. Brockington, *Kalamazoo College*
Russell E. Brown, *State University of New York, Stony Brook*
L. Cornick, *Old Dominion University*
Steve Dowden, *Yale University*
Kurt Fickert, *Wittenberg University*
Ruth V. Gross, *University of Texas, Arlington*
Peter Heller, *State University of New York, Buffalo*
Peter Hertz-Ohmes, *State University of New York, Oswego*
Kenneth Hughes, *Clark University*
M. Kuxdorf, *University of Waterloo*
Alan C. Leidner, *University of Louisville*
Siegfried Mandel, *University of Colorado, Boulder*
Horst Richardson, *Colorado College*
James Rolleston, *Duke University*
Judith Ryan, *Harvard University*
David Scarse, *University of Vermont*
Hugo Schmidt, *University of Colorado, Boulder*
Carsten Seekamp, *University of Colorado, Denver*
Roger Shattuck, *University of Virginia*
Margit M. Sinka, *Clemson University*
Walter H. Sokel, *University of Virginia*
Henry Sussman, *State University of New York, Buffalo*
Steven Taubeneck, *University of British Columbia*
M. D. Ticktin, *George Washington University*
Elizabeth W. Trahan, *National Coalition of Independent Scholars, Amherst, MA*

WORKS CITED

Aarne, A., and S. Thompson. "The Types of the Folktale." *Folklore Fellows Communications* 25 (1928): 123–24.

Abrams, M. H. "Coleridge, Baudelaire, and Modernist Poetics." *Immanente Ästhetik, Ästhetische Reflexion: Lyrik als Paradigma der Moderne.* Kolloquium Köln, 1964. Vorlagen und Verhandlungen. Ed. Wolfgang Iser. Munich: Fink, 1966. 113–38, 419–28.

Adorno, Theodor W. "Notes on Kafka." *Prisms.* Trans. Samuel Munchen and Shierry Weber. London: Spearman, 1967. 245–72. Excerpts rpt. in Bloom, *Kafka* 95–105.

Anderson, Mark, ed. *Reading Kafka: Prague, Politics, and the Fin de Siècle.* New York: Schocken, 1989.

Anthony, Katherine. *Margaret Fuller: A Psychological Biography.* New York: Harcourt, 1921.

Asman-Schneider, Carrie L. "From Agon to Allegory: Walter Benjamin and the Drama of Language." Diss. Stanford U, 1988.

Auden, W. H. "The I without a Self." *The Dyer's Hand and Other Essays.* London: Faber, 1963. 159–67. Partial rpt. in Hamalian 39–44.

Auster, Paul. "Kafka's Letters." *The Art of Hunger.* New York: Penguin, 1992. 134–39.

———. "Pages for Kafka." *The Art of Hunger.* New York: Penguin, 1992. 23–25.

Barthes, Roland. "The Death of the Author." Barthes, *Image* 142–48.

———. *Image Music Text.* Ed. and trans. Stephen Heath. New York: Hill, 1977.

———. "Introduction to the Structural Analysis of Narratives." Barthes, *Image* 79–124.

Bartning, C. O. Lithographs illustrating Kafka's "Vor dem Gesetz," "Ein Bericht für eine Akademie," "Das Urteil," *Der Prozess, Die Verwandlung. Phantastischer Realismus.* Ed. Wolfgang Thiede. Berlin: n.p., 1977. Exhibition catalog.

Bauer, Johann. *Kafka and Prague.* New York: Praeger, 1971.

Baum, Alwin L. "Parable as Paradox in Kafka's *Erzählungen.*" *MLN* 91 (1976): 1327–47. Rpt. in Bloom, *Kafka* 151–68.

Baumer, Franz, ed. *Sieben Prosastücke.* Dichtung im Unterricht 9. Munich: Kösel, 1965.

Beck, Evelyn Torton. *Kafka and the Yiddish Theater: Its Impact on His Work.* Madison: U of Wisconsin P, 1971.

———. "Kafkas 'Durchbruch': Der Einfluss des jiddischen Theaters auf sein Schaffen." *Basis: Jahrbuch für deutsche Gegenwartsliteratur* 1 (1970): 204–23.

———. "Kafka's Traffic in Women: Gender, Power, and Sexuality." *Literary Review* 26 (1983): 565–76.

———. "Kafka's Triple Bind: Women, Jews, and Sexuality." *Kafka's Contextuality.* Ed. Alan Udoff. New York: Gordion, 1988. 343–88.

Behler, Ernst. *Irony and the Discourse of Modernity.* Seattle: U of Washington P, 1990.

Beicken, Peter U. *Franz Kafka*: Die Verwandlung. *Erläuterungen und Dokumente.* Reclams Universal-Bibliothek 8155. Stuttgart: Reclam, 1987.

———. *Franz Kafka: Eine kritische Einführung in die Forschung.* Frankfurt: Athenäum Fischer Taschenbuch, 1974.

Beissner, Friedrich. *Der Erzähler Franz Kafka.* Stuttgart: Kohlhammer, 1952. Excerpts in English in Kafka, *Metamorphosis,* ed. Corngold, 187–88.

Belmont, Nicole. "Contes populaires et mythes." *Dictionnaire des mythologies et des religions des sociétés traditionelles et du monde antique.* Ed. Yves Bonnefoy. Paris: Flammarion, 1981.

Benjamin, Walter. "Franz Kafka: On the Tenth Anniversary of His Death." *Illuminations.* Trans. Harry Zohn. New York: Harcourt, 1968. 111–40.

———. "Some Reflections on Kafka." *Illuminations.* Trans. Harry Zohn. New York: Harcourt, 1968. 141–48. Rpt. in Bloom, *Kafka* 17–32.

Bernheimer, Charles. "Letters to an Absent Friend: A Structural Reading." A. Flores, *Problem of "The Judgment"* 146–67.

Binder, Hartmut. *Franz Kafka: Leben und Persönlichkeit.* Stuttgart: Kröner, 1983. Rpt. from Binder, *Kafka-Handbuch* 1: 103–584.

———, ed. *Kafka-Handbuch.* 2 vols. Stuttgart: Kröner, 1979.

———. *Kafka-Kommentar zu sämtlichen Erzählungen.* Munich: Winkler, 1975.

Binder, Hartmut, and Jan Parik. *Kafka: Ein Leben in Prag.* Munich: Mahnert-Lueg, 1982.

Bloom, Harold, ed. *Franz Kafka.* Modern Critical Views. New York: Chelsea, 1986.

———. *Sigmund Freud.* Modern Critical Views. New York: Chelsea, 1985.

Bödeker, Karl-Bernhard. *Frau und Familie im erzählerischen Werk Franz Kafkas.* Frankfurt: Lang, 1974.

Bonaparte, Marie. *Edgar Poe: Etude psychoanalytique.* Paris: Denoël, 1933.

Borges, Jorge Luis. "Kafka and His Precursors." Trans. James E. Irby *Labyrinths: Selected Stories and Other Writings.* Ed. Donald A. Yates and James E. Irby. New York: New Directions, 1964. 199–201. Rpt. in Hamalian 18–20.

———. "The Wall and the Books." Trans. James E. Irby. *Labyrinths: Selected Stories and Other Writings.* Ed. Donald A. Yates and Irby. New York: New Directions, 1964. 186–88.

Bradbury, Malcolm, and James McFarlane. "The Name and Nature of Modernism." *Modernism 1890–1930.* 1976. Ed. Bradbury and McFarlane. Sussex, Eng.: Harvester; Atlantic Highlands: Humanities, 1978. 19–55.

Brod, Max. *Franz Kafka: A Biography.* Trans. G. Humphreys-Roberts and Richard Winston. 2nd ed. New York: Schocken, 1960.

———. *Franz Kafka: Eine Biographie.* 1954. Frankfurt: Fischer, 1963.

———. *Über Franz Kafka.* Frankfurt: Fischer, 1976. Collection including *Franz Kafka: Eine Biographie, Franz Kafkas Glaube und Lehre,* and *Verzweiflung und Erlösung im Werk Franz Kafkas.*

Byrne, Richard. "German Cinematic Expressionism." Diss. State U of Iowa, 1962.

Calvino, Italo. *Invisible Cities*. San Diego: Harcourt, 1972.

Camus, Albert. "Hope and the Absurd in the Work of Franz Kafka." *The Myth of Sisyphus*. New York: Vintage, 1959. 92–102. Rpt. in A. Flores, *Kafka Problem* 251–61.

Canetti, Elias. *Der andere Prozess: Kafkas Briefe an Felice*. Reihe Hanser 23. Munich: Hanser, 1969.

———. *Kafka's Other Trial: The Letters to Felice*. Trans. Christopher Middleton. New York: Schocken, 1974.

Caputo-Mayr, Marie Luise, and Julius M. Herz. *Franz Kafka: Eine kommentierte Bibliographie der Sekundärliteratur*. Bern: Francke, 1987.

———. *Franz Kafkas Werke: Eine Bibliographie der Primärliteratur (1908–1980)*. Bern: Francke, 1982.

Carpenter, Edward, and George Barnefield. *The Psychology of the Poet Shelley*. London: Allen, 1925.

Carrouges, Michel. *Kafka versus Kafka*. Trans. Emmett Parker. Tuscaloosa: U of Alabama P, 1968.

Cassity, John H. "Psychopathological Glimpses of Lord Byron." *Psychoanalytic Review* 12 (1925): 397–413.

Citati, Pietro. *Kafka*. Trans. Raymond Rosenthal. New York: Knopf, 1990.

Cohen, Gary B. *The Politics of Ethnic Survival: Germans in Prague, 1861–1914*. Princeton: Princeton UP, 1981.

Cohn, Dorrit. "Kafka's Eternal Present: Narrative Tense in 'Ein Landarzt' and Other First-Person Stories." *PMLA* 83 (1968): 144–50. Rpt. in Bloom, *Kafka* 107–17.

———. *Transparent Minds: Narrative Modes for Presenting Consciousness in Fiction*. Princeton: Princeton UP, 1978.

Corngold, Stanley. *The Commentators' Despair: The Interpretation of Kafka's Metamorphosis*. Port Washington: Kennikat, 1973.

———. *Franz Kafka: The Necessity of Form*. Ithaca: Cornell UP, 1988.

———. "Kafka's 'The Judgment' and Modern Rhetorical Theory." *Newsletter of the Kafka Society of America* 7 (1983): 15–21.

———. "The Structure of Kafka's *Metamorphosis*: The Metamorphosis of the Metaphor." Corngold, *Commentators' Despair* 1–38.

Davey, E. R. "The Broken Engine: A Study of Franz Kafka's 'In der Strafkolonie.' " *Journal of European Studies* 14.4 (1984): 271–83.

Deleuze, Gilles, and Félix Guattari. *Kafka: Toward a Minor Literature*. Trans. Dana Polan. Theory and History of Literature 30. Minneapolis: U of Minnesota P, 1986.

Dietz, Ludwig. *Franz Kafka*. Stuttgart: Metzler, 1975.

Dooley, Lucille. "Psychoanalysis of Charlotte Brontë as a Type of the Woman of Genius." *American Journal of Psychology* 31 (1920): 222–23.

Dünnhaupt, Gerhard. "The Secondary Literature to Franz Kafka's 'Ein Hungerkünstler.' " *Modern Austrian Literature* 11.3–4 (1978): 31–36.

Eggenschwiler, David. " 'Die Verwandlung,' Freud, and the Chains of Odysseus." *Modern Language Quarterly* 39 (1978): 363–85. Rpt. in Bloom, *Kafka* 199–219.

Ellis, John M. "Kafka: 'Das Urteil.' " *Narration in the German Novelle*. Cambridge: Cambridge UP, 1978. 188–211.

Emrich, Wilhelm. *Franz Kafka*. Bonn: Athenäum, 1957.

———. *Franz Kafka: A Critical Study of His Writings*. Trans. Sheema Zeben Buehne. New York: Ungar, 1968.

Escher, Rolf. *Die Verwandlung: Sieben Radierungen zur gleichnamigen Erzählung von Franz Kafka*. Burgdorf bei Hannover: Steintor-Verlag, 1973.

Faber, Marion. "Kafka on the Screen: Martin Scorsese's *After Hours*." *Unterrichtspraxis* 19 (1986): 200–05.

Falk, Walter. *Franz Kafka und die Expressionisten im Ende der Neuzeit*. Beiträge zur neueren Epochenforschung 10. Frankfurt: Peter Lang, 1990.

Faulkner, Peter. *Modernism*. Critical Idiom 35. New York: Methuen, 1977.

Faynman, Asher Zelig [Zigmund Feinmann]. *The Viceroy; or, A Night in the Garden of Eden* [*Der Vitse-Kenig, oder a Nakht in Gan Eydn*]. Lvov, 1909.

Fetterley, Judith. *The Resisting Reader: A Feminist Approach to American Literature*. Bloomington: U of Indiana P, 1978.

Fickert, Kurt J. *Franz Kafka: Life, Work, and Criticism*. Fredericton: York, 1984.

Fingerhut, Karlheinz. *Franz Kafka: Klassiker der Moderne: Literarische Texte und historische Materialien*. 2 vols. Stuttgart: Metzler, 1981.

Flores, Angel, ed. *Explain to Me Some Stories of Kafka: "The Judgment," The Metamorphosis, "A Report to an Academy," "A Hunger Artist."* New York: Gordion, 1983.

———. *A Kafka Bibliography 1908–1976*. New York: Gordion, 1976.

———. *The Kafka Debate*. New York: Gordion, 1977.

———. *The Kafka Problem*. New York: Gordion, 1946.

———. *The Problem of "The Judgment."* New York: Gordion, 1977.

Flores, Angel, and Homer Swander, eds. *Franz Kafka Today*. Madison: U of Wisconsin P, 1962.

Flores, Kate. " 'The Judgment.' " Flores and Swander 5–24.

Fokkema, Douwe W. *Literary History, Modernism and Postmodernism*. Harvard University Erasmus Lectures, spring 1983. Amsterdam: Benjamins, 1984.

Fraenkel, Josef, ed. *The Jews in Austria*. London: Vallentine, Mitchell, 1967.

Freud, Sigmund. *Collected Papers*. Vol. 4. New York: Basic, 1959.

———. *Gesammelte Werke*. Vol. 12. London: Imago, 1947.

———. *The Interpretation of Dreams*. Vol. 4 of *Standard Edition*.

———. "The Relation of the Poet to Day-dreaming." *On Creativity and the Unconscious: Papers on the Psychology of Art, Literature, Love, Religion*. Trans. under the supervision of Joan Riviere. Ed. Benjamin Nelson. New York: Harper, 1958. 44–54.

———. *The Standard Edition of the Complete Psychological Works of Sigmund Freud*. Ed. and trans. James Strachey. 24 vols. London: Hogarth, 1953–74.

———. *Wit and Its Relation to the Unconscious*. Vol. 8 of *Standard Edition*.

Friedrich, Hugo. *Die Struktur der modernen Lyrik: Von Baudelaire bis zur Gegenwart*. Hamburg: Rowohlt, 1956.

Fronius, Hans. *Kafka-Mappe: Zehn Zeichnungen zu den Werken Franz Kafkas*. Vienna: Amandus, 1946.

———, illus. *Ein Landarzt*. Hildesheim: Schrift und Bild, 1966.

Gilman, Sander. *Jewish Self-Hatred*. Baltimore: Johns Hopkins UP, 1986.

Glaser, Hermann, et al. *Wege der deutschen Literatur: Eine geschichtliche Darstellung*. Frankfurt: Ullstein, 1986.

Glatzer, Nahum N., ed. *I Am a Memory Come Alive: Autobiographical Writings by Franz Kafka*. New York: Schocken, 1964.

Goldstücker, Eduard. "Kafkas Eckermann?: Zu Gustav Janouchs *Gespräche mit Kafka*." *Franz Kafka: Themen und Probleme*. Ed. Claude David. Göttingen: Vandenhoeck, 1980. 238–55.

———. "On Prague as Background." *Kafka-Studien*. Ed. Barbara Elling. New Yorker Studien zur neueren deutschen Literaturwissenschaft 5. New York: Lang, 1985. 81–86.

Gordin, Jacob [Jakov Gordin]. *God, Man, and Devil*. New York, 1903.

———. *The Savage One [Der vilde Mentsh]*. Warsaw, 1907.

Grabert, Willy, Arnot Mulot, and Helmuth Nürnberger. *Geschichte der deutschen Literatur*. 19th ed. Munich: Bayerischer Schulbuchverlag, 1978.

Gray, Richard T. "Biography as Criticism in Kafka Studies." *Journal of the Kafka Society of America* 10.1–2 (1986): 46–55.

Gray, Ronald. *Franz Kafka*. New York: Cambridge UP, 1973.

———. *Kafka: A Collection of Critical Essays*. Englewood Cliffs: Prentice, 1962.

Greenberg, Martin. *The Terror of Art: Kafka and Modern Literature*. New York: Basic, 1968.

Gross, Ruth V., ed. *Critical Essays on Franz Kafka*. Critical Essays on World Literature. Boston: Hall, 1990.

Grusa, Jirí. *Franz Kafka aus Prag*. Frankfurt: Fischer, 1983.

———. *Franz Kafka of Prague*. Trans. E. Mosbacher. London: Secker, 1983.

Hackermüller, Rotraut. *Kafka's letzte Jahre 1917–1924*. Munich: Kirchheim, 1990.

Hafrey, Leigh. Rev. of *Franz Kafka: Representative Man*, by Frederick Karl. *New York Times Book Review* 23 Feb. 1992: 7, 16.

Hamalian, Leo, ed. *Kafka: A Collection of Criticism*. New York: McGraw, 1974.

Hasselblatt, Dieter. *Zauber und Logik: Eine Kafka-Studie*. Cologne: Wissenschaft und Politik, 1964.

Hauptmann, Gerhart. "Fasching." *Erzählungen, Theoretische Prosa*. Vol. 6. Ed. Hans-Egon Hass. Berlin: Ullstein, 1963. 13–34.

Hayman, Ronald. *Kafka: A Biography*. New York: Oxford UP, 1982.

Hegel, Georg Wilhelm Friedrich. *Phenomenology of Spirit*. Trans. A. V. Miller. Oxford: Clarendon–Oxford UP, 1977.

Heller, Erich. *Franz Kafka*. Modern Masters M30. New York: Viking, 1975.

Heller, Peter. "Kafka as Story-teller." *The Dove and the Mole: Kafka's Journey into*

Darkness and Creativity. Ed. Moshe Lazar and Ronald Gottesman. Malibu: Undena, 1987. 61–69.

———. "On Not Understanding Kafka." *German Quarterly* 47 (1974): 373–93.

Herz, Julius M. "Franz Kafka and Austria: National Background and Ethnic Identity." *Modern Austrian Literature* 11.3-4 (1978): 301–18.

Heselhaus, Clemens. "Kafkas Erzählformen." *Deutsche Vierteljahresschrift für Literaturwissenschaft und Geistesgeschichte* 26 (1952): 353–76.

Hesse, Hermann. *Demian*. Ed. Robert Conrad. Boston: Suhrkamp, 1985.

Hibberd, John. *Kafka: "Die Verwandlung."* Critical Guides to German Texts 3. London: Grant, 1985.

Hiebel, Hans H. *Franz Kafka: "Ein Landarzt."* UTB 1289. Munich: Fink, 1984.

———. *Die Zeichen des Gesetzes: Recht und Macht bei Franz Kafka*. Munich: Fink, 1983.

Hiepe, Richard, ed. *Bilder und Graphik zu Werken von Franz Kafka*. Munich: Neue Münchner Galerie, 1966.

Hill, Claude. *2000 Jahre deutscher Kultur*. New York: Harper, 1966.

Hillmann, Heinz. *Franz Kafka: Dichtungstheorie und Dichtungsgestalt*. Bonn: Bouvier, 1964.

Hirsch, E. D. *Validity in Interpretation*. New Haven: Yale UP, 1967.

Hofmannsthal, Hugo von. "Letter to Lord Chandos." *Selected Prose*. Trans. Mary Hottinger, Tania Stern, and James Stern. New York: Pantheon, 1952. 129–41.

———. *Poems and Verse Plays*. Ed. Michael Hamburger. New York: Pantheon, 1961. Dual-language ed.

Holland, Norman N. "Shakespearean Tragedy and the Three Ways of Psychoanalytic Criticism." *Psychoanalysis and Literature*. Ed. Hendrick Ruitenbeek. New York: Dutton, 1964. 207–17.

Hoover, Marjorie L., Charles Hoffmann, and Richard Plant, eds. *Franz Kafka, Bertolt Brecht, Heinrich Böll: Erzählungen*. New York: Norton, 1970.

Horkheimer, Max. "Art and Mass Culture." Horkheimer, *Critical Theory* 273–90.

———. "Authority and the Family." Horkheimer, *Critical Theory* 47–128.

———. *Critical Theory: Selected Essays*. Trans. Matthew J. O'Connell et al. 1972. New York: Continuum, 1989.

Hughes, Kenneth, ed. *Franz Kafka: An Anthology of Marxist Criticism*. Hanover: New England UP, 1982.

———. "Psychoanalytic Criticism and Kafka's 'Das Urteil.' " *Perspectives and Personalities: Studies in Modern German Literature Honoring Claude Hill*. Ed. Ralph Ley et al. Heidelberg: Winter, 1978. 156–75.

Hutcheon, Linda. *A Poetics of Postmodernism: History, Theory, Fiction*. New York: Routledge, 1988.

Jameson, Fredric. "Beyond the Cave: Demystifying the Ideology of Modernism." *The Syntax of History*. Vol. 2 of *The Ideologies of Theory: Essays, 1971–1986*. London: Routledge, 1988. 115–32.

———. *Postmodernism: The Logic of Late Capitalism*. Durham: Duke UP, 1991.

Janik, Allan, and Stephen Toulmin. *Wittgenstein's Vienna*. New York: Simon, 1973.

Janouch, Gustav. *Conversations with Kafka: Notes and Reminiscences*. Trans. Goronwy Rees. New York: Praeger, 1953. 2nd, revised and enlarged ed. New York: New Directions, 1971.

———. *Gespräche mit Kafka: Aufzeichnungen und Erinnerungen*. 2nd, expanded ed. Frankfurt: Fischer, 1968.

Järv, Harry. *Die Kafka-Literatur: Eine Biographie*. Malmö: Bo Cavefors, 1961.

Johnston, William M. *The Austrian Mind: An Intellectual and Social History, 1848–1938*. Berkeley: U of California P, 1972.

Kafka, Franz. *America*. Trans. Edwin Muir. New York: New Directions, 1962.

———. *The Basic Kafka*. Ed. Erich Heller. New York: Pocket, 1979.

———. *Beschreibung eines Kampfes: Novellen, Skizzen, Aphorismen aus dem Nachlass*. Ed. Max Brod. Frankfurt: Fischer, 1954.

———. *Briefe, 1902–1924*. Ed. Max Brod. Frankfurt: Fischer, 1958.

———. *Briefe an Felice und andere Korrespondenz aus der Verlobungszeit*. Ed. Erich Heller and Jürgen Born. Frankfurt: Fischer, 1967.

———. *Briefe an Milena*. Expanded ed. Frankfurt: Fischer, 1983.

———. *Briefe an Ottla und die Familie*. Ed. Hartmut Binder and Klaus Wagenbach. Frankfurt: Fischer, 1974.

———. *The Complete Stories* [*CS*]. Ed. Nahum N. Glatzer. Trans. Willa Muir and Edwin Muir. New York: Schocken, 1971.

———. "A Country Doctor"/"Ein Landarzt." Steinhauer, *German Stories* 278–91. Dual-language ed.

———. *Dearest Father: Stories and Other Writings*. Trans. Ernst Kaiser and Ethiene Wilkins. New York: Schocken, 1954.

———. *The Diaries of Franz Kafka, 1910–1913*. Ed. Max Brod. Trans. Joseph Kresh. New York: Schocken, 1948.

———. *The Diaries of Franz Kafka, 1914–1923*. Ed. Max Brod. Trans. Martin Greenberg, with the cooperation of Hannah Arendt. New York: Schocken, 1949.

———. *Erzählungen*. Ed. Max Brod. Frankfurt: Fischer, 1952.

———. *"The Great Wall of China": Stories and Reflections*. Trans. Willa Muir and Edwin Muir. New York: Schocken, 1970.

———. *Hochzeitsvorbereitungen auf dem Lande und andere Prosa aus dem Nachlass*. Ed. Max Brod. Frankfurt: Fischer, 1953.

———. "A Hunger Artist." Trans. Harry Steinhauer. *Twelve German Novellas*. Ed. Harry Steinhauer. Berkeley: U of California P, 1977. 573–81.

———. "A Hunger Artist." Trans. Willa Muir and Edwin Muir. *The Norton Anthology of Short Fiction*. Ed. E. V. Cassill. New York: Norton, 1978. 714–21.

———. *In der Strafkolonie: Eine Geschichte aus dem Jahr 1914*. Ed. Klaus Wagenbach. Berlin: Wagenbach, 1975.

———. "In the Penal Colony." Trans. Eugene Jolas. *Partisan Review* 8 (Mar.–Apr. 1941): 98–107; 146–58.

———. "The Judgment." Trans. Malcolm Pasley. A. Flores, *Problem of "The Judgment"* 1–12.

———. "Ein Landarzt." Michalski 140–46.

———. *Letter to His Father/Brief an den Vater.* Trans. Ernst Kaiser and Ethiene Wilkins. New York: Schocken, 1966. Dual-language ed.

———. *Letters to Felice.* Trans. James Stern and Elisabeth Duckworth. New York: Schocken, 1973.

———. *Letters to Friends, Family, and Editors.* Trans. Richard Winston and Clara Winston. New York: Schocken, 1977.

———. *Letters to Milena.* Ed Willy Haas. Trans. Tania Stern and James Stern. New York: Schocken, 1962.

———. *Letters to Ottla and the Family.* Ed. Nahum N. Glatzer. Trans. Richard Winston and Clara Winston. New York: Schocken, 1982.

———. *The Metamorphosis.* Trans. A. L. Lloyd. New York: Vanguard, 1946.

———. *The Metamorphosis.* Ed. and trans. Stanley Corngold. New York: Bantam, 1972.

———. *The Metamorphosis/Die Verwandlung.* New York: Schocken, 1987. Dual-language ed.

———. *The Metamorphosis.* Trans. Stanley Corngold. *The Norton Anthology of World Masterpieces.* Vol. 2. 5th ed. New York: Norton, 1985. 1605–44.

———. *The Metamorphosis.* Trans. Willa Muir and Edwin Muir. *The Norton Anthology of Short Fiction.* Ed. R. V. Cassill. New York: Norton, 1978. 722–60.

———. *Parables and Paradoxes.* Trans. Willa Muir and Edwin Muir. New York: Schocken, 1961. Dual-language ed.

———. *"The Penal Colony": Stories and Short Pieces.* Trans. Willa Muir and Edwin Muir. New York: Schocken, 1976.

———. *The Penguin Complete Short Stories of Franz Kafka.* Ed. Nahum N. Glatzer. London: Lane, 1983.

———. *Sämtliche Erzählungen.* Ed. Paul Raabe. Frankfurt: Fischer, 1970.

———. *Shorter Works of Franz Kafka.* Trans. Malcolm Pasley. London: Secker, 1973.

———. *Tagebücher, 1910–1923.* Ed. Max Brod. Frankfurt: Fischer, 1949.

———. *Das Urteil und andere Erzählungen.* Frankfurt: Fischer, 1952.

———. *Die Verwandlung.* Ed. Marjorie L. Hoover. New York: Norton, 1960.

———. *Die Verwandlung.* Ed. Peter Hutchinson. London: Methuen Educational, 1985.

———. *Die Verwandlung.* Reclams Universal-Bibliothek 9900. Stuttgart: Reclam, 1978.

———. *Die Verwandlung.* Otten 117–78.

———. *Die Verwandlung.* Hoover, Hoffmann, and Plant 7–68.

Karl, Frederick R. *Franz Kafka: Representative Man.* New York: Ticknor, 1991.

Kobs, Jürgen. *Franz Kafka: Untersuchungen zu Bewusstsein und Sprache seiner Gestalten.* Ed. Ursula Brech. Bad Homburg: Athenäum, 1970.

Koelb, Clayton. *Kafka's Rhetoric: The Passion of Reading*. Ithaca: Cornell UP, 1989.

Kracauer, Siegfried. *From Caligari to Hitler: A Psychological History of the German Film*. Princeton: Princeton UP, 1947.

Kramer, Dale. "The Aesthetics of Theme: Kafka's 'In the Penal Colony.' " *Studies in Short Fiction* 5 (1968): 362–67.

Krusche, Dietrich. *Kafka und Kafka-Deutung*. Kritische Information 5. Munich: Fink, 1974.

Krutch, Joseph Wood. *Edgar Allan Poe: A Study in Genius*. New York: Knopf, 1926.

Kuna, Franz, ed. *On Kafka: Semi-centenary Perspectives*. New York: Barnes, 1976.

Kurz, Gerhard. "Nietzsche, Freud, and Kafka." Anderson 128–48.

———. *Traumschrecken: Kafkas literarische Existenzanalyse*. Stuttgart: Metzler, 1980.

Lacan, Jaques. *Ecrits: A Selection*. Trans. Alan Sheridan. New York: Norton, 1977.

———. *The Four Fundamental Concepts of Psychoanalysis*. Trans. Alan Sheridan. New York: Norton, 1978.

Le Roy Ladurie, Emmanuel. *Love, Death, and Money in the Pays d'Oc*. Trans. Alan Sheridan. New York: Braziller, 1982.

Levin, Harry. "What Was Modernism?" *Refractions*. New York: Oxford UP, 1966. 271–95.

Lindauer, Martin S. *The Psychological Study of Literature: Limitations, Possibilities, and Accomplishments*. Chicago: Hall, 1974.

Literary Review. Spec. issue. 26.4 (1983).

Lukács, Georg. *The Theory of the Novel*. Trans. Anna Bostock. Cambridge: MIT P, 1971.

Lyotard, Jean-François. *The Postmodern Condition: A Report on Knowledge*. Trans. Geoff Bennington and Brian Massumi. Minneapolis: U of Minnesota P, 1984.

Magny, Claude-Edmonde. "The Objective Description of Absurdity." A. Flores, *Kafka Problem* 75–96.

Mailloux, Peter. *A Hesitation before Birth: The Life of Franz Kafka*. Newark: U of Delaware P, 1989.

Mann, Thomas. *Tonio Kröger*. Prospect Heights: Waveland, 1992.

The Metamorphosis. Modern Critical Interpretations: Post-Enlightenment European Literature series. New York: Chelsea,' 1988.

Meurer, Richard, ed. *Franz Kafka. Erzählungen: Interpretationen*. 2nd, expanded ed. Munich: Oldenbourg, 1988.

Michalski, John. *Deutsche Dichter und Denker*. Waltham: Blaisdell, 1967.

Mitchell, Breon. "Kafka and the Hunger Artists." Udoff 236–55.

Modern Austrian Literature. Spec. double issue. 11.3–4 (1978).

Müller, Heiner. *Germania*. Ed. Sylvere Lotringer. Trans. Bernard Schutze and Caroline Schutze. New York: Semiotext(e), 1990.

Musil, Robert. *Der Mann ohne Eigenschaften*. Vol. 1 of *Gesammelte Werke*. Reinbek bei Hamburg: Rowohlt, 1978.

Mykyta, Larysa. "Women as Obstacle and the Way." *MLN* 95 (1980): 627–40.

Nabokov, Vladimir. "Franz Kafka: *The Metamorphosis.*" *Lectures on Literature.* Ed. Fredson Bowers. New York: Harcourt, 1980. 251–83.

Nagel, Bert. *Franz Kafka: Aspekte zur Interpretation und Wirkung.* Berlin: Schmidt, 1974.

———. *Kafka und die Weltliteratur: Zusammenhänge und Wechselwirkungen.* Munich: Winkler, 1983.

Neumann, Gerhard. *Franz Kafka, "Das Urteil": Text, Materialien, Kommentar.* Hanser Literatur-Kommentare 16. Munich: Hanser, 1981. Partial English trans. in Anderson 215–28.

———. "Nachwort." *Franz Kafka: In der Strafkolonie und andere Prosa.* Stuttgart: Reclam, 1990. 67–79.

Nietzsche, Friedrich. *Also sprach Zarathustra. Nietzsches Werke.* Vol. 1. Salzburg: Bergland, 1967. 303–588.

———. *The Birth of Tragedy and the Genealogy of Morals.* Trans. Francis Golffing. Garden City: Doubleday, 1956.

Norris, Margot. "Darwin, Nietzsche, Kafka, and the Problem of Mimesis." *MLN* 95 (1980): 1232–53.

———. "Sadism and Masochism in 'In the Penal Colony' and 'A Hunger Artist.'" Udoff 170–86.

Ortega y Gasset, José. *The Dehumanization of Art and Other Writings on Art and Culture.* 1925. Trans. Willard R. Trask. Garden City: Doubleday, 1956.

Otten, Anna, ed. *Meistererzählungen.* New York: Appleton, 1969.

Pascal, Roy. *Kafka's Narrators: A Study of His Stories and Sketches.* Cambridge: Cambridge UP, 1982.

Pasley, J. M. S. "Aestheticism and Cannibalism: Notes on an Unpublished Kafka Text." *Oxford German Studies* 1 (1966): 102–13.

Pawel, Ernst. *The Nightmare of Reason: A Life of Franz Kafka.* New York: Farrar, 1984.

Perloff, Marjorie. *The Poetics of Indeterminacy: Rimbaud to Cage.* Princeton: Princeton UP, 1981.

Pfeifer, Martin, ed. *Franz Kafka: Erzählungen mit Materialien.* Stuttgart: Klett, 1982.

Politzer, Heinz, ed. *Franz Kafka.* 2nd ed. Wege der Forschung 322. Darmstadt: Wissenschaftliche Buchgesellschaft, 1980.

———. *Franz Kafka: Parable and Paradox.* Ithaca: Cornell UP, 1962.

———, ed. *Das Kafka-Buch: Eine innere Biographie in Selbstzeugnissen.* Frankfurt: Fischer, 1965.

Pritchett, V. S. "The Logic of Franz Kafka." *New York Review of Books* 4 Feb. 1982: 6–7.

Quinones, Ricardo. *Mapping Literary Modernism: Time and Development.* Princeton: Princeton UP, 1981.

Raabe, Paul. "Kafka und der Expressionismus." Politzer, *Franz Kafka* 386–405.

Rasch, Wolfdietrich. "Aspekte der deutschen Literatur um 1900." *Zur deutschen Literatur seit der Jahrhundertwende.* Stuttgart: Metzler, 1967. 1–49.

Reiss, H. R. "Recent Kafka Criticism: A Survey." *German Life and Letters* 9 (1956): 294–305. Rpt. in Ronald Gray, *Kafka: A Collection* 163–77.

Rilke, Rainer Maria. *The Notebooks of Malte Laurids Brigge.* Trans. M. D. Herter Norton. New York: Capricorn, 1958.

———. *Selected Poems of Rainer Maria Rilke.* Trans. Robert Bly. New York: Harper, 1981. Dual-language ed.

Rimbaud, Arthur. "Lettre du voyant." *Oeuvres completes.* Ed. Antoine Adam. Paris: Gallimard, 1972. 249–51.

Robert, Marthe. *As Lonely as Franz Kafka.* Trans. Ralph Manheim. New York: Schocken, 1986.

Robertson, Ritchie. *Kafka: Judaism, Politics, and Literature.* Oxford: Clarendon–Oxford UP, 1985.

Rolleston, James. *Kafka's Narrative Theater.* University Park: Pennsylvania State UP, 1974.

Rorty, Richard. *Contingency, Irony, and Solidarity.* New York: Cambridge UP, 1989.

Roth, Philip. " 'I Always Wanted You to Admire My Fasting'; or, Looking at Kafka." *American Review* 17 (1973): 103–26.

Rothe, Wolfgang. *Kafka in der Kunst.* Stuttgart: Belser, 1979.

Ryan, Judith. *The Vanishing Subject: Early Psychology and Literary Modernism.* Chicago: U of Chicago P, 1991.

Scharkansky, Abraham Michael [Avraham Mikel Sharkanski]. *Kol Nidre; or, The Secret Jews of Spain* [*Kol Nidre, oder di geheyme Yudn in Shpanien*]. Warsaw, 1907.

Schild, Kurt W. "Formen des Verschlüsselns in Franz Kafkas Erzählkunst." Diss. Cologne, 1970.

Schnitzler, Arthur. "Der Witwer." *Die erzählenden Schriften.* Vol. 1. Frankfurt: Fischer, 1961. 229–38.

Scholz, Rüdiger, and Hans-Peter Hermann. *Literatur und Phantasie: Schöpferischer Umgang mit Kafka-Texten in Schule und Universität.* Stuttgart: Metzler, 1990.

Schorske, Carl. E. *Fin-de-Siècle Vienna: Politics and Culture.* New York: Knopf, 1980.

Schrey, Gisela. *Literaturästhetik der Psychoanalyse und ihre Rezeption in der deutschen Germanistik vor 1933.* Frankfurt: Athenaion, 1975.

Sheppard, Richard. "Kafka's 'Ein Hungerkünstler': A Reconsideration." *German Quarterly* 46 (1973): 219–33.

Sokel, Walter H. *Franz Kafka.* Columbia Essays on Modern Writers 19. New York: Columbia UP, 1966.

———. *Franz Kafka: Tragik und Ironie: Zur Struktur seiner Kunst.* Munich: Albert Langen Otto Müller, 1964. Paperback rpt. Frankfurt: Fischer, 1976.

———. "Freud and the Magic of Kafka's Writing." Stern 145–58.

———. "From Marx to Myth: The Structure and Function of Self-Alienation in Kafka's *Metamorphosis.*" *Literary Review* 26 (1983): 485–95.

———. "Frozen Sea and River of Narration: The Poetics behind Kafka's 'Break-through.' " *Newsletter of the Kafka Society of America* 7.1 (1983): 71–79.

———. "Kafka's Poetics of the Inner Self." *Modern Austrian Literature* 11.3–4 (1978): 37–58.

———. "Perspectives and Truth in 'The Judgment.' " A. Flores, *Problem of "The Judgment"* 193–237.

———. *The Writer in Extremis: Expressionism in Twentieth-Century German Literature.* Stanford: Stanford UP, 1959.

Spaethling, Robert, and Eugene Weber. *A Reader in German Literature.* New York: Oxford UP, 1969.

Spann, Meno. *Franz Kafka.* Twayne's World Authors Series 381. Boston: Twayne, 1976.

Sparks, Kimberley, and Constance Kenna. *Sechs kleine Morde.* New York: Harcourt, 1979.

Steiner, George. "Man of Letter." *New Yorker* 28 May 1990: 107–09.

Steinhauer, Harry, ed. and trans. *German Stories/Deutsche Novellen.* New York: Bantam, 1961. Dual-language ed.

———. "Hungering Artist or Artist in Hungering: Kafka's 'A Hunger Artist.' " *Criticism* 4 (1962): 28–43.

Stern, J. P., ed. *The World of Franz Kafka.* New York: Holt, 1980.

Stölzl, Christoph. *Kafkas böses Böhmen: Zur Sozialgeschichte eines Prager Juden.* Munich: Text & Kritik, 1975. Partial English trans. in Anderson 53–79.

Strindberg, August. *A Dream Play.* Ed. Jacques Chwat. Trans. Evert Sprinchorn. New York: Avon, 1974.

Sussman, Henry. *Franz Kafka: Geometrician of Metaphor.* Madison: Coda, 1979.

Swales, Martin. "Why Read Kafka?" *MLR* 76 (1981): 357–66.

Thiher, Allen. *Franz Kafka: A Study of the Short Fiction.* Twayne's Studies in Short Fiction 12. Boston: Twayne, 1989.

Thorlby, Anthony. *Kafka.* Students' Guide to European Literature. London: Heinemann, 1972.

Todorov, Tzvetan. *The Fantastic: A Structural Approach to a Literary Genre.* Trans. Richard Howard. Ithaca: Cornell UP, 1973.

Triffitt, Gregory B. *Kafka's* Landarzt *Collection: Rhetoric and Interpretation.* Australian and New Zealand Studies in German Language and Literature 13. New York: Lang, 1985.

Trilling, Lionel. "On the Teaching of Modern Literature." *Beyond Culture.* New York: Viking, 1965. 3–30.

Udoff, Alan, ed. *Kafka and the Contemporary Critical Performance: Centenary Readings.* Bloomington: Indiana UP, 1987.

Updike, John. "Reflections on Kafka's Short Stories." *New Yorker* 9 May 1983: 121–33.

Uppvall, Axel. *August Strindberg: A Psychoanalytic Study.* Boston: Gorham, 1920

Van Vliet, Claire, illus. *A Country Doctor.* West Burke: Janus, 1962.

————, illus. *Parables and Paradoxes*. West Burke: Janus, 1963.

Vietta, Silvio, and Hans-Georg Kemper. *Expressionismus*. UTB 362. Munich: Fink, 1975.

Wagenbach, Klaus. *Franz Kafka: Bilder aus seinem Leben*. 2nd, expanded ed. Berlin: Wagenbach, 1989.

————. *Franz Kafka: Eine Biographie seiner Jugend, 1897–1912*. Bern: Francke, 1958. Partial Engl trans. in Anderson 25–52.

————. *Franz Kafka in Selbstzeugnissen und Bilddokumenten*. Rowohlts Monographien 91. Reinbek: Rowohlt, 1964.

————. *Franz Kafka: Pictures of a Life*. Trans. Arthur S. Wensinger. New York: Pantheon, 1984.

Walser, Martin. *Beschreibung einer Form: Versuch über Franz Kafka*. 3rd ed. Munich: Hanser, 1968.

————. "Description of a Form." *Twentieth Century Interpretations of* The Trial. Ed. James Rolleston. Englewood Cliffs: Prentice, 1976. 21–35.

————. "On Kafka's Novels." Stern 87–101.

Weber, Albrecht, Carsten Schlingmann, and Gert Kleinschmidt. *Interpretationen zu Franz Kafka: "Das Urteil,"* Die Verwandlung, *"Ein Landarzt," Kleine Prosastücke*. Munich: Oldenbourg, 1968.

Weinstein, Arnold. "Kafka's Writing Machine: Metamorphosis in 'The Penal Colony.' " *Studies in Twentieth Century Literature* 7 (1982): 21–33.

Zweig, Stefan. "Der Amokläufer." *Die Mondscheingasse. Gesammelte Erzählungen*. Frankfurt: Fischer, 1989. 197–261.

————. *Die Welt von Gestern*. Frankfurt: Fischer, 1985.

————. *The World of Yesterday*. New York: Viking, 1943.

Audiovisual Aids

The Cabinet of Dr. Caligari. Dir. Robert Wiene. Goldwyn Pictures, 1919.

The Castle. Dir. Colin Nears. BBC. 17 Mar. 1974.

The Golem. Dir. Paul Wegener and Cor Boese. Hugo Riesenfeld, 1920. From the novel by Gustav Meyrink.

In Search of "K." Distr. Goethe Institute, 1014 Fifth Ave., New York, NY 10028.

Kafka. Dir. Steven Soderbergh. With Jeremy Irons. Baltimore Pictures (Miramax), 1992.

Ein "Landarzt" ["A Country Doctor"]. Read by Heinz Moog. Polyglotte D 7926.

Der Prozess [*The Trial*]. Read by Gustav Grundgens. Deutsche Grammophon 43 079, 1951.

Das Schloss [*The Castle*]. Dir. Rudolf Noelte. Zweites Deutsches Fernsehen. 7 June 1972.

The Stories of Kafka. Trans. Willa Muir and Edwin Muir. Read by Lotte Lenya. Caedmon LP 11 798, 1962. Also on cassette, CDL 51 114.

The Trial. Dir. Orson Welles. Syndicate Films, 1962.

The Trials of Franz Kafka. Distr. Goethe Institute, 1014 Fifth Ave., New York, NY 10028.

Die Verwandlung [The Metamorphosis]. Dir. Jan Nemec. Zweites Deutsches Fernsehen. 30 Oct. 1975.

The World of Mr. K. Distr. Goethe Institute, 1014 Fifth Ave., New York, NY 10028.

INDEX

Modern Language Association of America
Approaches to Teaching World Literature
Joseph Gibaldi, series editor

Montaigne's Essays. Ed. Patrick Henry. 1994.

Murasaki Shikibu's The Tale of Genji. Ed. Edward Kamens. 1993.

Pope's Poetry. Ed. Wallace Jackson and R. Paul Yoder. 1993.

Shakespeare's King Lear. Ed. Robert H. Ray. 1986.

Shakespeare's The Tempest *and Other Late Romances*. Ed. Maurice Hunt. 1992.

Shelley's Frankenstein. Ed. Stephen C. Behrendt. 1990.

Shelley's Poetry. Ed. Spencer Hall. 1990.

Sir Gawain and the Green Knight. Ed. Miriam Youngerman Miller and Jane Chance. 1986.

Spenser's Faerie Queene. Ed. David Lee Miller and Alexander Dunlop. 1994.

Sterne's Tristram Shandy. Ed. Melvyn New. 1989.

Swift's Gulliver's Travels. Ed. Edward J. Rielly. 1988.

Voltaire's Candide. Ed. Renée Waldinger. 1987.

Whitman's Leaves of Grass. Ed. Donald D. Kummings. 1990.

Wordsworth's Poetry. Ed. Spencer Hall, with Jonathan Ramsey. 1986.